With the Band

With the Band

Book Three in the Luminescent Juliet Series

Jean Haus

SKYSCAPE

SKYSCAPE

Text copyright © 2014 Jean Haus

Printed in the United States of America.

Published by Skyscape, New York

www.apub.com

Library of Congress Cataloging-in-Publication Data available upon request.

ISBN-13: 9781477847091
ISBN-10: 147784709X

Printed in the United States of America

To my father-in-law: I'll always remember listening to music with you—the Beatles, Lennon, Pearl Jam, Bush, and many more. Wish there could be more times and music with you. You are missed.

Chapter 1

L ike a stalker, I sit in my car waiting for *him* to come home. The apartment lot is only half full, and I'm parked on the far edge under the shade of a tree. It's the middle of the afternoon and things are quiet. I fight the urge to hightail it back to the university on the county road that brought me here. The steady beat of Breaking Benjamin's "I Will Not Bow" pounds from the car stereo. The song is supposed to be pumping me up, but my stomach is tight from nerves. Memories I've suppressed for over three years roll through me and set my pulse hammering like a war drum. Taking in a deep breath, I force myself to calm down and control my emotional turmoil. Older now, I'm stronger, wiser, and confident in myself.

I can do this.

An older Chevy Blazer pulls in front of apartment 5C. Clueless about what *he* drives, I lean forward, fists clenched so hard that my pink nails dig into my palms. When a guy bounds out of the driver's side, he's facing away from me. All I can make out is the back of his T-shirt, which says *Absolute Lawn Care.* I don't recognize the curly hair but as the guy starts walking, the swagger looks familiar. When he turns his head, I catch sight of his profile under the mop of curls as he unlocks the door to 5C.

Bingo.

The door closes and I draw in a deep breath. *Get your shit together, Peyton. You* will *do this.* Still, I sit. I flick off the radio and stare at his apartment door. Several minutes go by, yet other than gripping the steering wheel, I'm frozen.

Following a long internal pep talk, I glance in the mirror and then tuck the long layers of blonde hair sweeping across my forehead behind one ear. I consider applying lip gloss, maybe some powder, but don't reach for my purse. This isn't a social call.

I finally force myself out of my car and across the lot to apartment 5C. After straightening my tank top, smoothing my shorts, I take two deep breaths. Three loud knocks and several long minutes later, the door opens. The slight creak of its hinges might as well be the boom of a Pandora's box being opened.

I refuse to lower my gaze as *he* glares at me through the half-open door. He's wearing the same twisted expression that I recognize from the times we've crossed paths before—in the outdoor commons area or canteen or library—at random times over the past three years at the university we both attend. His clear disdain for me drips like venom into the bright Michigan summer afternoon. Mercifully, we've never had a class together.

I want to run back to my car, but I meet the loathing in his blue gaze without blinking.

His fresh outfit and wet curls tell me he just got out of the shower. He's got one hand holding the door open and the other clamped over a book opened against his thigh. The knuckles on both turn white as he stares at me.

"What do *you* want?" he asks icily.

"Hello, Sam," I say casually, ignoring the anxiety rushing through me. "We need to talk."

He starts to close the door as his lips twist into a scowl. "Still not interested in hearing anything you have to say."

Feeling a sudden surge of anger that overrides my anxiety, I push the door open with my foot, my flip-flop sliding across the glossy metal doorstep. "You think I'd wait over three years to come and talk about that? I'm here about your tour."

At the last word, he lets go of the door and the book drops from his hand and plops to the floor as I almost fall into the room. Onto him. Luckily, I catch myself on the door frame.

He points at me angrily, his finger stabbing the air. His dark curls flop over his forehead. "What about my tour? How do *you* know about the tour?" His voice rises in volume with each question. "We haven't even announced we're going on tour yet."

Two girls coming home to the next apartment watch us.

"Could you please let me in?" I say through clenched teeth.

Though his jaw tightens, he steps aside, bending to pick up the book. "Five minutes is about all I can take of you."

Shoulders back, I ignore the insult and march past him into a man cave. I'm surprised that the movie posters covering the walls are in frames. The sagging sofa and beat-up coffee table are used yet the huge flat screen on the wall is brand-new. Abandoned cups and food wrappers litter the tables. It's the standard male college apartment and has a familiarity that boosts my confidence for the awkward conversation ahead.

I hear the door click shut and turn around to find him leaning against it, staring at me with arms crossed and the book tucked under a biceps. I feel exposed under his cool regard. Like we've gone back in time and I'm about to be destroyed all over again. Forcing myself to push the thought away—I'm not that girl anymore—I cross my arms too, reflecting his pose. "Before I explain, I want you to know that Romeo came to me."

His eyes widen a bit. "What are you talking about?"

I had a long explanation rehearsed, but instead I blurt, "He wants me to go on tour with Luminescent Juliet."

Sam's face contorts in disgust and his arms drop to his sides. The book he's holding plummets to the floor again with a loud thud. "*You?* Hell no. Why?"

Though I expected it, his extreme dismay throws me. I force myself to remain calm and take a deep breath. "To take pictures, write a daily blog, and keep up on media accounts. Oh, and also to run the merchandise booth," I add absently. Though selling T-shirts doesn't appeal to me, gaining experience and, possibly, recognition as a music journalist does.

He pushes away from the door and in two steps he's standing less than a foot from me. "Why the hell would he ask you?"

Though the living room isn't that big, I hold my ground, refusing to back down, or escape into the connected kitchen, as he leans closer. In such close proximity, I become aware that he's not thin and lanky anymore. He has filled out and it's all muscle. One biceps has a black, curling tattoo. Or tattoos? I can't tell from this angle, but either way, it surprises me for some reason. The book he's holding has a picture of Steve Martin on it, and that fits the old Sam—he always used to read funny stuff. The T-shirt he's wearing, with its simple graphic lettering that says *The Doors,* also fits the old Sam. A tattoo does not. "Come on, Sam. Don't pretend you haven't noticed my work in the school paper."

"I don't pay attention to that shit, but yeah, I've heard." He runs a hand down his face. "Damn. I don't know why I'm surprised. It's just like Romeo to use someone from school. Just like he hired the audio-visual team to launch us," he adds absently, as if talking to himself. He rubs his jawline before his gaze comes back to me. "You told him no, right?"

"I told him yes already."

"Without talking to me?" he asks incredulously.

I shake my head and resist the nervous urge to gnaw on my lip. Then a wave of irritation washes over me. My emotions are like a seesaw. "Really? Are you saying I need your permission?"

He crosses his arms again. "I *am* in the band."

I consider his pull in their college band, which I've recently researched to death. Sam plays bass. Justin sings. Gabe is on drums. And Romeo plays guitar. From what I've seen, he also runs the show. "I have a hard time believing you really want to explain our past to your bandmates. I have an even harder time believing they'll care about us cheating on your brother over *three* years ago."

His upper lip curls at me. "Are you doing this just to piss me off?"

"Get over yourself," I snap, finally losing a bit of my cool. "I don't want to be around you either, but it's a great opportunity. Whatever coverage I write will go national. Maybe there's a book in it."

"A book?" Sam's eyebrows shoot up.

I nod. "Romeo agreed if you guys get big, I can use whatever blog stuff I write for a book about the tour."

"Riding on our coattails," he sneers.

"Working hard and promoting you," I say.

Sam stares at me in anger, his muscular body so still it's eerie. At last he asks, "Did you tell Romeo anything about us?"

The word *us* grates on my nerves. "Why would I tell him about the past? About Seth? I didn't even tell him I knew you, and that's the reason for my little visit. As far as I'm concerned, we're strangers."

Sam's lips twist into a thin, mocking line and his eyes slowly rake over me. "Strangers, huh?"

Gah. I want to smack that look off his face. "It's been more than three years, Sam. That's a long time. Almost the span of high school or college," I say flatly. "So yes, *strangers*."

We're both silent, staring at each other, when the door behind him opens.

"Hey, dude," the tall guy says, nearly colliding with Sam as he walks in. "I got your shit for the tour—" He pauses when he notices me and utters a slightly confused-sounding "Hey." Then he turns to Sam. "Sorry, didn't know you had company."

"It's all right," Sam says, still staring at me. "Could you give us a minute, Jeff?"

"Yeah, no problem," Jeff says, striding past us into the connected kitchen.

At the thud of a door closing down the hallway off the kitchen, Sam says, "So you came here to tell me we're going to pretend to be strangers. Anything else?" His expression is cold.

"I wanted to warn you and clear the air. I'm hoping we can agree to get along over the next six weeks."

"Like friends?"

"Yeah, like friends," I say, unable to keep the sarcasm from my voice. "I don't want to make things hard for you, and I'm hoping you won't make my job unpleasant for me."

He raises an eyebrow. "So I'm supposed to just accept that we're stuck together on a bus for six weeks straight?"

"Ignore me if that's what it takes, but being a dick isn't going to change the past."

His expression turns condescending. "Ah, so you think *I'm* going to be the problem."

"Yes, Sam, I'm worried you haven't grown up and will act like an ass instead of an adult. Should I be?"

He shrugs, leans against a chair, crosses his orange-socks-clad feet, and gives me a wry look. "Probably."

Anger shoots through me. Feeling like I might combust, I clench my fists beneath my folded arms. It takes a few moments, but I push down my anger and coolly say, "I'm doing this, even if I have to deal with you being a jerk. This has the possibility of opening doors for me."

Still watching me, not blinking, Sam slowly moves forward until his thickly muscled body is just inches from mine. "You're probably right," he says. "The past isn't going to change anyone's mind about letting you on the tour. But you're right to feel worried. I'm going to make the next six weeks hell for you every chance I get." He smirks at me. His gaze is furious.

An angry "f-you" almost escapes from my mouth. Instead, I swallow the expletive and say evenly, "You assume I'm just going to take it? No retaliation?" I step around Sam and open the door to the apartment. Looking back over my shoulder, I say, "Paybacks are hell, and hell is usually a two-way street. Think about that." Then I step out into the summer sunshine, slamming the door behind me.

I don't rush to my car, but instead stroll casually across the parking lot. But once I'm in the driver's seat, my entire body trembles from adrenaline. My fingers shake as I push the key into the ignition. Gripping the steering wheel, I force myself to breathe in deeply through my nose and let out air slowly through my mouth.

Repeat. Repeat. Repeat.

When Romeo called me, it had come out of the blue. And his news—that Luminescent Juliet had been invited on a national tour with two other major bands—had stunned me. I knew the band was huge on campus. And I knew they had released an indie album a few months before. But during those first few minutes of talking to him, I'd been surprised the band was hitting the big time—and caught equally off guard that he was calling to tell *me* about it. Sure, I'd written one piece about them for the school paper, back when they'd first started drawing big crowds. But it wasn't like I was a groupie or anything. Actually, just the opposite. I'd seen them play only once, at the beginning of sophomore year. And the instant I'd recognized the bass player was Sam, I'd vowed to stay away from all things Luminescent Juliet.

The minute Romeo offered me the job—to go on tour with them and chronicle their every move—I realized that he'd obviously researched my credentials but not my personal life. I could tell that he knew nothing about the past Sam and I shared. Not that the past would have mattered to Romeo—because my work is good. Professional. Smart, with just enough edge. It turned out that Romeo had interviewed everyone who was going to be on the school newspaper's editorial team in the upcoming year. My obsession with music was the deciding factor between me and the other two people he interviewed. Luckily for me, our interview had veered off course and into a deep conversation about the merits of '70s punk versus '90s grunge rock. I'd worried that my very vocal opinions had screwed up the interview up. Instead, they had sealed the deal.

As soon as Romeo made me an offer, I took the job. My goal was to become a music journalist. I'd been seriously into music since I was twelve, so touring with a band and writing about it was like a dream come true. Finally, my work would be seen beyond the pages of a college newspaper. I just didn't want to deal with Sam. Or the past.

But now that my conversation with the jerk is over, I feel certain that even dealing with him will be a small price to pay for a huge step forward in my career. I'm pretty much over the past. I was never the girl they made me out to be, and I've come a long way since the days when a hateful rumor was enough to level me. I've slowly learned how to rise above the rumors and not look back.

I turn the key in the ignition with a feeling of resolve.

The past will not affect my future.

I drive away without looking in my rear-view mirror, back at Sam's apartment.

Chapter 2

Standing in the middle of my bedroom, I read over the long list of what to pack for the tour—more like an instruction booklet—in my hand again:

One small suitcase

One backpack

Fifteen pairs of socks

Fifteen pairs of underwear

Laundry bag with name on it

No more than three pairs of shoes

One box of nonperishable groceries

On and on it goes. Romeo is one thorough guy—although it has crossed my mind that *anal-retentive* might be a better descriptor. When I met him and Justin to review preparations for leaving, I'd been unable to hide my surprise at the pages of instructions they'd handed me. Justin had laughed when my eyebrows rose, but Romeo explained that he'd spent hours researching the best tricks for surviving a band tour, and that these seemingly small things turned out to be big issues. He wanted to take care of the details in advance so everything could go smoothly on the road, so the band could just focus on playing.

One thing I could tell from his list—the guys in Luminescent Juliet were slobs. There was a whole section of bullet points about who was supposed to clean up what . . . and when. I wrinkled my nose at that part. There were definitely going to be drawbacks to my spending the next six weeks with four musicians on a bus. Especially given that one of them couldn't stand me.

I tap my foot to Nirvana's "All Apologies" playing from my iPod deck on the desk and glance over the huge pile of things on my bed. I've gathered everything on the list, plus my camera gear and computer, and I can already imagine Romeo, the apparent micromanager, saying something about all the stuff. Just as I'm debating whether I can squeeze one more outfit into my suitcase, my roommate and cousin, Jill, comes into the room, holding two frosty margaritas.

She wiggles her blonde eyebrows at me.

I smile. Starting when Jill and I were both about eight years old, we got into the habit of telling people we were sisters. Since we both have brown eyes and blonde hair, everyone usually believed us. Then, by the time we were around thirteen, I started putting on weight. We didn't look like sisters again until our senior year of high school, after I got serious about dieting and exercising. Of course, these days we don't tell anyone we're sisters, but we still look alike. We both keep our long, straight blonde hair cut a few inches past our shoulders. We dress similarly, partly because we share our closets. I fit into most of her things but not all. And unless I starve myself, which I refuse to do after too many years of strict dieting, I'll always weigh more than she does. Jill is an inch shorter than me, and she's built thin. I'm a little curvier. But after struggling with my self-image for years, I'm okay with my curves. So what if I have to buy bigger-sized jeans in certain styles? Size is just a number. There are worse things than being bootylicious. Like being obsessed with what a scale says.

Jill goes over to my desk and turns down the music. "The girls are coming over," she says, holding a margarita out for me.

I don't reach for the glass. "I'm supposed to go out with Bryce," I say. "He'll be here any second." I'm already dressed in a gauzy, flowing, sleeveless dress, and all that's left for me to do is to put on mascara.

Jill pushes the drink into my hand. "Practice always runs over," she says, rolling her eyes. "Baseball is so boring that I don't know how it can run late, but it always does. You can have a few while you wait."

I take the drink from her.

"He'll like you nice and easy," she says with a wink.

I give her a dirty look and take a sip. "I'm never easy."

She smirks and tosses her hair back on one shoulder. "Didn't seem like it that time I walked in on you two."

"The infamous Saint Patty's Day session," I say, rolling *my* eyes. "You're never going to let me live that down." I don't regret it, exactly, but I'm still embarrassed that Jill had walked in on us after we'd done several rounds of green beer pong and were in a full make-out session on the couch, with various pieces of clothing removed. Bryce and I had waited another month until we had sex. Thoroughly still embarrassed, I flick some salt from the rim of my glass at her. "Who's coming over?"

She swirls a straw in the slush of her drink. "Ashley and Jules, of course, and probably Sara. Maybe Gwen."

"Fun," I say. "Almost wish I could skip the date and hang out with you guys." It's true. I love our group of girlfriends. It's made up of Ashley and Jules, who lived across from us in the dorms freshman year—and whom we still see all the time, partly because Jill works with Jules at the student coffee shop. I met Gwen when I started working at Tony's, a local Italian restaurant, making desserts and occasionally waitressing. She instantly fit in with our group and started hanging out with us all the time. She almost killed me when

I told her I was temporarily leaving the restaurant job to tour with Luminescent Juliet. It's possible they'll hold my job until I get back, since I've worked there for three years. But I'm not worried either way. My future career as a journalist is far more important than making giant-sized portions of spumoni and cannoli or serving up heaping plates of spaghetti.

"We'll just be forced to get smashed without you," says Jill, laughing.

Usually, we reserve Fridays for our ladies' nights, no guys allowed. Sometimes we hang at one of our apartments. Sometimes we go out. Tonight is a Wednesday, so it's a spur-of-the-moment gathering.

I take a long sip of the frozen drink. A few moments later, brain freeze has me rubbing the bridge of my nose. I sit down on the edge of my bed.

Jill's expression is curious. "Are you okay?"

I admit, "I'm still nervous about Sam."

Jill's upper lip curls. "Please. What's he going to do? Destroy your reputation on a bus? Make you cry? You're over all that. Definitely tougher now."

Jill, of course, knows about everything that destroyed my senior year. She had gone to high school with Seth and Sam, had been the one to introduce me to the fraternal twins. Back then, her life had seemed so much more fun than mine, even though she lived in serious farm country in the thumb of Michigan while I lived two counties over, in a town that drew tons of tourists each summer. But the fact was, Jill was just more social than I was. She had way more friends, and got invited to all the parties. So after I'd lost weight my senior year, I made the drive to her parents' place on weekends and let her drag me around with her. And on one of those nights, I'd met Seth, at a barn concert.

"Seth was the one who ruined my reputation. Sam was just an asshole," I recall, though both had hurt me in one way or another.

"Still is," Jill says. "He's an ass of the highest degree, like ass to the power of infinity. Ignore him."

I sigh. "I plan to. I just don't like remembering all that drama, and hurt." The giggles behind my back throughout the day at school, the nasty comments on Facebook, the writings on bathroom walls, and my self-confidence in the gutter are painful memories I don't like to linger on.

She plops down next to me, wrapping an arm around my shoulders. "Fuck Sam. Fuck Seth. You were young, screwed up, and those two were to blame for everything that went down. Especially moody, stupid, egomaniac, rumor-spreading Seth." She clinks her glass with mine. "So let it go." She flutters her lashes at me. "I'll always love you."

Grinning, I clink my glass back. "Love you too."

She glances at the huge pile of stuff I still have to pack, behind us on the bed. "This summer is going to suck without you here."

"I wish you could come with me." I smile. "But honestly, other than dealing with Sam, I'm so excited to be going on a tour. With three bands!" I say, lifting my glass and clinking it with hers again.

She shakes her head and smiles. "You're one lucky bitch, but who better than you?" She waves a hand at the wall by my desk, which is plastered with old concert posters, guitar picks, an original Ramones T-shirt, and several album covers, including a signed copy of the Stooges' *Raw Power*, all framed and sealed under glass. My grandfather was a bouncer at a punk club in Detroit years ago, and he gave me all the stuff. He met and saw many of the early bands perform live, from the Clash to Black Flag.

A knock sounds at the door, and Jill hauls me off the bed.

"Come on, that has to be Ashley," she says. "You can at least hang out with us for an hour until loverboy gets here."

Two margaritas later, Jill and Ashley are reenacting my first meeting with Bryce in the middle of the kitchen while Sara, Gwen, and I sit at the counter bar on the other side in the dining area. Jill, wearing a baseball hat, smacks into Ashley, whose features twist in terror. She lets out a yelp, falling clumsily onto the floor. Jill immediately drops to her knees and starts waving her arms frantically. I can't stop myself from laughing.

It's a perfect rendition of when Bryce and I met. And so romantic. *Not.*

Our run-in, literally, had happened in late autumn last year, when I was covering a benefit baseball scrimmage for the school paper. I'd been shooting photos from the sidelines when the heavily muscled third baseman had knocked me over while going for a fly ball. In retrospect, I shouldn't have been so close to third base, but I'd been getting such good shots with my camera that I hadn't wanted to move an inch. So our collision had pretty much been my fault. Even though it wasn't romantic, Bryce was. He was seriously worried about me through the whole thing. We'd exchanged numbers after our crash, and he'd called me that night to ask if he could come by and make sure I was okay—and he'd even brought flowers. He kept up the phone calls and visits, and a few months later, he'd asked me out. I liked him well enough, and because we both seemed to be equally busy, we fell into an easy routine of casual dating that's worked for us ever since.

"So that is how Barbie met Ken," Jill says, bowing. I curl my lip at her and jokingly narrow my eyes. Because Bryce, like me, has blond hair, she's been referring to us as Beach Barbie and Ken since our first date. The other girls laugh. I take a long, brain-freezing sip from my margarita and ignore her comment.

As Jill helps Ashley off the floor, there's another knock at the door.

"Oh, let me get it!" Jill runs across the living room and whips open the door, smirking at us over her shoulder. Her entire body freezes as she says, "Holy shit!"

Holy shit is right. Instead of Bryce, whom we were all expecting, Sam stands in the doorway. His gaze travels past Jill to me and then over the other girls. He puts on a slick grin. "Hello, ladies," he says smoothly, leaning casually against the door frame and giving the girls with me at the bar a wink. "Is this a bad time?"

He's dressed in long shorts and a faded black tank. His dark curls are a sexy mess under a baseball cap turned backward. He should look like a loser slob, but with his skin tanned golden-brown from lawn work, his muscular arms on display, and his toothy white grin, he looks like a sloppy, college hottie—and I suppose he is, given the way all my friends except Jill are hungrily checking him out.

Sam's hotness, which I'd ignored when I'd been so obsessed with his brother, Seth, is magnified now. His body looks as chiseled as that of a professional athlete. Sam had always been the one of the two who looked sweet and searing, like a poet. But with his build now adding another layer of gorgeous to his square jaw, sharp cheekbones, and deep-set blue eyes, his looks are as killer as the flirtatious smile he flashes. I'd forgotten that grin, because for the past three years the only expression I'd seen him wear was one of contempt.

Jill looks at me, waiting for me to answer him as her foot taps impatiently on the carpet.

Gwen, Sara, and Ashley continue to stare at Sam with wide, hungry gazes.

I slowly slide off my stool. "What do you want, Sam?"

He glances at the other girls sitting at the counter/bar and grins sexily before saying, "Could I talk with you for a minute?"

Since he appears sincere, I move toward the door. "All right."

Jill's look is level as I pass her. Because Sam's crooked grin is still in place, I wonder if maybe this will be a first step toward resolving our mutual dislike. Maybe he's ready to be mature. I pry the knob from Jill's hand, ignore her pointed stare, and step outside, shutting the door behind me.

Sam leans back against the railing of the porch to our apartment, his biceps flexing as he props himself up, his ankles crossed. He is the picture of disheveled cool. "Listen, I'm sorry," he says. "I was a dick the other day at my apartment. You caught me off guard. Romeo didn't give any warnings about you or anyone else coming on the tour."

I nod, hopeful we can find a way to get along.

He lets out a sigh as his eyes roam over me in the dress. "I still don't think you should come on the tour."

Now it's my turn to sigh. Perhaps we're really going to be stuck in the past forever, our distrust of each other like an angry, thrashing metal song that never ends. I don't say anything, just raise an eyebrow.

"Consider it, Peyton," Sam says. "Six weeks on a bus ignoring each other. Do you really want to deal with that?"

"I've already explained my reasons for going," I reply. "Your last-ditch effort here isn't going to work."

His ankles uncross as he pulls away from the railing and stands up straight. His full lips become a thin line. "Why do you have to be so fucking difficult?"

Unable to control my anger, I snap, "Difficult? Because I'm not doing what *you* want?"

He lifts the cap and runs a hand through his curls. His wide shoulders sag. "This whole thing is difficult. You have no idea how difficult it is for me."

His tone, his words, and his stiff body language signal that there's more going on than that one past incident concerning us. Something is weighing on him so heavily that it strikes a chord of sympathy in me. "Maybe you should explain."

"I . . ." His eyes are troubled and clouded by a shame that not only confuses me but tugs at my heart. He glances toward the parking lot of the apartment complex and lets out a short breath. When his gaze comes back me, he says, "You know I can't stand you."

Asshole. I'm aware he can't stand me, but his aversion didn't feel like the issue a few seconds ago. Though I can't imagine what his emotions are, I'm sensing more than simple dislike. "Well, I can't stand going to early morning classes or serving crappy-looking pizza or talking to guys with stupid opinions. Yet I deal with all that." I reach for the door handle. "So my suggestion to you is to deal with it."

His jaw clenches and his mouth twists, but before he can blow up at me, Bryce steps out of the dusk and onto the porch. Wearing jeans and a fitted T-shirt, he looks good—ready for a night out. Though at six one he's over two inches taller than Sam, Sam's heavy muscles make him appear larger than lean Bryce. He gazes from Sam to me. "Hey, Peyton. What's going on?"

His voice is calm yet tense in a way that tells me he has noticed Sam's rigid posture and angry eyes.

I feign indifference and shrug. "Nothing much. This is Sam, the bassist from Luminescent Juliet." I gesture to Bryce. "My boyfriend, Bryce Hanson."

Bryce gives Sam a skeptical look. I let go of the door handle and move close to my boyfriend's side. "Sam came to double-check on everything for the trip tomorrow, but he was just leaving."

Sam nods casually but I notice his fists are balled tightly at his sides. "Guess I'll see you tomorrow."

Bryce watches him go, then turns to me. "What's his problem?"

I tilt my head as if I'm lost in thought. "Nerves? They want everything to be perfect." There is no way in hell I'm explaining my past with Sam or that dark time in my life to Bryce. We kind of date in the moment. Sharing our pasts has never been part of our relationship.

As Sam pulls away in his Blazer, Bryce stares down at me. His gaze turns troubled. "You sure you want to do this?"

I bump his arm with my shoulder. "Yes, I'm sure. I'm going to miss you and Jill, but it's too good an opportunity to turn down." I put my hand on his chest. "Besides, you'll be gone half of the time at away games over the next two months."

He puts one strong hand over mine and the other on my waist, drawing me close. "Gone, yes, but missing you." His sweet words have me leaning in faster for his kiss as he bends toward me, but the door whips open.

"Oh, hey, Bryce." Jill looks to me. "Where's Sam?"

Bryce and I reluctantly step apart.

"Had to go," I say. "He was just checking that I have everything ready for tomorrow." My pointed look at Jill says, *Keep your trap shut*, before I turn toward Bryce. "Let me get my purse and we can go," I say.

"Sure," he says with a quick smile, and follows me back into the apartment.

"Hi, Bryce," Gwen and Ashley say in unison, their voices friendly and just a little flirtatious. As I go to my room, I can hear them asking about the baseball team, then their questions about where he's taking me. I hear something about a sushi bar, which surprises me. Bryce rarely moves out of his comfort zone. And sports are pretty much the extent of it. Nine times out of ten, we go to Lucky's, a local sports bar. I don't mind since it's a college hangout too, but obviously Bryce is trying to do something special to send me off.

In my bedroom, I pick up my purse and take a deep breath, trying to forget about Sam. I'm going out with my boyfriend of seven months, and not only is he looking good, he's taking me to sushi. This is going to be our last night for the next six weeks, so I want to enjoy it.

Screw Sam.

Screw the past.

Tomorrow I'm leaving town to tour with not only Luminescent Juliet but also two other bands. Bands signed to major labels. Bands that get national coverage. Everything in my life—excluding Sam—is going perfect right now. No one can take that away from me.

Chapter 3

The front of a dusty antique store seems like a strange place for a band tour to begin, but that's exactly where Jill and I find ourselves standing the next day. Apparently, Luminescent Juliet practices in the space above the shop. Since it's where they keep all their gear and instruments, it's where the huge, intimidating black-and-gray tour bus is picking us up. According to Romeo, producers usually fly in bands when they join a tour, but because the most recent stop was Chicago—the tour has been going for five weeks already and the last three shows didn't have an opening act—the manager decided to have the bus pick us up and drive us to Denver.

We try to stay out of the way as the chaotic scene unfolds. Packed duffels, boxes of food, instruments, and people fill the sidewalk between the store and the bus. I already put my suitcase near the baggage slots below the bus, and added my backpack and food box to the pile by the front door. The only thing I'm holding on to is my camera bag, since I have no desire to see it get manhandled.

As we watch things slowly get loaded, Jill makes a commentary out the side of her mouth like a sportscaster—*Score! Two suitcases are now on the bus!* I bite my lip so I don't burst out laughing.

Once everything is loaded onto the bus, I sense the reluctance hanging in the afternoon summer air. It's clear that some of the good-byes taking place aren't easy. Romeo bends his dark head and talks softly to a pretty, petite college girl with a two-toned—blonde and brown—ponytail. A small boy hangs on to Justin's tattooed arm while his other arm wraps around a stunning auburn-haired young woman with a sleeve tattoo. A blonde chick dressed in a tight tank top and Daisy Dukes presses against Gabe, the one band member I've never met, wrapping her fingers in his shoulder-length hair while her lips form a pout. Sam stands a little ways off, on his own, smoking a cigarette and staring at the ground. Strange, I don't recall him being a smoker.

As I continue watching the scene, I start unzipping my camera bag. I'm not an amazing photographer or anything. I've taken a few classes, and I'm aware of the whole angle and light thing. I'm just not a wizard with the whole angle and light thing. My talent is recognizing the right time to catch emotion. And I'm glimpsing a perfect time.

After pulling my camera out and then pushing the bag at Jill, I start moving around and snapping pictures. Romeo and the petite girl gazing at each other, forehead to forehead, with the bus looming in the background. Justin holding the tattooed girl in a tight one-armed hug while the boy clings to his other arm. Gabe being pulled into an aggressive kiss by the scantily clad blonde. And lastly, Sam staring at the ground as cigarette smoke floats in a hazy swirl around him. His brows are low. His lips flat.

When I come near him, he looks up and scowls at me, jerking the black-and-orange striped beanie down over his curls to his eyebrows. "Keep that shit away from me," he snarls.

I lower the camera and try to push down my irritation. "Onstage? Can I photograph you onstage at least?" My tone is curt. Guess my irritation won out.

"Yeah, whatever." He drops his cigarette in a can by the door and stalks past me.

I put the cap on the camera lens and smooth the anger from my expression. I will not let Sam get to me.

When I sidle back over to the bus, Romeo introduces me to his girlfriend, Riley. I shake hands with Justin's girlfriend, Allie, the woman with the tattoo sleeve. I shake hands with Gabe too, since we're meeting officially for the first time, and I can't help but notice that nobody introduces his girlfriend. When the last farewells recommence, Jill gives me two hugs. One from her and one from Bryce—he's at practice. Then, finally, the band and I climb onto the bus.

The bus is rocker-style and awesome. It's split up so there's one big room in the front, with a compact kitchen and two leather sofas, and a small room in the back with a wraparound sofa. In between the two rooms are closets, two sets of bunks, and a tiny bathroom. There are flat-screen TVs in the front and back, plus each bunk has its own tiny TV. Since there are only four bunks, I offer to sleep on the couch in the back when we're on the road. All four band members—surprisingly, even Sam—offer me their bunks. But I insist. Really, it's more private in the back anyway, even if each bunk has a curtain.

Gary is our bus driver, a short older guy with gray hair and thick glasses. Thus far he's been quiet and accommodating. Romeo took charge after we got on board and made sure we all stored our things neatly. Now, as the bus is rolling down the highway, all five of us are gathered in the front room. I'm next to Gabe on one of the leather couches while Romeo and Justin sit together on the couch facing us. Sam is by himself at the small kitchen booth. Romeo is reciting his list of rules aloud, reading from a notebook in his hands. Justin looks annoyed. Gabe is motionless and quiet. Sam leans his head back against the booth, covers his forehead with his beanie, and looks visibly annoyed too.

The rules are never ending. Be respectful to Gary. No groupies on bus. (Yes!) If people are sleeping, keep it down. Clean up messes. (I'm alarmed that these two are needed.) Since the water supply is limited, shower on the bus only if necessary. Anyone can eat what's in the fridge and cupboards, because it's paid for with band funds. All other food is on your own. Make sure the AC is off before using the microwave or a breaker will blow. Open flame on the stovetop is not allowed while on the road.

On and on he goes. I zone in and out, trying not to notice that Sam has started to sarcastically orchestrate Romeo's never-ending monologue, moving two fingers in the air like a conductor. Being in the same space as Sam is making me nervous, which makes me pissed off at myself. So I breathe deeply and make myself listen to Romeo drone on about laundry. According to him, we'll each take a turn, every week if possible. I suppose between the bus travel and hotel stays, laundry might become an issue. However, none of these four men are washing my underwear.

Um, just no and never.

I raise my hand as if I'm in high school. Romeo's expression is odd, but he nods.

"You guys are going to be far busier than me, and, well, this is your tour, so I can do the laundry."

Justin grins. "Sounds good. How nice of you."

Romeo glares at him through the dark hair falling over his forehead. "Thanks, Peyton." He gives both Sam and Gabe a stern look. "But I'd like everyone to be aware that Peyton has a job to do, and it has nothing to do with laundry. She's here to promote us, not take care of us." He lowers the notebook he is holding. "Tomorrow night is our first show. First thing in the morning, we'll go over the set."

Apparently, that means this meeting is adjourned, because within seconds everyone is out of their seats. Justin and Gabe immediately head to the flat-screen TV at the front and start hooking up a gaming system. Sam goes to the fridge and pulls out three beers.

Romeo glances at me and gestures to the back room. "You ready for interviews?"

"Sure," I say, standing up. I'd sort of forgotten until now that Romeo and I had talked about me interviewing each band member to get material for the first blog posts of the tour.

Romeo nods in Sam's direction. "He's up first," he says.

I feel my stomach drop.

Sam looks up at us with a sour expression. "Why me?"

"Because I need to go over some things on the phone with the concert manager," Romeo says, looking darkly at Sam.

Without saying anything, Sam puts the beers in the fridge and marches to the back room.

We sit on opposite sides of the low square coffee table. I'm glad to have a piece of furniture in between us. Pretending nonchalance, I get out my voice recorder, a pen, and a notebook while he stares out the tiny window above my head. Invisible tension crackles in the air. We're both as stone-faced as a couple of rockers hiding behind sunglasses on the red carpet.

Ugh. Do I really want to do this?

When Romeo had initially called me, he'd explained why he wanted me to cover the tour. He'd thought a blog with professional pictures and creative posts at least every other day would keep his current fans entertained and attract new ones. Always the skeptical journalist, I'd asked why the guys in the band couldn't handle a blog on their own. Well, for starters, he'd said sardonically, they couldn't take their own pictures, especially onstage, and besides, they're not professional writers. He wanted things creative but polished.

I'd liked his answer.

Once we'd hammered out everything—my minuscule pay, his expectations, my expectations—I told him I wanted to interview everyone before the tour began. I wanted to hear the story of how Luminescent Juliet landed on this national tour from the different perspectives of each of the band members. But instead of giving me access, Romeo had insisted on putting off the interviews until the tour kicked off. Beforehand, everyone was too busy getting ready and practicing, but once we were on the bus, there would be lots of time. Instead of doing the interviews then, I'd created the blog so eventually all I had to do was plug in my first post. And I'd generated lists of questions. Needless to say, my questions for Sam were the least thought out.

Since I don't want to start with anything personal, I ask, "How is it that Luminescent Juliet ended up on the Summer Tour of Rock?" I hit record on my machine and wait.

He shoots a skeptical look, first at me, then at the tiny recording machine. He says in a flat tone, "There are basically two reasons. One, our album made it into the top one hundred on a couple of different indie charts last month, and two, the opening band pulled out of the tour. I'm not sure if we were the only band they considered as a replacement, but when they called, it took us about two seconds to say yes."

"Why such a quick yes?"

"This tour is major," he says, sitting up from his slouch. "We'd been considering putting together a small tour by ourselves. It would have involved a couple of vans and us doing all the legwork. We wouldn't have played any big arenas or made any money, so the main point would have been to build a bigger fan base On this tour, we'll actually make some money *and* have the opportunity to build a bigger fan base. It was like getting a huge present dropped in our laps."

"Though you're all in college, would you say that Luminescent Juliet is your first priority?"

"We're—wait." He raises his eyebrows. "You're running all the blog posts by Romeo before you put them up, right?"

Guessing he's not sure how honest to be, I nod reassuringly. "Absolutely. Having Romeo approve all the posts was part of our agreement."

"We're playing it by ear," says Sam, looking slightly reassured. "Band and school are both priorities right now."

I tap my pencil on my notebook, searching my list for a neutral question. "So *what* is your college major?"

"English," he says, an evasive tone returning to his voice. He slouches back into the couch.

I stop myself from curling my upper lip. I'd thought for a second that he was warming up, but now it's obvious that I was just hoping. Boy, this is going fan-super-fucking-tastic. I look down at my notebook again. Since I don't have any more specific questions for Sam, I glance at the list I made for Gabe.

"How long have you been playing the drums—I mean *bass*?"

His gaze meets mine. "Only three years."

Clearing my throat, I glance down at the notebook page. "Any experience with music before that?"

"I played the guitar in another band. A garage band. Or since we lived in the middle of butt-fucking farmland, maybe you could call it a barn band." He gives me a piercing look, his eyes narrowed. "What was the name of that band, Peyton?" he asks in a low tone.

The pen tightens in my grip as he waits for me to answer. "Bottle Rockets," I say in a tone as low as his.

His gaze bores into mine. "Why are you asking me these stupid questions?"

Though I don't want to, I flinch. "I want a bit of background on each of the members."

He yanks that damn beanie down over his eyebrows, sits back, and crosses his arms. "You know my background."

No. Not really. I knew him for about six months, and most of that time I was infatuated with his brother, Seth.

"Shit, Peyton, we slept together."

Jerked out of my thoughts, my eyes flash fire at him. "Do. Not. Ever. Bring that up again," I force out through clenched teeth. Talking about the past with Jill was hard enough. Talking about it with Sam will never happen.

Something blazes in his gaze but disappears too quickly for me to read it. "I think we're done here," I say coldly. "I'll assume that all you want your background information to say is that you played guitar in garage band with your brother, who was the singer, before you joined Luminescent Juliet."

"Don't include the part about my brother," he says so icily that my own former cold tone seems warm and fuzzy.

I want to know why he's refusing to let me mention his brother, but I'm aware that he's going to get super pissed if I ask. I'm also aware there's no way he's going to explain anything.

I stand up and put my hands on my hips, then glare down my nose at him. "Great start," I say sarcastically. "Why don't you send someone else in?"

His expression is level while I smile pleasantly at the asshat.

There's no way I'm going to let him see how much he gets to me.

Chapter 4

I wake up in the middle of the night, startled that the bus isn't moving. A peek outside my window produces a view of a shadowy rest area. After tiptoeing to the bathroom and then to the fridge for a bottle of water, I realize Gary is sleeping on the couch in the main room. Stupidly, I had thought we would drive through the night. As if Gary, the middle-aged man of few words, doesn't need to sleep. It takes me forever to fall back asleep. When I wake up in the morning, we're rolling again.

I tend to be an early riser. I usually have to get up at five in the morning three days a week to go make desserts at Tony's. So it's not surprising that all the band members are still asleep as I tiptoe past the bunk area with a notebook in hand. I find a plastic bowl—not too hard with only four cupboards—and pour cereal and milk. While eating breakfast, I make a list of what I need to accomplish prior to the concert tonight. Interviews took up most of yesterday—all the other band members were more talkative than Sam. Justin and Romeo gave me a ton of information. Both of them seemed super excited about the tour. Gabe wasn't as open, but he was nowhere near as defensive as Sam was. After eating a ham sandwich for dinner, I'd called Jill, then Bryce before laying out a blanket and pillow on the couch.

My first goal is to use the interviews to create bios for the band members to go with their pictures. I also want to finish the first tour post about leaving home.

I'm still digging into my Cheerios when Sam stumbles into the kitchen area. One side of his head is springy with curls. The hair on the other side is flat and he is dressed in a faded Jimi Hendrix T-shirt and flannels. He searches in the cupboards. Froot Loops in hand, he opens the fridge.

Clearing my throat, I push the milk to the edge of the table.

Sam finally notices me sitting behind him and scowls. I'm not sure if the frown is because of me or because he's not a morning person. As he collapses across from me in the booth and drops the cereal box on the table between us, I'm guessing both.

I tug my pen from the spiral of the notebook. He stares out the window. I work on my list. He shoves in cereal.

The uncomfortable breakfast continues, with the hum of the highway below us and cereal crunching until Sam unexpectedly asks, "How'd you sleep back there?"

Shocked that he's talking to me, I nearly drop my plastic spoon. "All right. You?"

He pours another bowl of cereal. "Like shit. Those bunks are narrower than hell."

"The back couch wasn't too bad, but I was startled to wake up in the middle of the night at a rest stop."

He finishes chewing. "Pulled into it around midnight."

"You nervous about the concert tonight?" I ask. I'm not sure if I keep the conversation going because he's actually talking to me or because it's become my habit to ask questions.

He shrugs and scoops up more cereal. "We've played some big shows."

"When the crowd is more than five thousand?"

"No, but I'm thinking it's all the same if I'm up onstage."

My head tilts as I imagine the excitement of performing live. "I suppose."

The bass line from "Higher Ground" by the Red Hot Chili Peppers rings from the pocket of his flannels. He sets his spoon down and digs out the phone. He scowls at the screen and then answers, "What's going on?"

His gaze wanders to the window as creases form between his brows.

"Why would you assume that? I wouldn't do that." He shoves his cereal away. "I haven't forgotten you."

I pretend to be immersed in my list and not listening, but it's hard to ignore the one-sided conversation. Like most waitresses, I'm good at ignoring people, especially customers arguing across plates of pasta, yet Sam's frustrated tone catches my attention.

"No. No. No. That's not true." He rubs his temple. "Are you listening to what you're saying? What you're suggesting?" The temple rubbing continues as he listens. "It's not that I don't trust you." Sam pauses, as if suddenly remembering he's not alone. "Just a minute." He scoots out of the booth. "Hey, hey, you need to calm down," he says, marching toward the back of the bus.

I tap my pencil on the notebook, thinking that Sam has one demanding girlfriend. I wonder what she looks like, if she's a student, and whether I've had any classes with her. Irritated at myself, I toss my pen down. Who cares? I certainly shouldn't. Still, I can't stop thinking about it. I wonder why she wasn't there yesterday to see him off. But then again, Bryce couldn't make it because of practice, so maybe she had prior commitments too. I glance out the window and wonder why I'm contemplating Sam's love life.

I don't want to contemplate anything about Sam.

Within the hour, Romeo holds his morning meeting. I'd hoped to get some material out of it, but the meeting is pretty boring. The guys talk about a song list until they all agree. Romeo reminds Gabe about keeping the tempo so they don't "crash," whatever that means. I'm guessing the implication is that he and Sam won't be able to stay with the beat unless Gabe provides a strong lead. They spend another twenty minutes choreographing Sam's, Romeo's, and Justin's onstage movements. Although not every second is accounted for, I'm surprised at how much they do plan out, even moving around to show and explain to one another what they envision.

Lunch is another round of sandwiches. I opt for peanut butter and jelly this time, with a side of raw carrots. There's not much junk food on the bus. I guess that's not surprising, given all of Romeo's research. He probably read somewhere that bands don't perform well if they live on Cheetos and canned ravioli for six weeks.

I spend the rest of the afternoon in the back room, working on the bios and the blog post. I look through the pictures I took yesterday and decide which ones to put up. Only one shows a girlfriend. From ages twelve to sixteen, I was in *luuuve* with a whole bunch of hot musicians, and I never wanted to know if the objects of my affection were in relationships. I'm guessing that filling up the posts with lovey-dovey pictures isn't the thing to do. Especially because Luminescent Juliet is composed of four hot guys.

I'm aware their looks are part of their appeal. Romeo with his swoop of dark hair and intense dark eyes. Justin's gorgeous model look, complete with blond hair and tattoos. Gabe's lean, rocker body and harsh face framed by brown shoulder-length hair. And Sam, with his sculpted profile, curls, and muscular build. They're like a grown-up boy band that's way past cute and into full-on sexy. Luckily, I have a great boyfriend. Though he's good-looking too, I learned long ago that looks aren't everything. Real communication is more important. So I'm completely immune to hot-looking guys, especially to Sam.

Late in the afternoon, I go to the front room to show Romeo the first post, but he is on the phone, his face angry and tense. With an equally strained expression, Justin paces the length of the aisle from the kitchen to about five inches behind Gary's seat, then back again. Gabe is attacking the couch with his drumsticks. Sam sits in the kitchen booth with his feet up and his head back, looking unfazed, reading a book. Since he's the only person not in the middle of a freak-out, I'm guessing he's the best one to talk to.

"What's going on?"

He lifts a brow at me and tilts his head toward the window. "You haven't noticed the lack of speed?"

I glance out at the bumper-to-bumper traffic around us, and realize that we're moving at the pace of a turtle. I shake my head. "Guess I was too absorbed in my work." When Justin paces past me to the end of the bus for the second time, the implications hit me. "Are we going to make the show?"

Sam shrugs, then yawns. "Not sure, but there's not much we can do now, is there?"

Ignoring his nonchalance, I do the math. We left Michigan yesterday at one. Even with a long stop for gas, we must have done ten hours yesterday. The trip to Denver takes eighteen hours. We were supposed to get there at four o'clock, which would have given the band three hours to do sound checks and get ready before going onstage at seven. I glance at the time on my phone. Three o'clock. Denver has to be hours away, because the landscape around us is rolling hills. Out the front window, the mountains are visible in the distance, but getting to them might take forever.

Romeo glances out the window and swears. I shut my laptop. I'm guessing he's not going to be interested in checking the post right now. Sam goes back to his book. Justin continues pacing. Feeling a little anxious, I head to the back room and put away my computer. The bus comes to a complete stop and someone up front yells out, "Fuck!"

Sitting on the couch, I use my phone to check our distance from Denver. According to the map, the journey there should take a little less than two hours. I glance out the window. The horrendous traffic could easily eat up the next two hours. Whoever made this schedule is an idiot. It doesn't allow much time for error.

The bus doesn't move. I look at my phone again, glance out the window, and then clench and unclench my hands repeatedly. There's nothing else to do.

Sam comes into the back room. He nods toward the TV and puts his book on the table. "Mind if I watch? Gabe's couch drumming and the nonstop bitching up front is getting on my nerves."

"Be my guest," I say, shaking my head. How can he be so calm? This is their first show. "This really isn't fazing you?"

"Nothing I can do. I can't worry about everything in life," he says absently, grabbing the remote and starting to flick through channels. He props his feet on the table, next to his book. I glance at the cover: *The Hitchhiker's Guide to the Galaxy*. It must be funny, because I faintly recall that Sam used to carry around books, even at parties, and they were always humorous. He would read lines to me from them. Sometimes I would get the humor; other times I just laughed at the goofy way he read the lines. I'm suddenly annoyed that the only side of him I ever see is the grumpy one. The fun-loving side of him seems to be gone.

"What do *you* have to worry about?" I ask, ticking off the options in my head. Getting laid? Partying? Maybe grades?

"You still interviewing, Ms. Couric?" he asks snidely.

Yup. He's nothing but a total jerk when he's around me. Twisting away from him, I check my phone. We haven't moved much.

Sam keeps flicking through channels.

I watch too. Well, kind of. Mainly I'm trying to understand his indifference. I'm betting his demanding girlfriend sucks all the energy for worrying out of him.

An hour passes with me checking my phone and glancing at the latest channel Sam has landed on. The bus alternates between a stop and a crawl, once in a while rolling forward suddenly in a spurt. As it nears five o'clock, we're a little less than an hour away. We could make it. Like minutes prior to seven.

Sam gets a call and within seconds, he's arguing again about trust.

Feeling as if I'm unintentionally eavesdropping on his dysfunctional relationship, I decide to get ready for the show. My suitcase is under the bus, and my backpack has a limited wardrobe, but there's not going to be enough time to unload the suitcases, which are behind the instruments, before showtime. I'll have to make do with what I've got.

In the bathroom, I drag on a pair of low-riding jeans and a Clash T-shirt emblazoned with the cover of *London Calling*, which I usually use for sleeping. The shirt is big, so I tie it at one corner, leaving a slice of my stomach showing, which I never do, even though Jill is constantly telling me to show off my abs. They're quite toned because I've been working out three times a week since senior year of high school. After sliding my flip-flops back on, I wash my face with as little water as possible and then apply some makeup. Lastly, I scrunch my hair and add gel. Without electricity, there's not much else I can do with it.

When I head out to the front room, the guys are still despondent about the traffic jam. Justin now sits on the couch across from

Gabe, whose sticks continue thudding on leather. Romeo's still on the phone. Since there's no sign of Sam, I'm guessing he's still watching TV in the back room.

I see mountains surrounding us when I look out the window.

I check my phone for the time and the distance. Ten after six and only twenty-two miles left.

"You should get ready," I announce to no one in particular.

Justin's expression is mocking. "Our clothes are underneath the bus."

"You don't have anything up here?"

Gabe hits his sticks together with a loud *thwap*. "No stage clothes."

"Well," I say, lifting my backpack to my shoulder, "maybe you'll have to go for the college student look tonight." I glance at my phone. "We should make it. We have a little over twenty miles left, and we're moving now." I look again at the traffic outside. It's not fast, but it's moving.

Romeo puts down his phone. "She's right. Get dressed."

"What about a shower?" Justin asks.

Turning toward the front window, Romeo says, "There's enough water for everyone to have just one. Pick before or after."

Frowning, Gabe says, "Definitely after playing the drums."

In the back room, I find Sam dozing, legs propped on the table, his hands folded across his lap. Seeing his face so tranquil startles me for a moment. With his long, dark lashes and his full, chiseled mouth, he's all male but somehow sweet.

Using my foot, I tap his foot resting on the table. His eyes flutter open, then his gaze turns hard as it focuses on me.

Sweet? Please. What was I thinking?

"You have about forty minutes to get ready. Forty-five minutes until you'll be onstage."

His eyebrows shoot up in a question.

I gesture to the pajama bottoms he's still wearing. "What I'm saying is, you might want to change."

I move to the corner where my stuff is piled, but stop just short of bending down when I sense his gaze on me. When I glance over my shoulder, his eyes are roaming my body.

My gaze turns pointed. "You need something?"

His eyes continue to travel over me slowly—too slowly. My arms itch to wrap around my body for cover because his deliberate gaze is starting a flutter in my stomach, butterfly wings gone crazy . . . I resist tugging my shirt down over the inch of skin showing above my belt and glare at him.

"Nice shirt," he says with a grin.

Though I know he's a Clash fan too, it's completely obvious that my shirt is not what he's checking out. "Thanks," I say, my tone laced with sarcasm.

His gaze sweeps over me again. "You've filled out since high school, huh?"

When he met me during my senior year, I was living on carrots and celery. My goal now is to eat reasonably and maintain a healthy weight, not to look as skinny as a teenage model. But he'd better not say I'm bigger or something. My body image issues from high school still linger, and they can creep up on me.

"What does that mean?"

He shrugs. "You've finally got an ass."

My jaw drops and I grab the remote from the tabletop to throw at him, but he's up and off the couch before I can toss it.

"A seriously hot ass," he says under his breath, then steps through the door.

Shocked, I drop the remote, which lands on the floor with a thud.

Chapter 5

I miss their first two songs because it takes forever for me to sign in and get the backstage pass. With a pass around my neck, I head down a hallway, passing locker rooms along the way—this arena is usually used for sporting events—until I end up behind the raised stage. The music and the volume of the crowd, along with palpable energy in the air, hit me as I come around one side of the stage. Security guards stand in a line, forming a wall in front of the stage. A few glance over their shoulders at my pass but maintain their impassive faces and crossed arms as I keep moving between them and the stage. The floor beyond the bouncers is packed, yet the seats beyond the floor aren't even half-filled—unfortunately for Luminescent Juliet, an unknown opening band is good inspiration for a beer run. Except for the diehards standing on the floor. They're camped out for the duration.

I glance up onstage, still amazed that all four band members were able to get their gear out of the bus and start performing within a half hour of our arrival. Dressed in the worn, baggy shorts, T-shirts, and tennis shoes that they wear to lounge on the bus instead of their usual rocker jeans and boots, they're definitely sporting the college look tonight, but they still look hot. As their song "Bleak Moon" pounds in my eardrums and rumbles in my chest, I take a closer look at each of them, starting with Romeo. He's at the corner of the stage, playing a solo. Justin is hanging out near Gabe and the drums. Sam is plucking his bass in the other corner. I walk the length of the front of the stage, between it and the bouncers, overwhelmed at my closeness to the band. I could reach out and touch Romeo's shoe. For several minutes, I'm caught up in the lights, the music, the roar of the crowd, and my proximity to the band. An excited giddiness rolls through my stomach as I'm immersed in the moment and the intensity of it all. I've never been this close to the action at a concert. What makes it even more amazing is that, in a small way, I'm part of it.

The guitar solo ends. Justin jumps to the center of the stage and starts singing. I grab my camera just in time to catch him in another jump. The song is energetic, with a hint of blues. Before I was asked to join the tour, I'd always avoided Luminescent Juliet's music, mainly because I didn't want to be reminded of Sam. It took some work, considering how popular their songs have been at our school for the past two years. Once I'd agreed to come, though, I bought their new album and made myself listen to it. I was a bit shocked by how good they sounded. How well they mixed punk, folk, and blues into a rock sound all their own. That talent had strengthened my resolve to come on tour.

Done with "Bleak Moon," they roll right into another song. I'm aware, after listening in on their last meeting on the bus, that they have thirty-five minutes to perform. It's smart that they opted to keep playing instead of switching out instruments and going acoustic.

As the rhythm builds, I catch a great photo of Gabe in a drum fill. Then I shoot a picture of Romeo standing before a gathering crowd, the fans lifting their hands to him. Justin raises the microphone stand above his head. The pose makes a unique photo from my angle below. After getting a bunch of good shots of everyone else, I turn my attention to Sam.

He bounces, sings the chorus, and points to the crowd when he's not plucking on his bass strings. He looks like he's having a blast, and I'm reminded of the happy-go-lucky Sam I used to know. The Sam who is apparently gone. I lift my camera and catch him winking at a girl in the front. Next I take a picture of him and Justin sharing a microphone as they sing the chorus. When he's done singing, he steps back and concentrates on playing his bass. The energy and playfulness he shows onstage come across as unconsciously sexy. I'm not sure if that's a new part of his performance, or if I was too obsessed with Seth or just too young and immature to notice it before.

They end their set with their biggest indie hit, "Inked My Heart." At the first notes, a murmur of excitement flows through the crowd on the floor. The song is popular enough that some of them must know it, but it also causes a hush because it starts in a slow, dreamy, melodic way that's distinctly different from the songs they've played so far. Justin sings the lyrics with real emotion and I can feel the crowd respond. I let my camera hang from my neck and reach for the notebook in my back pocket. Instead of taking pictures, I jot impressions. The crowd swaying in sync with the melody. The band under the dimmed lights, a haze of stage fog behind them. The perfection of the music and the clearness of Justin's voice. His sad, somber expression as he sings. The pure concentration Romeo and Sam are giving to their instruments. Gabe's visible restraint behind the drums. I tend to catch the details better in words when I'm in the moment. I want to use my initial impressions when I write the blog post later. The song ends and the crowd goes wild.

Though I've heard from the other band members that Justin can sometimes ramble behind the microphone, he wraps up perfectly this time. He simply leans forward and says, "Thank you."

The band clears the stage, and takes the energy hanging in the air with them.

As the lights come on, I tuck my notebook in a pocket and move to a roped-off area on the side of the floor where backstage ticket holders sit. Some guy comes by with a box strapped around his neck that's stocked with beer. Crazy thirsty after the exhilaration of the performance, I buy one and start sipping as I wait for the next band. While my main reason for coming was to get experience as a journalist, seeing rock bands for free—in the backstage area no less—is a huge, awesome-ass perk.

Griff, one of the bands on the tour, opens with a loud, rowdy song that gets the crowd going again. Their sound is more heavy alternative rock, whereas Brookfield, the last band to play and the one with the biggest name, is more folky. Style-wise, Luminescent Juliet is kind of between the two, and suddenly I realize why the tour manager wanted them even though they had recently hit the big time by rising up the indie charts. Of course, I'm a fan of both of the other bands, and many of their songs are on my playlists.

I'm swaying to the music when Justin appears at the entrance of the gated area. Spotting me in the back, he waves for me to come over. I silently laugh as the girls around me give me cold, envious looks, thinking I'm about to hook up with a super-hot lead singer. *Not.* Once I get to him, he starts striding down the long hall.

"Come on. Romeo sent me to get you. We're in a suite on the top floor."

Dang. I almost stop and turn around. I was enjoying the concert, the close proximity to the stage, yet I'm here to chronicle Luminescent Juliet and do a job. So I force myself to follow Justin to the elevator. A security guard simply nods to us as we go inside.

On the top floor, we head down another hall and enter a dimly lit room full of people lounging on couches and sitting at long tables. Gabe and Sam sit with a bunch of girls in one corner. Justin points to a counter with buffet trays and leans close when he speaks so I can hear him over the music of the concert, which is loud even up here.

"Grab something to eat, then come watch the show." He gestures across the roomful of people to rows of seats in front of a glass wall. Beyond the glass, a shadowy sea of people's heads provides a stark contrast to the brightly lit stage at the bottom of the arena. He also points out the door leading to a private bathroom in the back of the room.

I slowly realize that we're in one of the glassed-in suites at the top of the arena.

Justin heads to an empty seat next to Romeo while I reach for a plate. As the scent of meatballs, cheese-filled potato skins, and chicken wings hits my nose, my stomach grumbles. I'd been so entranced by the music, I forgot I hadn't eaten a thing since my peanut butter sandwich at lunch. I take a little something from each tray, then fill the rest of my plate with raw veggies. Dieting like a madwoman on and off for almost two years sucked. I now concentrate on being healthy in order to stay in size six jeans instead of obsessing over calorie counts.

Once my plate is full, I notice the only spot open is at Sam's table. I'm hit by a wave of anxiety. Irritated by my own reaction, I move toward the empty seat anyway. I need to be fearless when it comes to Sam, for my own mental health. Otherwise, it feels like I'm not over the past, and I am, dammit.

I sit at the far end of the table. One of the girls scans me dismissively and Sam smiles coldly at me. "How'd we do?"

He knows they're good, and I'm not about to lie just because we don't like each other. "Great. If I didn't know, I would have never guessed you're a college band."

His cold smile turns into a sneer. "Just a college band, huh?"

My mouth twists. I grumble, "Quit, Sam. I didn't mean it like that. Everything I say to you isn't calculated to come out bitchy."

We stare at each other, firing eyeball missiles, and a hush comes over the table.

Out of the corner of my vision, I notice Gabe watching us.

Sam must notice too, because he leans back. "Touchy," he says, then turns to the girl on his right. He twists her long hair, gives it a slight tug, and whispers something in her ear that elicits a loud laugh. Sam grins cockily.

I roll my eyes and reach for a chicken wing. Luckily, the band performing beyond the glass gives me something to look at, so it's easy to ignore *him*.

After I finish eating, I sip a bottle of beer until I realize this is a great time to grab my camera and take pictures covertly. I snap a few of Justin and Romeo concentrating on the concert. Gabe and Sam never glance up as I capture them sitting with a tableful of chicks. I'm careful not to get the girls' faces, which isn't easy since two of them are sitting on Gabe's lap. Unless I get them to sign waivers since they're not in the crowd, it could be a problem to post their photos, so it's best to avoid the issue. Gabe is clearly having fun. So much for the blonde "girlfriend" wearing the Daisy Dukes on the day we left town. Sam also looks relaxed. His mood appears so flirty and light, it's almost hard to believe he's the same guy who is usually such a dick to me. Seeing him act so pleasant, talking and laughing with three women, I'm suddenly pissed that he can't let the past go. He is clearly determined to be a jerkwad to me.

The members of Griff come in, and I notice that the stage is being changed over. I put down my camera and go lean against the far wall, watching the band members as they start to unwind.

Surprisingly, the members of Griff don't seem much different than Gabe or Sam. They stand around drinking beer and talking. Though they're sweaty and flushed, girls hang on them. A bottle of whiskey makes a round. I'm kind of let down. I'm not sure what I was expecting. Maybe something more wild and crazy? Other than the plethora of black clothes and rocker hair, this suite resembles a fraternity party. A boring one at that.

I pick up the camera again and take some more pictures, but when Sam and the girl move to a couch, irritation boils inside of me. I let my camera hang from my neck and get a second bottled beer. Leaning against a chair behind Romeo and Justin, I gulp half of it down. Sam was right. This isn't going to be an easy six weeks.

I concentrate on watching Brookfield, the best-known band on the tour, and by the time a guy leans on the chair next to mine, my anger is pretty much under control.

"Hello there," he says. His sultry tone is impossible to miss.

"Hi," I say slowly, trying to place him because he looks familiar.

"Couldn't help but notice you over here all alone." His smile is warm yet somehow sly.

The black jeans and buttoned-up shirt have me guessing he is from Griff. I search his long face with its slightly crooked nose. He has that thin, sexy rocker look that dismisses good-looking. Finally, I put the pieces together and recognize his black, wild hair. He's the guitarist for Griff.

He brushes a silver-ringed finger on my arm. "You the shy type?"

I lightly tap the camera around my neck. "No. I'm the at-work type."

His head tilts in a question.

"I'm with Luminescent Juliet. Kind of their personal promoter."

"Really?" His dark eyes travel the length of me, pausing at the slice of naked midriff. He inches closer. The tips of his black boots brush my flip-flops. "You're going to be with us the whole tour, kitten?"

Leaning away from him *and* the kitten reference, I nod. Like the others in Griff, he appears to be in his late twenties, but his pervy comment makes him sound older. Even too old to be in Brookfield. Those guys are actually in their late thirties.

He takes a long draw from his bottled beer, then frowns. "You with one of them?"

I shake my head. "I have a boyfriend at home."

His thin lips curl into a satisfied smile. "At home, huh?"

"Yeah, we've been together for almost a year," I say, exaggerating my relationship with Bryce, hoping this guy will back off.

"Ah, but he's not here." He puts out a hand. "Name's Rick. Guitarist of Griff."

His egotistical tone implies my panties should drop now that he has announced who he is, but I keep a straight face. "Yeah, I saw the concert," I say, shaking his hand. "I'm Peyton. Your set was great but I should get going. Long day of travel tomorrow, you know?" I step back, unexpectedly longing for the couch at the back of the bus, but he doesn't release my hand.

He tugs on it. "Where you going? It's early, not yet midnight, Peyton." His voice purrs over my name.

"Lots of work to do tomorrow," I say, trying to pull my hand from his grip. He's about to find out that this kitten sometimes has claws.

He tugs me closer. "How about one more beer?"

"I—"

"What's going on, Peyton?" Sam asks, suddenly appearing next to us.

Rick releases my hand and stares at Sam with narrowed eyes. Sam stares back with a tight jaw.

Testosterone hangs in the air between them. I force a relaxed expression. "Nothing much, just heading back to the bus."

Sam tilts his head toward the exit. "Let me walk you there." He is not asking. He is commanding me. Yet my desire to get away from Rick overrides the irritation from Sam giving me orders.

"All right," I say, taking in Rick's frown. "Nice meeting you. See you around."

Watching me with a gleam in his gaze, he nods, lifting his beer as a good-bye.

In the hallway, Sam asks in a furious tone, "Was that jerk hitting on you?"

Not wanting to start anything, I shrug. "He just wanted to have a beer with me."

"Yeah, that's all he wanted," Sam says as we step onto the elevator. He pulls the striped beanie out of his back pocket and yanks it on.

I cross my arms in front of me and lean against the back wall. "I can take care of myself, Sam."

His hand grips the elevator rail. "Did you want to have a beer with him? Should I walk you back up?"

Ah, how quickly my savior returns to being a dick. *I will not lose my temper. I will not lose my temper. I. Will. Not. Lose. My. Temper.* "Yeah, you ruined everything, couldn't you tell I was playing hard to get?"

I glare at him as the elevator doors open. "He's so famous, I'd do anything to sleep with him, even forget about my boyfriend." I breeze past him into the hall.

"You do have a past with the whole band thing," he says, catching up to me.

Keeping calm. "Sure, I dated a singer. I liked him." Actually, I thought the sun rose and set on his stupid ass, and believed I was in love. Teenagers are dumb. "There's a bit of difference."

We step out into the cool night. Apparently, high altitudes allow for hot days that turn chilly after sunset, and I shiver as we talk under the glow of the lights in the parking lot. With Sam following a few steps behind, I march past the other bands' buses—they each have two—then the roadies' buses. Of course, because we arrived so late, our bus is the last in the long line.

"So, what about me?" Sam asks.

I keep moving, don't turn around to look at him. "What about you?"

"Why did you sleep with me?"

I nearly trip as my body seizes up from a mix of anger and embarrassment, but I force myself to keep my cool. I will not let Sam get to me.

"I told you never to bring that up again. It was a mistake. We both know it." I reach for the little flap of a door handle. "Alcohol and heartbreak were to blame." *Fuck!* The handle doesn't move, which means the bus is locked. I give the door a quick rap with my knuckles.

Sam grabs my hand to stop my knocking and presses both of our hands against the fiberglass door as he leans forward, his body shadowing mine, so close I can feel his warmth. Although he's behind me, I catch the scent of whiskey. "So you used me?" he says harshly. His mouth is inches from my ear.

"What are you talking about?" My voice breaks on the last word. I'm nervous about his closeness.

"You and Seth broke up, then you used me to get over him."

"What?" I gasp and half turn, forcing him to step back a little. "No. It just happened. You know that. Or were you that wasted?"

He releases my hand and moves away. "I know you never considered me as anything more than a friend before that."

I rap on the door again, and say over my shoulder, "You still can't be pissed at me about that night."

"Pissed? No. Aware of what kind of person you are, yes."

"And what kind of person am I?" I ask, my teeth clenched.

"Self-centered. Bitchy. Stuck up." His tone is laced with spite.

"Because you think I used you?" I bark, turning to face him. "You are a hypocrite. We go to the same college, asshole. How many coeds have you been with? Even *I* know some of the girls you've slept with." My tone is spiteful too when I add, "Or shall we say *used*?"

He glares down at me, his lips tight. "They know what they're getting into."

"And you knew how I felt about Seth!" I roar, and start pounding on the door.

At last, the lock rattles from the inside and the door opens. Gary is already going back up the stairs as I step up into the bus. From the bit of interaction I've had with him, it has become apparent that he doesn't consider socializing part of his job.

I turn around. "Good night, Sam," I say snottily. Then I shut the door in his face.

Chapter 6

The sound of Gary's faint snores fills the bus as he sleeps on one of the couches in the front room. Meanwhile, even though I set up my bed, brushed my teeth, and took a very quick shower, I can't fall asleep. Since Sam opened his stupid mouth, my mind can't stop straying to the past.

To Seth. That name was once elation and pain wrapped in one. I rarely let myself think of him. When I do, I remind myself that everyone has growing pains and difficult passages in life. That's what Seth was for me, and remembering that fact helps me deal with the memories. He was the first boy who ever chased me, my second kiss—my first had been a sloppy affair after a freshman homecoming dance—and my first boyfriend. Though we went to different high schools, we spent hours texting and talking on the phone. I lived for Saturdays then. Thought about nothing but being with him.

I was euphoric that he wanted me. He was the lead singer of the Bottle Rockets, the popular band that played at all the parties that summer and autumn, and so girls hit on him all the time. When he'd first declared his love, I lived in a haze of teenage hormonal love for months. It was a change to be adored. At the start of high school, I'd been chubby, and the stigma had stayed. No boy in my school had ever shown any interest in me. Seth, on the other hand, treated me like a prize. Bought me flowers. Took me to dinner twice, and serenaded me once. Showed me how sensual kissing could be while being patient with me.

Then, after three months of bliss, everything changed. He became more persistent about sex. It didn't feel right—I was still too self-conscious about my body—and I became more resistant. Then our conversations turned difficult. He started accusing me of talking behind his back, mocking him to our friends because he couldn't get me to sleep with him. He even insinuated I was cheating on him, his tone so angry that it set my heart trembling. Still in love, I'd beg forgiveness even though his attacks were based on nothing. Round and round the cycle went for two months. Until the night the whole thing exploded and we broke up, and my choosing Sam's shoulder to cry on turned out to be the final nail in the coffin, and the intro to six months of rumors and hurt.

I've always refused to think of that night. At first it was connected to my desire to bury the Seth breakup, because thinking about it hurt too much. Then, as I started putting the painful episode in the past, it seemed stupid to dredge it up and try to process the whole thing. But now it's almost four years later and I can't sleep because Sam's accusation stings so badly. Did I use him? No. We were both drunk. We both let things go too far. And that's it.

At least, I always believed so.

Clutching the blanket wrapped around me, I roll over miserably.

Maybe it's time to face that night, reconsider it now that I'm older, and try to truly move the fuck on. I close my eyes and, for once, don't block the memories. Instead, I allow my mind to dredge up every painful detail.

Jill was in the farmhouse, partying, and I was outside in the cold winter night, crying. I walked to her parked car, the gravel of the driveway

crunching under my feet, then leaned against the side door and sobbed.
The smell of cow patties hung in the cool air. The darkness and silence
of the winter night was intensified by the lights and laughter coming
from inside the house. The full, shining moon created eerie shadows in
the apple orchard along one side of the driveway.

Seth was making me crazy. All week, he'd been texting me, calling
me, telling me how he couldn't wait for the weekend, and couldn't wait
to see me, yet within the first hour of my arrival at the party, he'd started
slinging his accusations until we were in a full-blown shouting match in
the kitchen. It had started with him saying I was a bitch who was hold-
ing out on him. At first, I'd tried to reason. But he'd kept it up, heaping
on more abuse, not caring that everyone at the party could hear. Finally,
something snapped. Instead of taking my usual approach, denying every-
thing and dissolving into hopeless tears, anger rose up in me.

"Seth," I'd said, "who the hell do you think I'm cheating on you
with?"

"Half of the guys at your high school, you slut!" he'd screamed, his
face twisted in an ugly sneer.

Something had gone dead in me then. I'd looked him in the eye.
"It's over, Seth," I'd said. Then I'd run outside before I burst into tears.

I silently pleaded with the universe to send Jill outside. When Seth
had started his verbal attack, she'd had been in the living room. Was
it possible she hadn't heard? Then I realized that she might have gone
upstairs, hooking up with the guy from college she'd been watching for
months. If that was the case, I was going to be out there forever.

A car pulled up and parked at the end of the long line. I stooped
down, hoping the newcomers wouldn't spot me. One person's footsteps
came closer, crunching across the gravel. When it was clear the lone per-
son was going to walk right past and spot me either way, I straightened
up, tugged out my keys, and pretended I was finding the right key to
open the door.

"Peyton?" a male voice asked.

Crap. I let go of the handle.

"Just getting some air," I said, trying to steady my voice and hide that I'd been crying.

"It's a bit cold to be getting air."

In seconds, Sam stood in front of me. A fifth of something dangled from one hand, a book from the other. Parties sometimes bored Sam, so he always brought something to read. "You and Seth fighting again?"

I nodded and sighed, then looked at the ground.

He stepped closer. "You okay?"

"I'm all right," I said tightly, still refusing to lift my head.

He stepped closer. "Hey, you want me to get Jill for you?"

"No." Jill's last three weekends had been ruined by Seth and me fighting. Each time, she'd left the party with me, then listened to me cry all night. If she was hooking up with college boy, whom she'd been flirting with for weeks, I wasn't going to ruin it.

"Well, you can't sit out here. It's too cold. Come on, I'll walk you in."

"Thanks, but no," I said. Sam was always helping me too, after these stupid fights. Seth made me cry. Sam helped me laugh. *"I'm not going in there. We fought in front of everyone. Broke up in front of everyone."*

He sighed. "Okay, come on. We can hang in the barn." Though it was dark outside, he somehow read the confusion on my face. He laughed. *"No worries. We won't be hanging with the cows. There's a small office in the back with a space heater."*

I shook my head. "Um, aren't you supposed to play tonight?" People flocked to every party the Bottle Rockets played at. I knew that as soon as they started the first song—and usually they played only three or four—the house would be packed wall-to-wall. All the band members got some attention, but it always seemed to me that more than half of the girls were in love with Seth.

"*Midnight. Seth wants a big crowd, but everything's set up in the basement since Wes's kit is already there.*" *He nodded toward the barn.* "*Come on.*"

I reluctantly followed him past the other cars and across the drive-way to the barn.

"*You'll see,*" *Sam said over his shoulder, leading the way.* "*The office really isn't that bad for being in a barn. Wes's dad even sleeps back here sometimes when a cow is sick or whatever.*"

We went in a side door and down a dark hallway, where the scent of cows got stronger with each step. Sam stepped inside a dark room at the end of the hall and tugged on a chain hanging from the ceiling, and the space was then encased in a soft glow. There was a desk, shelves behind it filled with books, an old couch covered with afghans, and a space heater that Sam flicked on before shutting the door and turning to me.

At the sight of my tears in the light, he shook his head. "*Seth's an asshole.*"

Seeing the pity in his light blue eyes sent more tears falling down my cheeks. He set the fifth on the desk, then pulled me onto the couch and into his arms as usual. I was always crying on Sam's shoulder. It had become so constant, just the feel of him was comforting. After letting me cry against his coat for a few minutes, he asked, "*What was it this time?*"

"*Same old stuff,*" I mumbled into his coat. "*I'm a cheating, rumor-spreading bitch.*"

He sighed into my hair. "*I'm not sure where he gets this shit, but my blind brother needs his ass kicked.*"

My fingers curled around the lapel of his jacket. "*I don't want to talk about him.*"

"*All right.*"

I glanced around the room. "Thanks for showing me this place. I was freezing my ass off outside. But you don't have to stay in here with me."

"Maybe I want to stay in here with you."

A cow's muted moo filled the silence until Sam said, "'She Don't Use Jelly' by the Flaming Lips."

A sad giggle escaped me. I could always expect a laugh with Sam around. "'Satan Gave Me a Taco.' Beck."

He smirked down at me. The first few times we met, Sam and I had tried to one-up each other on musical knowledge, but we soon became convinced neither of us knew more than the other. Then Sam started this game of trying to match songs. No one else seemed to get it but us.

I sat up a little but Sam's arm stayed around my shoulders. "Are we supposed to be in here?"

"Wesley doesn't give a shit, and his parents are in Florida for the winter. He turned eighteen this year, so they pay him to keep up the farm for a few months."

"Huh, I can't imagine my parents taking off for the winter, and I've been eighteen since September." I glanced at the fifth sitting on the desk. To avoid extra calories, I normally only allowed myself two drinks at any party—and I'd already had those inside—yet something about the fight with Seth made me want to ignore my usual limits. "Can I have a drink?"

"It's tequila."

I shrugged.

"I brought it to pass around, but sure, let's have our own party." Sam leaned over me and grabbed the bottle. The sensation of his body sliding across mine made my breath hitch for a second, which seemed strange. After shucking our coats, we passed the bottle back and forth— the first couple of sips were tough to hold down—and talked music, laughing as we argued about whose taste in bands was better. Flipping

pages, he read some lines from the book he'd brought with him, which was called High Fidelity *and set in London. From what I was hearing, the novel sounded like a mix of music and heartache. I didn't get all the sarcastic humor, but Sam's lame British accent made me laugh as hard as the quotes. I felt strangely calm and free, until half the fifth was gone and the conversation led back to the Bottle Rockets and Seth.*

"You guys going to keep the band going at Michigan?" I asked, my voice breaking at "guys" because it included Seth.

Sam lifted my chin with a finger. "Hey, Peyton. He'll come around. He always does."

I shook my head. "I can't do it anymore," I said in a raw whisper.

"Do you want to do it anymore?" Sam whispered back.

"No. No, I don't," I said, truly believing it in that buzzed moment.

The whispering somehow made the moment intimate, created a connection that wasn't there or made me aware of one that I'd previously ignored. My breath hitched again.

Sam leaned closer, his eyes searching mine. "Seth and you are truly over?"

"Yeah, I think so," I said softly, feeling caught in Sam's gaze. "I told him so."

Before I realized what was happening, his arms were around me, and his lips were on mine. More startling than his kiss was my reaction to it. The soft demanding pulse of his mouth set me on fire. His slow searching tongue was a driving burn that made me want to explore. I locked my hands behind his neck and kissed him back. The kiss was long and hot and air draining, and drew me into a cocoon of lust.

Warm and languid, I floated through sensations that I hoped would never stop. Soft lips gliding across the contours of my neck. Calloused fingers easing under my shirt and caressing my waist, gliding up to my ribs. The silky whisper of a tongue following the curve of my ear. Palms, so searing that I felt their heat through the silk of my bra, cupping my breasts. A warm, wet mouth trailing across my cheek.

Breathless, yearning for more, I felt free of the inhibition and apprehension that had so often marred my intimacy with Seth. Though I'd lost weight, I was still extremely conscious of my body. Jill had always told me that any man was lucky to be with me, no matter what my size, but I always worried about not being good or beautiful enough for him. In theory, I knew Jill was right, but I could just never relax enough to let things go further. Yet everything about being with Sam on the couch felt so fluid and natural that self-consciousness about my figure was the last thing on my mind.

Unable to stop myself, I turned my head and caught that mouth with mine, aching to lose myself in the sensations Sam was creating.

After the heated meeting of our mouths, I lay back, pulling him closer. My need turned frantic with his weight on me. I clutched his arms. He slid his hands down to my hips. We each tugged the other closer. As our tongues knotted together, his erection pressed between my spread legs, and I just about incinerated at the feel of him against me.

I whimpered into his mouth.

He pulled away slightly, propping himself up on one arm and looking down at me. He was raised above me, his harsh breath fanning and warming my skin.

Suspended in a haze of lust that I didn't know was possible, I watched him with heavy-lidded eyes. I refused to contemplate the confusion in his gaze. Instead, I wrapped a leg around him and reached my hand to the back of his neck, then yanked him down to me.

He came down with a groan, covering my lips with his. Mouths locked together, we rocked against each other. We both panted at the delicious friction. Rocked. Panted. Rocked. Groaned. The mounting desire had us mindlessly tugging and hauling down each other's jeans and underwear until there was nothing between us but the hard feel of him against my skin.

I felt him press into me. Just a bit.

"Peyton?" he panted, rising up on his elbows.

My body didn't want his question. It didn't want any distractions from the lustful cocoon we had weaved. It wanted to forge ahead with a fierceness I didn't know was possible. Letting need take over, I lifted my hips and brought him farther into me.

We both gasped. We both trembled. We both moved closer.

There was a sharp burn, but even that didn't deter me from wrapping my legs around him and sinking him fully in.

Sam drew his head back, the muscles of his neck straining. I quivered at the beautiful masculine sight above me as heat burned below. Then his head dropped, his mouth covered mine, and he started moving.

And the cocoon spun shut. His mouth, his hands holding my jaw, his moans, his movement inside me, left me mindless. We arched and grasped and clutched each other, senseless as the cocoon burst open, and pleasure like a newly born butterfly soaring in the bright sunshine floated through me. He fell against me, his face on my chest, his body warm and heavy on mine.

As the moments ticked past, reality slowly began to set in. What the hell did you just do, Peyton? *Before I could collect my thoughts, before I could comprehend what had happened, the door flew open.*

Seth stood there, tall and lean. His long hair practically hid his eyes as they traveled the length of our bodies sprawled on the couch. His expression conveyed a look of hurt as his mouth twisted into a snarl. "I knew it. I knew you were just some dumb slut holding out on me."

"Seth . . ." Sam said in a warning tone as he tugged the afghan under us.

Every trace of lust seeped out of me, and I felt instantly, dreadfully sober. Sam's weight on me was an anvil of regret. Tugging the blanket around me, he pulled himself up, yet regret still pressed heavily on my chest. "Leave her alone," Sam said, his tone hostile, dragging up his pants.

"Seriously?" Seth shouted. "What the fuck? How can you defend the bitch?" He spun around and flew out the door, kicking it with a combat boot as he left.

Shame and guilt twisted inside me as the door banged shut. His look of hurt hammered regret through me. I'd been angry with Seth, but I'd never, ever wanted to hurt him.

"Seth!" I yelled, pushing Sam away. "Wait! This was a mistake! A crazy mistake!" I jerked my pants up, grabbed my coat, and ran after him. Outside, I yelled his name again, but he was already entering the house.

Tears started falling as I rushed across the wide driveway of gravel and burst into the house. I didn't care about being embarrassed by tears. I had to talk to Seth, had to explain. More people had arrived. I was shoving my way through the crowd in the kitchen when the music was cut off and I heard vicious shouting that included the words "slut," "bitch," "fuck you," and "asshole." By the time I muscled my way into the living room, Jill and Seth were standing a few feet apart, glaring at each other.

Seth flicked his head toward me. "Ask the cunt who she just fucked five minutes ago."

"You're nuts!" Jill yelled, turning toward me. "Tell this asswad he's out of his mind!"

People moved away from me, and it was as if I were standing on an island instead of at the edge of the living room. When I saw Seth's cold, angry face, my bottom lip started to quiver.

Jill's angry expression softened as worry lined her face. "Peyton?"

Everyone's eyes were now on me.

"*She's been fucking my brother,*" *Seth snarled, crossing his arms over his black T-shirt. "And I'm betting it's been going on behind my back the whole time. They're always together. Constantly hiding and fucking in corners.*"

I violently shook my head as more tears escaped. "No. It was never like that."

His upper lip curled at me. "Screw off, Peyton. You're a lying cum-sucking slut."

"*Shut your sick mouth!*" *Jill shouted in his face, and several people gasped. She marched over to me. Putting an arm around my shoulders, she said, "Let's go. The shit is getting too deep in here."*

The crowd parted like we were on script in some stupid teenage movie.

Jill hauled me toward the kitchen, yet I couldn't help glancing over my shoulder at Seth.

Standing with his arms still crossed, Seth smiled cruelly at me. "Ever heard the saying, Don't look back? Get the fuck out of here!"

"*Come on,*" *Jill growled near my ear. "Before I turn around and bitch-slap his face."*

Though I wanted to plead with him, I allowed Jill to lead me out of the house. Sam stood outside the door. His gaze tore from the bright full moon and narrowed as he watched us pass.

"*What the hell are you looking at?*" *Jill snapped.*

"*Nothing,*" *he said with an air of indifference while his eyes burned into me. He then turned and walked into the house.*

The sound of one of the guys going into the bus bathroom pulls me back into the present. My entire body is shivering and I pull the blankets up. What in the world made me think I'd processed that night and gotten over it? I still feel awful that I cheated on Seth, with his brother no less, but I wasn't playing the temptress.

I wasn't using Sam. I was hardly aware of what I was doing. We both played a part. I cringe a little when I think how I dismissed him right after—I now realize that probably came across as totally bitchy—but did he actually expect something else? Why would he? We were just friends.

At least that's what I've always thought.

Chapter 7

The next day, I focus on writing and don't stray from the back of the bus. I can't look Sam in the face after recalling the passion we shared—when I hear his voice, a rush of heat warms my cheeks. I'm stuck in a state between embarrassment and awe. I'm not sure how I kept that memory buried so long; yet bringing it back up doesn't change anything, especially the rumors that followed me for the rest of senior year, the months of heartache over Seth, and the overwhelming desire to avoid Sam once I realized we shared a college campus. Desperate to stop thinking about the whole thing, I try to dismiss it from my mind.

I was distraught.

I did not use Sam.

Letting out a sigh, I pull myself together. I change some wording to make the first post I'm finalizing sound more upbeat, weeding out the sad tone that Romeo didn't like. I wrote about the band's leaving like I saw it. However, Romeo wants me to portray their departure as mainly filled with excitement for the tour. After I change the post, I upload it and then post some pictures from the concert to Facebook and Twitter.

I'm finishing everything when we pull up in front of the hotel in Austin, Texas. Half of the long drive was while we slept, but even half a day on a bus was too much. The bus space felt huge yesterday, but after being in it for two days straight, it has gotten smaller by the hour. I've never been so excited about the prospect of a shower in my life. After the unsatisfying experience of rinsing off in the shower for no more than two minutes last night, standing under a steady stream of hot water sounds awesome.

After check-in, my excitement about the shower dims when it becomes apparent that my rollaway is going in Sam and Justin's room—apparently Justin and Gabe don't get along, and Romeo wants a break from Justin, his roommate at school. Not sure how it was decided, but unless I want to bring up That Which Shall Not Be Spoken, I'm stuck in a room with Sam the Asshat. Great. Along with the fact he's always an asshat, I'm now living with my freshly recovered and incredibly hot memories of sex with him. Awkward? Yes. And then some.

Of course, the two more famous bands on the tour, Griff and Brookfield, get suites for each of their members.

As Justin, Sam, and I take the elevator up and head down the hall to our room, we're all quiet. It's strange how traveling wears a person out. We've hardly stepped into our standard-sized double when Justin heads for the shower. Double great. I'm rooming with asshat *and* selfish. We have to be at a local radio station's party for the tour in less than thirty minutes. I bite back the urge to yell after him, "Hey, jackass, girls take longer to get ready!"

Instead, I unzip my suitcase to search for an outfit. I'm concentrating so hard on trying to find something clean that I almost jump when Sam says quietly, "I'm sorry about last night, Peyton."

My suitcase, along with my jaw, almost falls to the floor as I turn around. I push down the intimate memories that have been trying to bubble up all day. The slob is still wearing flannel pajama bottoms and a tank top. I meet his light blue eyes. A rush of heat sizzles through me before I lock down the thoughts and get myself under control.

I draw in a short breath. "Um, okay. Thanks for apologizing."

Sam plops on the end of a bed and tosses the book in his hand onto the nightstand. "It's—well, between the alcohol and the . . . I got pissed for no reason." He runs a hand through his dark curls. "I don't know why I brought up our past. I'll try to stop being a jerk, okay?"

I want to chastise him, and question what he was going to add after "alcohol," but his offer is too good to turn down. And maybe it's enough to help us move on past that crazy night. "I would appreciate the effort," I say in the lightest tone I can muster.

"It's not really you." He sighs. "It's more me. I just—just have a lot of shit to deal with."

Like the night at my apartment, I'm getting the sense there's something I'm missing. Yet once again I'm clueless. Staring at his striking profile, I push my hands into the back pockets of my shorts and rock on my cheap flip-flops. "Is it your girlfriend? The one who calls you all the time?"

"Huh?" His eyes crinkle in the corners as he looks up at me in confusion. "What are you talking about?"

A blush flushes my cheeks. "The calls you got during breakfast and when watching TV. I—I wasn't trying to listen. You were just so loud."

He stares at me in confusion, then laughs sadly. "Yeah, my crazy girlfriend. She drives me nuts."

Feeling lucky that I have Bryce, I say, "That's too bad."

He sighs. "Yeah, it sucks sometimes."

Justin comes out of the bathroom dressed in only boxers. He's not my type, but fan girls would be swooning right now at his wet hair and perfect, tattooed pecs. The intricate black designs remind me of his girlfriend, Allie. He told me she owns a tattoo parlor back home and that's where they met. I wonder how much of his tribal body art was done by her.

"Hey, bitch," Sam says to Justin, leaning back with his palms on the bed. "Don't be a gentleman and let the lady go first or anything."

Justin looks at me, surprised. "Shit, Peyton. I'm sorry. It's usually just me and dickhead here," he says, jerking his chin in Sam's direction.

"It's okay," I say politely.

Sam flips him off, then falls back on the bed. "I'll be the gentleman. Shower's all yours, Peyton."

"Thanks," I say as Justin whips a pillow at Sam's head.

Of course, Sam and I are late getting to the limos. Gabe comes out the hotel doors the moment we're about to leave, so the three of us share the last limo. Gabe and I sit on either end of the backseat, my camera case between us, and Sam sprawls across the opposite seat. They're both dressed as rockers in black jeans, shirts half buttoned with tanks underneath, and boots. I feel lucky since I imagine the other limos must have been stuffed full of rockers. I'm in capris and a sequined tank top, maybe a little beachy for the occasion but the best I could pull off.

As soon as we're on the road, Sam reaches for the glass container on the bar next to him. Lifting it, he says, "Gabe?"

"Yeah, make that shit a double," Gabe says, watching the passing scenery.

"Peyton?" Sam asks, opening the ice chest.

My nose wrinkles at the amber liquid. "Ah, straight liquor? No."

He removes a beer from the ice and holds it up in a question.

I nod and he hands it to me. After opening the beer, I sip at it and, like Gabe, watch the scenery fly by as night begins to fall. Austin is brown and barren compared to the lush green of Michigan. I take in the faded yellow grass and sun-bleached houses as the sound of clinking ice echoes in the limo.

We turn a sharp corner and I slide toward Gabe. With my chest pressed against his arm and my camera case digging into my stomach, I quickly push away and mumble, "Excuse me."

As I scoot back to my side of the leather seat, Sam stares at Gabe with narrowed, angry eyes. Gabe laughs. Sam hits the button to lower the glass partition between us and the driver.

"Watch the fuck how you're driving," Sam says, then hits the button to send the partition up again. He takes a swig of whiskey then says lazily, staring at me, "'Sunday Bloody Sunday.' U2."

Startled, I can only return his stare as memories of the game fill my head. His expression is calm and solemn, even patient. After dipping a toe into the past last night, and being overwhelmed by the memory of our passion, I suddenly flash on our moments of friendship—the extensive conversations about music and lyrics, long hours spent playing our game.

In burying that night, did I submerge everything that happened between us? How much is my brain capable of almost erasing? As our gazes stay locked, I'm starting to wonder.

"You high again?" Gabe asks.

Sam shakes his head. "Well?" he says, looking at me. He pours another glass of whiskey from the glass container, this time for Gabe.

I blink at him. This comment, I'm aware, is an offering of peace even more potent than his sincere apology. I force myself to link the song to another while he stares at me expectantly. "'Zombie.' Cranberries."

His full lips form a slow, authentic grin.

I'm caught in the beauty of that grin until Gabe's voice disrupts the moment. "Cranberries? You have to be joking!" He leans forward and snatches the glass of whiskey and ice from Sam. "Something from Coldplay would be closer to U2 than the pussy Cranberries."

Still grinning, Sam raises his glass to me. "'Zombie' is a perfect match."

Gabe's brows lower. "How?"

Sam tilts his head toward me, taking a long, slow drink of whiskey.

I consider how to explain our long-forgotten little game. "The match is about the feel and meaning of the song. It's more complicated than just choosing two bands that sound alike. Both songs are angry about war."

Gabe still looks confused. "Give me another one."

"All right." Sam lowers his drink to one knee as his fingers drum on his other knee. "'Rush.' Big Audio Dynamite."

"That's too easy," I say.

"Huh," Gabe says, swirling the ice in his drink by rotating the glass. "Nothing goes with that weird shit."

I take a sip of beer and wait, but when Gabe continues to appear lost, I say, "'Story of My Life.' Social Distortion."

Sam grins again. "Perfect."

Gabe's glance at me is cynical. "What are you, a fucking walking music library?"

A laugh escapes me. "Kind of. I've been obsessed with music since my grandpa, who worked at punk clubs in Detroit in the seventies, gave me his record player and albums when I was twelve. Overnight I went from a huge fan of boy bands like the Backstreet Boys to liking the Clash, the Ramones, Devo, the Dead Kennedys . . . anything hardcore punk or rock from about the seventies and after."

"I think music sounds like shit on old-fashioned records," Gabe says, still swirling the ice in his glass. "At least on the ones I've heard."

I shake my head. "Not at all. There's something so raw about old vinyl. All the fast punk stuff sounds better."

"What about your dad?" Sam asks.

"What *about* my dad?" I ask back.

"Why didn't your grandpa give his music to him?"

I smile at the thought. "My dad is pure country. Hank Williams. Johnny Cash. He wouldn't have listened to the albums. But me . . . Well, my grandpa made up his mind to pass down his taste in music. When my grandma died, he moved in with us, and the music I was playing in my bedroom drove him nuts. Incredibly irritated, he started playing his old favorites, hoping to change my tastes. And he did," I add, suddenly wishing I were back in Michigan and visiting my family.

I love them all, but my grandfather and I have had a special connection. I know he wouldn't love me any less if I'd continued with my boy band obsession. He's not a music snob. He believes whatever music touches you is fine, as long as *he* doesn't have to hear it.

Sam laughs, pulling me back from my thoughts. "Just what every twelve-year-old should be listening to."

"What?" I ask.

"'Too Drunk to Fuck' by the Dead Kennedys."

I shrug and smile. "The language may have been part of the allure."

Sam smiles back at me. "Exactly what I thought."

The limo slows along the side of a huge building. A huge crowd waits in front of it to get inside. As we pull into the back lot, to an area that is fenced off with orange construction mesh, I set my half-full beer in a cup holder and haul the camera over my head as

Sam and Gabe drain their glasses. The driver opens the door and we emerge to see a girl in the shortest shorts in the world—paired with the highest heels—waiting next to a rusted metal door.

She glances over the clipboard in her hand as we step closer. "The last two members of Luminescent Juliet, the indie band?" Her sultry black-lined eyes roam over Sam and Gabe. When Gabe nods, she looks to me. "And you are?"

"She's our promoter," Sam says levelly.

"Oh," she says with a slight frown. "I didn't know indie bands had *those*. Well, I'm Kayla from WZIK Rock." She holds her hand out in a dainty manner. Both Sam and Gabe stare at the hand like it's a foreign object. The indie comment may have hit a few nerves.

Holding in an offensive giggle, I shake her hand and introduce myself and the guys.

She lets out a small huff. "Okay, follow me. We're going in the back."

Sam and Gabe give each other a look, then follow Kayla as she opens the door. We step into a long, dark hall. Kayla's heels echo on the tile until she stops and opens another door. As Metallica's "Enter Sandman" blasts at us, Kayla shouts, "This is the VIP area! You have about a half hour before signings and pictures start. Drinks and food are complimentary. The radio station is footing the bill." Her expression is smug.

Sam and Gabe breeze past her without a glance.

Even though she has a bug up her ass, I say, "Thanks," as I enter the bar. The decor includes steer horns mounted all over the walls and strange lighting from a mix of disco balls and spotlights. Western chic? More like the seventies on crack on a ranch. The VIP area, located in the back and raised a few steps higher than the front, is half full of people. I recognize some of the other bands' members and a few roadies. The bar beyond the wooden rail that separates the VIP area is packed. People lean over the rail and point at band members like they're watching animals at the zoo.

Sam and Gabe are already at the bar. Instead of joining them for a drink or filling a plate with food, I pull out my camera and wander around taking pictures. I catch Romeo talking to a guy dressed in a suit, who I'm guessing is the tour manager, and Justin talking with some of Griff's members. Then I turn and capture Sam and Gabe doing shots with a couple of scantily clad girls.

Maybe Sam's girlfriend has a reason to be bitchy.

As Sam leans down and whispers something to one of the girls, a burst of annoyance shoots through me. Perplexed, I lower my camera and let it hang from my neck. What's my deal? I try to think logically. My frustration has to be confusion. Of course it's hard to know how to feel now that he's gone from being a dick to being a nice guy—and back again, judging by the way he's about to cheat on his girlfriend.

I scan the crowd until the irritation passes, then glance at a clock and realize the half hour warm-up is over. All the band members are rounded up—the phrase is a perfect pun, given our surroundings— and seated at tables in the front of the VIP area. Lines have already formed, with people waiting to get pictures, autographs, and meet the musicians.

After taking a few out-of-focus shots of the crowd, I decide it's time to get a drink and a plate of food.

The night drags as I sip Diet Coke and watch Kayla direct the madhouse. The crowd of girls in front of Luminescent Juliet's table grows by the minute. The band might not be well-known, but the guys' hotness creates a draw that soon enough makes their line longer than the others.

The guys sometimes take breaks and join me at the bar to bitch about how dumb the event is, but I'm mostly alone and horribly bored. I do meet several members of the other bands as they come up for breaks. Most of the guys in Brookfield seem reserved and almost businesslike compared to the guys in Griff, who dress *and* act like rockers.

Near the end of the event, I head for the back door to get away from the noise and to call Bryce from the parking lot. When I step outside, the smell of weed is unmistakable. Spotting Kayla and Sam amid a haze of smoke a few yards from the building, I nearly drop my phone as I step back, stunned by the sight of them together. I feel a burst of annoyance like the one from earlier. I immediately justify it as shock that they're getting high in the middle of a promotional event.

Kayla giggles at my look of surprise.

Sam pinches off the joint's red, burning cherry and stalks toward me. "Go inside," he orders Kayla, stepping up to me and tossing the butt onto the cement.

Her bottom lip juts out in a pout, but she does what he asks.

Though I haven't seen him smoke since the day we left, Sam digs out a pack of cigarettes from his pocket. "Don't say anything to Romeo."

He is not asking. He is telling me. I clench the phone in my fist. "So you're assuming I'd go and tattle? I'm not like that, Sam."

He taps a cigarette on the side of his wrist. "Peyton, I'm not trying to start an argument or be a dick. Romeo gets in my business too much, and I don't want to deal with it. I didn't expect you to run to him, just maybe to say something in passing."

"I wouldn't say anything." Obviously, Sam must smoke pot somewhat regularly for him to be this adamant about Romeo not finding out about it. Still, I'm surprised. From what I recall, he never used to. He didn't drink much when we'd hung out in the past either. Sam and I had usually been the most sober ones at high school parties. Fear of too many empty calories had always kept me from overindulging. I'd never been sure why he'd steered clear of partying. But it's clear he doesn't anymore. Really, though, his partying habits are none of my business.

"Thanks," he says, lifting his lighter. A flame brightens his face as he lights his cigarette. His eyes are glazed and red.

I cock an eyebrow. "You don't think Romeo's going to notice?"

He blows out smoke, then laughs. "This tour has him wound tighter than a coke fiend. He doesn't pay attention much anymore."

The bass line of "Higher Ground" rings out of Sam's pants.

He digs his phone from a pocket and sighs at the screen. "Yeah?" he answers in an irritated tone.

Even before he starts talking, the pained look on his face tells me his psycho girlfriend is on the other end of the line. Not wanting to eavesdrop again, I rush to the back door as he says, "Stop it. That shit isn't true."

Though I'm annoyed with him right now, a surge of protectiveness hits me. He needs to break up with this woman. Constant arguing isn't a relationship. Been there. Done that. It sucks. As I step into the hallway, I wonder if this girl is the reason Sam drinks more now and smokes pot. Or why with other people he pretends to be the happy-go lucky-guy I used to know, when I can see that guy is mostly gone.

Chapter 8

I t's a bit odd waking up in a room with two men, especially knowing they stayed out late partying. I'm kind of wired to think of others—sometimes it turns into my downfall—so I try to be quiet when I wake up and sneak from my tiny rollaway into the bathroom. I'm certain Sam and Justin need their sleep. After we all came back from the radio station event, I called Bryce and went to bed, but Justin and Sam went to the hotel bar. I woke up briefly when I heard Justin come in around one. I woke up again when Sam stumbled into our room hours later. But now, as I tiptoe out of the bathroom, he is sitting up at the edge of his bed. He's bent over his knees, with his hands covering his face.

"Sorry if I woke you," I whisper. "I'm heading out to do laundry so you guys can sleep."

Glancing at me through splayed fingers, he shrugs.

I grab my card key and quietly exit the room. At the bus, I give Gary a bag of bagels for meeting me and opening the bus, then drag our five half-full laundry bags to the laundry room, which is in the far recesses of the hotel. Given our limited clothes supply, I'm planning to take advantage of the washing machines at every hotel stop, even though we're barely four days into the tour. Just as I finish dropping each bag in front of a machine, Sam waltzes in with two steaming cups.

As I stand there surprised, he holds out a hot coffee. "Thought you might like some company and some coffee."

I practically snatch the drink from his hand. "Thanks," I say, and take a long sip of the caffeinated goodness. Did he remember that I like it black? Or was he just guessing? Though I was planning to head to the exercise room for a half hour on the treadmill once the machines were going, Sam's offer of company is too thoughtful for me to turn down. Besides, I'm only half awake.

After gulping down more coffee, I dig quarters out of my pocket and make a pile on the counter. "I was going to wash them all in cold. I planned on dumping them in without separating colors." I wrinkle my nose. "I'm not touching dirty man underwear."

Letting out a laugh, Sam sets his coffee down on a chair. "Sounds like a plan."

We load the machines with clothes and quarters, then sit together sipping coffee in the line of plastic chairs. Water blasting into the machines fills the silence. I try to think of something neutral to talk about, something that doesn't have to do with the past. Then I think, *Screw that*. Maybe it's better to stop pretending there isn't a past between us—well, except for that one night. That is *so* off-limits. But if we're going to get along for real, pretending we weren't friends just isn't going to work anymore.

"So how is Seth doing?" I ask nonchalantly, and notice Sam's grip around his cup tightens.

"He's all right."

"Is he at the University of Michigan?" Both Sam and Seth were supposed to go to school in Ann Arbor, which was why I'd dropped my purse freshman year when I saw Sam in the commons at our university. I'd never expected to run into him at college.

"No."

"Where'd he go?"

"He went to the U of M for a semester and came home."

"He isn't going to college?"

"Nope."

"Why?"

"Seth found out college isn't for him."

"But he was so excited when he got accepted."

Sam shrugs.

His short or lame responses are starting to get on my nerves. "Is he working, then?"

He shifts, turning halfway toward me. "He cooks at a diner on Main Street. Why are you still interested in Seth?" he asks evenly.

I put my hand up, palm toward him. "Don't. I'm not hung up on Seth. How could I be after the way he treated me? Almost everyone who lived within a hundred-mile radius of the party where we broke up thought I was a cheating skank or a whore slut. In the months before all *that* happened, he'd turned from the perfect boyfriend into a jealous, possessive nut. I should have broken up with him months before that night."

"*Don't* call him a nut, but since you're bringing it up—why didn't you break up with him when he was treating you like that?"

The nut reference must have hit a nerve. I decide to ignore his response. "Besides the fact I wasn't the most self-assured girl then, it was hard to let go of the Seth I knew at the start. The boy who showed up at my school with flowers. The boy who threw pebbles at my window and sang to me at midnight. He was the first boy who ever really liked me."

Sam's confused gaze searches mine. "What are you talking about? Every guy in our group wanted you at the first party Jill brought you to."

Suddenly, I'm confused. Did Sam want me? He had never acted like it until maybe that ill-fated night. "I'd been—overweight through most of high school. The summer before we met, I lost over thirty-five pounds. The guys at my school who'd never looked at me didn't change their minds, even after I'd lost the weight." My thumb absently rubs the side of the coffee cup. "If I'm being honest, I have to admit that Seth's attention went to my head."

He studies me. "The guys at your school were idiots even before you lost the weight."

I smile at that. "I liked to think so."

He watches me with a slow burning gaze. "I wonder if you'd never . . ."

"What?"

With the shake of his head, his gaze returns to normal. "Nothing. No use wondering over the past. So your new boyfriend doesn't have any issues with you being on tour with four guys?"

"He wasn't super keen on the idea, but he trusts me," I say, feeling a little uncomfortable talking to Sam about Bryce. Still, I did ask about Seth, so I guess we're opening the floodgates. Kind of. "Plus, he's on the baseball team, and will be gone for half the summer anyway."

"So, what, if he wasn't busy all summer, would you still have come?"

I tap my cup on my knee and seriously consider the question. "Probably. I'd like to work in the music business as a journalist eventually. This opportunity was perfect for me."

"So your career comes ahead of your boyfriend?"

I shrug. "I don't know. I've never thought about it like that. I like him a lot but we're not engaged or anything. There wasn't some dramatic choice involved. It wasn't like coming on this tour would mean us breaking up."

He tilts his head in something like a half nod, and then the room is filled with the sound of whirling water as both of us stare at the washing machines.

"So you like our album?" he asks, breaking our silence.

"It's good," I say with a smile. "Real good. I'll admit I was surprised. The mix of folk, blues, and punk really works."

"Except for the surprised part, I'll take that as a compliment coming from you."

I nudge his arm with my elbow. "What surprised me was the complexity of the music. You guys go to my school. You're a band from mid-Michigan. It's just unusual to find such awesome talent so close to home. When I first listened to the album, it seriously impressed me."

"That just came out. You never came to see us before we released it?" His tone is incredulous.

"Once," I admit, then decide to be totally honest. "It was the U-Palooza at the beginning of sophomore year, and I still wasn't over the whole Seth thing. When I saw you playing onstage, I kind of went into shock. The only band member I'd heard about in advance of the show was Romeo. I made sure not to go to any more shows."

"Hell," he says, running a hand through his messy curls. "You must have been really hung up on Seth."

I shake my head. "It wasn't actually about Seth. It was more about me. The whole thing hurt me more than it should have, probably because I was so vulnerable from the start. The whole weight thing . . . and finally getting attention . . ." I don't finish. I've said enough. A conversation about my body image and self-esteem issues? We're just not going there.

He stares at me for a long moment. "Well, that sucks. I'm sorry. I never meant . . . Things were a bit tense after that—that night."

We stare at each other and emotions churn in my stomach, both from the release I feel from talking honestly and because his confused frown makes me want to reach out to him.

The whirl of a washer halting its spin cycle fills the sudden silence between us.

He stands and tugs a rolling wire cart over to a machine.

I get the other cart and push it next to his, filled with fresh resolve that it's time to get over the past. "It's been nearly four years," I say, opening a washer while trying to separate my emotions from the facts. "We were all kids. Somehow, after seeing you at the U-Palooza, I started feeling ready to let go of the what-ifs."

Without looking at me, he heaves clothes from the washer into the cart. "Yeah, it's better for you to move on. I guess with things fucked up between Seth and me, I didn't consider how much everything might have affected you." He pauses, pulling out more wet clothes, and focuses on me. "It's just that when you showed up at my door before the tour, all that shit resurfaced, and I went into dick mode."

Nodding, I reply, "For one quick second, I was overwhelmed with the past too when Romeo called me. I'm just not that person anymore." My lips press together as I glance at the wet pile of clothes in the cart. "I never was the person Seth made me out to be after that night."

I glance up and he's frowning at me. "Peyton, for what it's worth, I never thought you were that person." He rolls the cart over to a dryer.

I'm left standing there, staring at the muscles of his back move as he shoves clothes in a dryer. Sam should be the one person who was aware I wasn't a slut. Usually virgins aren't considered sluts.

I too toss wet clothes into a dryer while my mind churns in confusion. If he knew I wasn't a lying, slutty bitch, why all the condescending glares over the past years? Why so much silent hate? I slam the door of the dryer.

Maybe because you came between him and his twin brother, Peyton?

The thought hits me like a bolt of lightning. Like Sam, I've been regarding what happened through how it affected me. I'm not entirely dense. I was aware to a certain degree that night pitted brother against brother—but I never considered how it might have torn two brothers apart who'd once been inseparable. Maybe the rift had even sent Sam to a different college. Instead, I imagined him hating me because his brother did. Not because of what happened afterward or how it changed his life.

The past, the fallout, my hurt, *everything* suddenly shifts, and the laundry room feels like it's on a tilt as I push my cart back to another washer that just finished its spin cycle. Though I hadn't been a lying, slutty bitch, I may have been a bit self-centered. Or maybe a whole hell of a lot. Less than an hour ago, I wanted to confront the past head-on. Now scared that night might have ruined Sam and Seth's relationship, I'm thinking *Screw that.* At the same time, I've learned that denial just prolongs things, makes them fester. I don't want to be a coward any longer.

I open a washer as Sam moves to the machine next to it. "So you and Seth are still close, right?" I ask.

The tumble of clothes in the dryers becomes loud. I clench the wet clothes in my hands when I glance at him. As I take in the bleakness of his gaze and the tightening around his mouth, which convey complete sadness, the wet clothes drop to the floor. "Sam?"

His gaze snaps to mine and his expression clears. He reaches into the washer and jerks out a wad of wet clothes. "We talk every day, and I go home about every other month. We're fine, good."

I'm *not* a coward about probing a little more, but as he drops the clothes into the cart, pushes his shoulders back, and turns the cart toward a dryer, his body language clearly signals he's done talking about Seth.

My mind stuck in a knot, I pick wet clothes up off the floor and stuff them into a dryer. Apparently, if Sam's body language means anything, things aren't right with the brothers. After all this time, I'm sincerely hoping their issues have nothing to do with me.

I'm starting to wallow in that old guilt when I'm swept off my feet and my butt lands in a wire cart.

Lips brush against my ear as he says, "You ready for a ride?" He shakes the cart like he's revving up an engine.

"No!" I yell, my voice garbled with laughter.

Sam pushes me across the small laundry room.

"Stop!" I try to shout, but I'm breathless with giggles. Before I crash into the wall, he spins me around and around, again and again. My vision swirls. "Ahhh, stop or I'm going to puke on you!"

He spins me faster.

"Sam!"

He halts the cart suddenly and hauls me out. I take a shaky step and almost fall against his muscular chest. His hands wrap around my waist to steady me.

Looking up at him and leaning like the Tower of Pisa, I laugh. "You're an idiot."

He grins at me. "What's that saying?" His square chin angles as he pretends to think. "Takes one to know one?"

My fingers grip his shirt as I lean the other way. "The saying is false."

Sky-blue eyes crinkling, he laughs.

Suddenly, Gabe pops his head into the room. "Hey, we're all meeting for breakfast." His mouth curves into a knowing smirk at the sight of our near embrace. "To go over the set for tonight."

I push away from Sam and stumble against a dryer.

Gabe looks to Sam. "You coming?"

"Yeah, we need to finish loading the dryers."

Snorting, Gabe shuts the door.

Sam wheels the cart toward the last washer that contains our clothes.

"I can finish," I say, regaining my balance while trying not to get peeved about Gabe's knowing look.

"One more load and we can both go to breakfast."

"Just grab me a muffin or something." I tow his cart closer to me. "But you need to go." I wave my hand toward the door like I'm dismissing him.

He lowers his chin and peeks at me through his lashes. "You want to touch my underwear in private?"

The joke wipes away my irritation. With a buttload of concentration, I keep my expression neutral. "How'd you know?"

"I'm good at spotting closet perverts."

I whip a wet shirt at him and he catches it. He's about to toss it back when his phone goes off. His grin dies and he drops the shirt into the cart.

Reaching into the pocket of his flannels, he says, "I'll stop back with the muffin." Then he answers his phone sharply with "What's going on?" and walks out the door.

I don't know why, but I'm saddened at the thought of him having such an awful girlfriend.

Chapter 9

Despite being an arena, the venue in Austin has great acoustics. On the floor, in between the stage and the line of security guards again, I watch the guys onstage while music at megawatt volume vibrates in my rib cage. It's loud, it's in my face, and I love it. This is my sunny day. Sleeping in. Chasing butterflies. Making snow angels. Riding a roller coaster. The live music is all awesome things rolled into one.

Simply standing here and being a part of it is like a natural high. I'm a frickin' kite. I take a deep breath and force myself to get to work. Taking photos doesn't feel like too much of a chore—not when there are so many amazing images to capture.

Onstage, the members of Luminescent Juliet look rocker hot. Instead of shorts, T-shirts, and tennis shoes, they're dressed in stage clothes. Wearing a cowboy hat, Justin's in an unbuttoned white shirt and tattered jeans. I take several pictures of him in all his tattooed glory. Romeo's sporting all black. Behind the drums, Gabe is wearing just a leather vest, low-riding jeans, and a massive studded belt. Even Sam, who in all the pictures on their former website wore old, baggy clothes, is sporting frayed jeans, a fitted gray T-shirt, and low boots. But always a bit goofy, he sprayed a strip of orange hairspray through his curls that matches the color of his bass.

The chicks in front of the stage are swooning like sixties school-girls at a Beatles concert. I take a picture of them screaming and fanning themselves.

The band is in the middle of the song "Trace," which from what I can gather is about memories of a girl. The lyrics resonate with emotion, but instead of being predictably layered over slow and melodious music, the song has a fast, driving beat. It works. "Trace" is one of my favorite songs by the band.

The stage lights flicker and change color and intensity as I shoot a photo of Sam jumping to the last beat of the song with the flare of the lights bright behind him.

Their next song, "Midnight," has a bluesy, folk feel. The lyrics in this song are about the dark moment when partying changes from fun to desperate, which doesn't seem like something Romeo would write, but he obviously did since all the lyrics except "Inked My Heart" are credited to him.

Romeo steps to the edge of the stage, lifting his guitar, playing the long opening riff. I crouch and get a kick-ass angle from below. When I move to the other side of the stage and take a picture of Sam, the camera catches him winking at me. After glancing at the small digital screen, I can't help giving him a grin.

Once again, I let my camera hang from my neck and drag the small notebook from my back pocket. I jot notes about the crowd's excitement, about the intensity of the music and the energy of the band. Then I watch the band perform "Inked My Heart." Every time he sings it, Justin is captivating. It's hard to pay attention to anyone but him. From the emotion on his face to the passion in his voice, it's obvious the song means something to him—and I'm guessing that something is Allie. It seems things worked out, because although the song is full of sad, raw feelings, it was apparent on the day I saw them together that they fell in love despite the heartache.

Of course the crowd goes wild. Well, the fans who are paying attention. Again, about only half the seats are full since these guys are the opening act. By the time Brookfield starts playing, the crowd will be at maximum capacity.

When they're done playing, the guys head backstage to the press room, which I've learned is called the green room. Some random DJ from WZIK Rock interviews the band members, then has pictures taken with them. No surprise, Kayla and her clipboard hover nearby. Because the whole WZIK event left a bad taste in my mouth, I stand on the sidelines, clicking through the photos I took. When a reporter from the local newspaper interviews the band, though, I do shoot some pictures.

After one more interview, this time for a local magazine, the band hightails it to their shared dressing room while I head to the tables in the back. Although there is a daily allowance from the tour for food, it isn't much for five people, and it's mainly used to stock the cupboards on the bus. From the beginning, Romeo has made a point of reminding us to take advantage of the free food available at the concerts and promotional events.

I grab a wilted sub and an apple. A little ranch helps the sub, but it isn't exactly tasty. I have gotten a bit spoiled working for an authentic Italian restaurant for the past three years. Food should have layers of flavor and taste good. I love to eat now that I'm finally off the diet train. Dieting like that sucked ass. Then again, starting to overeat again because I was depressed after the breakup with Seth also sucked major ass. The worst was having to go back to dieting to get rid of the ten pounds of depression weight I'd put on. After being on a diet roller coaster for years, I've learned that eating reasonable portions of the food I want and exercising three or four times a week, if possible, maintains my weight. Maybe it's not my dream weight, but I've learned to accept it—as Jill says to me sometimes, "What's wrong with a size six, you crazy woman?" So, yeah, the sub is pretty close to awful, but I try to enjoy it.

Some of the roadies are also eating, and their plates are loaded with two or three sandwiches each. I've noticed they'll eat anything because they've been here since morning, setting up, and will be here until after midnight, taking everything down. Two of them come over and introduce themselves as Chris and TJ. I'm asking them questions about the concert setup when my phone vibrates in my pocket.

I dig it out and see a text from Sam. Wow. He's texting me now. We must be getting along.

We're on the bus. Gary's ready so we're taking off early.

Whoa. I'd planned to watch the next two concerts, but I drop the last bite of sandwich, tell the roadies good-bye, and head out of the stadium into the parking lot.

Inside the bus, Green Day blasts from the stereo dock. Gabe and Justin are already playing a video game. Romeo is in the back room on the phone, talking to Riley, I'm guessing. And Sam is at the counter, mixing drinks. Big shocker there. Well, at least this new Sam I'm getting to know.

"Whiskey and Coke?" Sam holds up a glass in my direction. I frown as I sit down on the couch under the TV. I try to steer clear of sugary drinks made with hard liquor. "No, thanks. Not in the mood to puke."

He rolls his eyes. "Beer, then?"

I give him a thumbs-up. The bus starts rolling and he pulls a Corona out of the fridge. He pops the cap, and a second later my hand is freezing from holding an ice-cold beer.

"Dude," Gabe says to Sam, "you ready?"

Sam hands him a drink in a plastic cup. "Slow your roll. Set Peyton up with a player." He hands another drink to Justin.

Beer catches in my throat. "What? I have no idea how to play."

"It's just a fighting game. You kick and punch." He sets his drink behind the couch. "Scoot down, Justin."

They all move down, saving the end of the couch for me.

Reluctantly, I go over to the couch across from the TV and sit next to Sam, since the TV is swiveled toward the longer couch. I know next to nothing about video games.

"Here." Sam hands me a controller and his leg brushes mine. "Just push the *X* to kick and the circle to punch."

Ignoring the strange sensation along my thigh, I stare at the cartoon-looking characters on the flat screen. "Who am I?"

"Fat Princess," Gabe says with a laugh.

"*Fat Princess?*" I say, instantly recognizing the character in a pink dress and crown in between a muscled man and some other guy in a flowing cape.

"Hey," Justin says, "she's the only girl."

I hit *X* and my character's short leg hits the caped guy. "This fat girl is going to kick some butt, then."

The fighting commences. I lose big, every time. But they keep bringing me back. Finally, after three more beers and five lost fights, I move on to the next round.

"Suck on that, Ninja Justin."

Justin snorts, stands, and heads off for another drink.

I'm pushing buttons furiously, fighting caped man, when raccoon guy—Sam—helps me destroy Gabe.

"Okay, jackass," Gabe says, throwing his controller on the opposite couch. "She ain't gonna give it up 'cause you let her win."

"Fuck you," Sam says.

"Yeah, fuck you," I say. "He's not going to 'let' me win, because I'm going to legitimately kick *his* butt. And no one's getting laid on this bus, so keep the giving-it-up comments to yourself."

"I don't know about that," Sam says. "Romeo's getting phone sex as we speak." On the screen, Sam's muscled guy smacks my princess in the chest.

"Gross. I sleep back there, you ass." My Fat Princess kicks his raccoon guy in the face. "Like I want that visual in my head. I need some brain bleach now."

Sam's jump knocks my pink princess over, and she lands on her well-padded belly. "Now that's gross. I didn't say he was spanking it, just talking it."

"Spanking it?" Since I know zero sweet moves, I power up on the weird orb things I've been collecting and saving. "What are you, fourteen?"

"Twelve." His character hits mine again. "My brain is forever stuck at age twelve."

"Well, I was trying to be nice, but I *was* thinking twelve." I let my Fat Princess's power loose, and Sam's character flies off my chest, slams into the wall, and falls down. I jump off the couch, bouncing up and down. "I did it! I won! Me! The worst suck-ass player of video games in the world won!" I do a little dance, shaking my elbows and butt, then toss the controller on the couch before I gulp down the rest of my beer.

Romeo comes out of the back room. "Turn the music down. Gary doesn't need to hear that shit."

Gabe flips him off, then turns down the volume on the console next to him on the wall.

Sam stands. "You ready to lose some money, bitch?" he asks Romeo.

Romeo jerks open the fridge and pulls out a beer. "Get the cards. Talking smack ain't going to save your ass."

Sam looks to me. "You in, Peyton?"

I raise a brow.

"Poker?"

I laugh. "Ah, no, I work my butt off for my money." Literally. Waiting tables can be harsh. "I'd rather play it safe. Plus," I say, setting my empty beer bottle in the sink with the others, "I need to make a few calls." My mother and grandfather first, then Jill and Bryce.

Sam's mouth thins as I walk toward the back. Before I can pull the curtained door shut, I hear him and Justin arguing about who's going to deal first. Gabe joins in and the argument turns into yelling.

Sometimes I forget I'm on a bus with four college guys. Other times . . . they are all such boys.

Chapter 10

When I wake, the bus is still. I stretch until the leather beneath me creaks, and my body slips off the couch. I get up and peek out the little window and immediately start squinting. We're parked outside a hotel, and bright sun gleams off the marble entrance. Bellhops in burgundy suits and little hats are hauling out suitcases from the storage compartment of the bus to a grand revolving door. I pull the blind shut.

New Orleans!

And we'll be here four days. The past few days passed in a whirl of bus, sandwiches, sound checks, concerts, and back to the bus for a crappy shower and then bed. Dallas, Oklahoma City, and Little Rock passed by in a blur. The pace was exhausting, and I wasn't even performing. Though traveling in general is exciting, New Orleans and New York are highlighted in bright pink in my copy of the itinerary. Other than fulfilling my band responsibilities, I plan to spend the next three days sightseeing.

Making a quick trip to the bathroom, I see the guys are still sleeping, so I'm quiet as I pack up my stuff and get dressed. When I head out of the back room again, everyone is up. Bags and other items are already piled by the front of the bus. Romeo's up there by the driver's chair, talking with Gary. Sam and Gabe stand in the kitchen area, digging cereal out of bowls.

"Room's not ready," Gabe says through a mouthful of cereal as soon as I step into the main room.

"I didn't expect them to be," I say, scooting around him and Sam. I dump my stuff onto the pile.

Gabe shrugs. "Guess the king rooms are."

"King rooms?" I ask in confusion.

Sam pours me a bowl of Cheerios and hands me the jug of milk. He points a plastic spoon toward Romeo. "We're with Gabe this round. Riley and Allie are flying down today. Justin and Romeo went in on another room, since the tour only pays for one room, so they could each have their own."

"Oh," I say, doing the math in my head and taking a bite of cereal. They've been apart from their girlfriends for over a week and a half. Geez, hooked at the hip much? How are they going to last six weeks? Maybe the ladies wanted to visit the Big Easy. I know if I were going to visit my rock star boyfriend, it would be here or New York. I'd have to toss a coin to decide. I lift my cereal bowl to Sam. "Thanks."

He nods as Romeo comes over to us.

"They have only king rooms ready," Romeo says. "They're putting your stuff in our rooms so you can take showers and change. Your room won't be ready until after four."

The bellboys start moving our stuff and we finish clearing out of the bus because Gary has to fill it with gas and water before parking it at tomorrow's concert venue. Everything belonging to Sam and me ends up in Justin's room on the ninth floor. We take turns in the bathroom while Justin talks to room service. I hear words like "flowers" and "champagne" and "chocolates" being thrown around as he paces the length of the room. I turn on my laptop and finalize a new blog post while Sam showers. I want to get out of this room and into the city streets. Obviously, Justin has some serious romantic plans happening, and I'm eager to give him some space.

Sam comes out of the bathroom and gives Justin crap about being pussy whipped, then we head to Romeo's room on the twelfth floor.

Gabe and Romeo are watching TV, but it's obvious that Romeo is distracted. He hardly says a word when he reads over my blog post—unusual, to say the least—and he's constantly checking the time on his phone. He must be waiting for a text from Riley. Once he okays the post and I load it for the legions of fans, Gabe, Sam, and I make a quick exit.

"It's eleven o'clock," Gabe says as we get into the elevator. "What the fuck are we supposed to do for five hours?"

Sam and I both look at him like he's nuts.

"Dude," Sam says, "we're in New Orleans. Music, booze, tits, gambling, food . . . twenty-four/seven. You name it, they got it."

"Yeah," Gabe says in a sarcastic tone. "You looking to get high?"

Sam shoots him a scornful look. "Like I'm going to walk around the streets of New Orleans and ask about scoring. I may be a dumbass, but I'm not that fucking stupid, asshole."

Scoring? Pot seems a little out of the realm of scoring.

Adjusting his ball cap, Sam turns to me. "Where do you want to go, Peyton?"

Everywhere. "How about we start with the French Market?"

"All right," Sam says, pulling out a little guidebook from his back pocket.

"French what?" says Gabe.

All of us pause as we step out of the elevator and into the huge, ornate lobby. Crystal chandeliers hang from the ceiling. Satin couches and wingback chairs fill the space. And a small fountain gurgles in the center. I may be sharing a room with two idiots, but for a minute I'm filled with gratitude to be here. I'd never be able to afford to stay in this place on my pathetic restaurant salary. I don't even want to imagine the price of one night, let alone three.

Sam reads over a page in the book, then glances at Gabe. "French Market," he says. "Sounds like it's basically got tourist junk and food."

Gabe curls his upper lip in revulsion.

As we pass the fountain, I'm seriously contemplating taking off by myself if everything we do is going to trigger an argument.

Sam taps a map in his book with his finger. "It's not too far from Bourbon Street."

Gabe's face is blank.

"Tits and booze."

Gabe nods, slowly agreeing. "All right, let's go."

We catch an old-fashioned trolley that runs along the edge of the river to the French Market. The thing is fabulously antique-looking but has air conditioning, lucky for us. Late June in Louisiana feels worse than August in Michigan. Humidity hangs like a limp rag in the ninety-degree heat.

After roaming the stalls at the market, where I buy my mother a key chain shaped like a fleur-de-lis—the flower that represents New Orleans—and a Jazz Festival T-shirt for Jill, we decide to try the various food booths. We each pick something to sample and share. I go with boiled jumbo shrimp. Gabe picks crab hush puppies. And, of course having to be goofy, Sam brings back fried alligator. It's not too bad, but the thought that it may have originated in a swamp has me washing each bite down with a gulp of water.

Gabe whines about the heat the whole time we're eating.

"Dude," Sam says, setting down his beer, "we're in the South. Like the bottom of it. Deal with it or go back to the hotel and crash on a couch in the lobby."

Gabe drains the rest of his beer. Sweat is dripping down the sides of his face. "The couch it is." He stands. "I'll check out the strip clubs later. After the temperature drops." He grabs the last hush puppy, pops it into his mouth, and gives us a wave as he heads toward the nearest trolley stop.

Sam and I each get a bottle of water to go and start walking. Near Jackson Square, he catches me watching one of the many horse-drawn carriages that tour the French Quarter. Before I can agree, he drags me to one of the carriages lined up along the street.

Our driver, dressed in a white shirt and black vest, tips a worn straw hat and tells Sam he should sit on the backseat, next to his pretty lady instead of across from her. A grin spreads across Sam's face, and in seconds he is next to me with his arm around my shoulders. His body feels burning hot next to mine in the ever-increasing heat, so I nudge his side with my elbow until he pulls back a little. Just a tiny bit. The carriage driver smirks, says something about young love, tugs at the horse's reins, and we're off.

As we pass Creole homes with ornate balconies, our driver describes various significant aspects of the architecture. When he explains that the spikes on some of the balcony poles are called Romeo spikes, Sam chuckles. He further explains they were to stop a woman's suitors from climbing onto the balcony. Sam reaches for my hand and makes a stupid comment about how spikes couldn't hold him back from true love. The driver grins wide and knowingly. I squeeze the crap out of Sam's sweaty hand and he releases mine. But even though I don't want to hold his hand, I'm having fun.

The tour takes us past an Ursuline convent, several celebrity homes, the oldest bar in the United States, some narrow shotgun houses, and along the way, we hear several ghost stories. Sam makes wide eyes at the scary parts and hugs me closer. I nudge him away each time. My elbow is getting quite the workout on this carriage ride.

When we return to Jackson Square, Sam refuses to let me pay. So I leave the tip instead. Then we head to Bourbon Street. We argue as we stroll. I'm adamant about not going into any strip clubs—unless he's willing to check out a nude male revue with me.

He laughs and shakes his head.

"Fine, then, we'll find something else to do," I say. I drag him into some shops that we pass, including a voodoo store, an art studio, and a T-shirt place. At a store that sells miniature versions of everything, he puts his foot down: no strip clubs for him, no stores with miniature crap for me. Unless I want to make a deal? I walk away. Miniatures are cute but not that cute.

Our first stop on Bourbon Street is the Hard Rock Cafe. We spend an hour wandering around and studying all the memorabilia. The next stop is an absinthe bar with walls covered in old newspaper clippings. Excited to try the famous drink, Sam orders an absinthe for each of us. The bartender pours cold water over a sugar cube in a slotted spoon perched over each glass, and after the cube melts into the liquor below, we each try a sip. It has a strange flavor, like licorice mixed with herbs.

Sam takes a long sniff of the liquor. "Absinthe was banned around nineteen hundred in a shitload of countries, including ours. Lots of people thought it was a drug. A psychedelic one." He takes a long sip.

Recalling the moment I saw him smoking the joint at the WZIK Rock event in Texas, I stare at the green liquid in my glass. "Is that why you wanted to try it?"

He shrugs. "Well, yeah, but I know it's just alcohol."

His disappointed tone has me wondering if he wishes it weren't "just alcohol." "Do you like it?"

He shrugs. "It's okay."

I gulp down the rest of the licorice-tasting liquid to get it over with. "So where to now?" I ask, setting my empty glass down.

"If a strip club is out of the question"—he gestures across the street—"how about some karaoke?"

"Um, no, never. Just *no*," I say, vigorously shaking my head.

He finishes the absinthe and pushes his glass across the bar. "Let's just check it out."

"I'm not singing," I say stubbornly. But it's hard to resist Sam's enthusiasm as he nearly drags me across the street. When we step inside, the bar is half-full, even though it's the middle of the afternoon. On the small stage, a middle-aged white guy is destroying the tune of "Sweet Home Alabama." I go to the ladies' room while Sam finds a table.

When I get back, I find him at a small round table, sitting on a vinyl stool. He's lifting a pencil to a karaoke list. I sit down across from him. "Don't even think about it," I say.

He taps the pencil tip on the paper. "Is it okay if *I* sing?"

"Oh yeah, sure. Of course." I wrinkle my nose as I glance at the small stage and its bright yellow backdrop covered with cat paws painted in black. "Why would *you* want to? Not enough that you've spent the last week and a half on a real stage?"

"This is different from performing. Cheesy fun," he says with an offhanded shrug that makes him look young. Suddenly, I'm charmed. He seems so easygoing, like his old self. The waitress drops off our drinks. Two shots and two beers. Sam digs into his leather wallet, flipping out money, and I notice a picture sticking out of one overstuffed pocket. The photo of two preteen boys, holding bats and wearing baseball caps backward, causes a tiny knot to form in my stomach. After a deep breath—and Sam handing the waitress a five for her tip—the knot loosens. Sam told me that he and Seth are doing fine.

My brows rise once the waitress leaves and I ask, "Shots?"

He shoves one at me. "We're in New Orleans, baby, live a little."

I ignore the "baby" and reach for the shot. He lifts his and we both swallow them, staring at each other.

Fire burns down my throat. Coughing, I slam the shot glass onto the table. "What the hell was that?" I ask in between gasps.

He grins. "151."

"Sam! It's only . . ." I dig my phone out of a pocket in my shorts and look at the screen. "Five thirty in the afternoon!"

"We're in—"

"Don't say it," I warn.

The rum goes straight to my head and creates an instant buzz. He smiles and pushes a beer at me. We sip suds and watch the caterwauling onstage, grinning every now and then at each other over a missed note or a screech. My toes tap to the singing, which by the time I'm halfway through my beer doesn't sound *that* bad anymore.

We're on our second beer, and I'm feeling rather mellow when the announcer calls out, "Next up, Sam and Peyton!"

"What?" My voice comes out as a screech, and the plastic beer cup in my hand wobbles. Beer splashes onto the table.

Sam removes the cup from my hand and tugs me up.

"Come on."

"I told you no karaoke!" I hiss.

He keeps pulling me, saying over his shoulder, "It will be fun. Besides, you'll never see any of these people again."

As we near the stage, I try to escape his grip, but he holds me tight and leads me up the stairs.

A girl in a short skirt hands us microphones as the announcer says our names again along with "Here to sing 'You're the One That I Want'!" The announcer points to the screen across from us, then steps offstage.

Oh fuck. Could Sam have picked a worse song? It's the epitome of cheese *and* it's not exactly easy to sing.

The bouncy music starts, and I swear a groan goes through the crowd as they conjure up memories of John Travolta and Olivia Newton-John in *Grease*. Sam turns his baseball cap backward, struts toward me, and starts to sing without looking at the screen. The dork must know the song by heart.

Walking around me, he nails the first line perfectly. Damn. He can actually sing. I mean, more than backup. Compared to the crap we've been listening to the last hour, he sounds like a professional. Well, I guess he is. Everyone in the room turns toward us.

Oh double fuck. So much for "Danny." It's "Sandy's" turn.

Pissed that Sam got me up here, I belt out the words, keeping an eye on the screen as I stalk toward him. He shuffles backward and the crowd goes nuts. At the edge of the stage, he leans toward me, and *I* shuffle backward. Even my buzzed brain realizes we're kind of imitating the movie.

By the middle of the song, we've got our routine down, circling each other and shooting fireworks into each other's eyes. I stop worrying about how badly I sing and start having fun.

The song ends with us staring at each other, both breathing heavily. The crowd goes nuts, clapping and whistling. Someone shouts, "Kiss her!"

More people join the chant.

Sam grins at me, and though I lean away, his hand catches the back of my head and his lips descend. His hot mouth covers mine, moves over my closed lips, and sucks at them before letting go. The kiss is quick but sets my wet lips tingling and my heart racing.

My temper flares and I pull away, but the crowd goes more nuts as the announcer repeats our names. Sam grabs my hand and tugs me down into a bow.

"Paybacks are hell," I remind him as we're bent over. He grins at me, then pulls me off the stage.

Chapter 11

I'll have a water," I say to the bartender.

"Wussy," Sam says to me, then lifts his beer glass to the bartender for another.

I slide my empty beer glass back and forth over the wooden bar top. We sit in an open courtyard with a bar in the center. It's almost nine p.m., but the heat and humidity are still fierce. "Whatever. I have to pace myself or you'll be carrying me back."

He looks at me innocently. "How do I get to carry you?"

I pause, still sliding my glass back and forth. "What do you mean?"

His eyes twinkle at me. "Let's go for piggyback, so your breasts are pressed against my back all the way to the hotel."

I toss my beer-soaked cocktail napkin at him. "Shut up, you pervert."

Catching the napkin, he ignores me. "Let's do shots."

"No. More. Shots." We'd downed some Jägermeister about an hour before to help me forget my kiss-induced bad temper. Guess it worked, because I've stayed in that warm, happy place ever since and almost forgot about planning his payback. Thing is, I don't want to get way too drunk, which is why we'd also split a shrimp po'boy. After eating it, we decided to skip the dinner the tour promoters are putting on tonight at the hotel. I check my phone. Five more minutes until the jazz band we're waiting to see will come on. "Ready to move up front?" I ask.

Sam hands me my water and a beer. Taking the beer I didn't want, I give him a dirty look. He shrugs and heads to a table near the dancing area in front of the stage. Minutes later, the stage lights up and the band, a group of older men, comes out. Unfortunately, after a few songs, Sam and I are frowning at each other. Though the band clearly has some good musicians in it, they start with Sinatra and segue into Louis Armstrong. I like both just fine, but in New Orleans, I want to hear something more than a cover band.

Since the music is loud, especially the horns, I point to the exit and lift my brows. Although he can take it out to the street, Sam points to his beer. I sigh, and turn back toward the stage.

A woman comes out and a hush falls over the crowd. She steps in front of the microphone, and the drummer hits a beat while the guy playing the upright bass plays a low tune. The rest of the band members don't touch their instruments, and instead only snap their fingers into the microphones. Before I can figure out what the song is, Sam hauls me up. "We have to dance. I *love* this stupid song."

He drags me to the flagstones in front of the stage. The woman starts singing, and I slowly realize the song is "Fever" by Peggy Lee.

Holding my hands, Sam shimmies away from me, moving to the beat of the music. Then he draws me close, like body-to-body close. I can feel the muscles of his chest and his thighs, pressed for several long seconds against mine. Then our bodies part, moving to the slow, hypnotic beat and the woman's lush voice. Until he pulls us flush again, and the fever she's singing about feels all too real as I press against him. This time he doesn't let me go. Instead, he tugs my hand up to his shoulder, wraps an arm around my back, and holds our joined hands up, swaying his hips to the rhythm perfectly.

Damn, this boy can dance. The hand on my back slides to grip my hip, and he shows me how to move with him.

Now our hips are moving to the slow, lush beat. Together. In perfect rhythm.

Fever escalating.

I try to cool down the lust rushing through my body, but . . .

Moving with Sam to the hypnotic beat and listening to the woman's sumptuous voice—maybe under the influence of too much alcohol—hurls me into a sensual stupor. Everything except the music and the press of our bodies fades to the background. Our dancing has me drunker than all the alcohol I've consumed. I'm suddenly intoxicated by lust.

The song ends. It takes me a few seconds to stop moving, to wake up. The loud thunder of clapping wrenches me from the sensual haze, and I nearly jump away from Sam, who's watching me. His gaze makes my memories of our night together feel all too real. Memories I thought I'd buried. I turn away from him and stumble to our table. After gulping the rest of my beer, I smack my empty glass on the table and point to the exit.

"Let's go," I say.

He taps the side of his glass, reminding me he's not done with his drink, and starts to sit.

"Take it with you," I say, pushing my chair under the table. "We're in New Orleans, baby."

I'm grateful they allow people to walk around with alcohol in the Big Easy, because I know Sam hates to leave a drink behind. But after that sensual dance, I'm determined that we are leaving. As in now. I don't wait for Sam to follow me. I make way through the tables to the sidewalk outside.

He catches up with me halfway down the block. "What's your rush?"

"It's after ten. You have a photo shoot tomorrow and a concert."

"Oh, I can hang."

"Well, I guess I'm a lightweight, because I can't."

He rolls his eyes. I march toward the hotel. Well, what I assume to be the direction of the hotel, anyway. I'm rather buzzed. Realizing I may be wandering aimlessly, Sam removes the map from his back pocket to make sure we're headed the right way. Once he is done studying the map—and he guides us to the right path—a song title comes whipping out of his mouth. I counter each time with a title that has him grinning. Though our walk probably lasts over a half hour, it feels like we arrive back at the hotel in mere minutes.

After checking in at the reception desk for our room keys, we sneak through the lobby quickly, afraid someone might drag us to the dinner probably still going on. Besides being slightly too loaded to deal with a roomful of rockers, the day of sightseeing and drinking in the heavy humidity has left us sweaty and exhausted. I have no idea if Sam has been affected by the strange roller coaster of emotions the day has produced. But I know that I, for one, need a breather.

We race up to our room, and Sam goes directly to the little fridge filled with booze.

He lifts two small bottles. "Nightcap?"

The man is trying to kill me. "On ice. No shots. And give me something that won't make hair grow on my chest."

Sam smirks. "Now that's something I'd like to see."

I reach into the ice bin on the table next to me and chuck a cube at him.

Bending to duck from the icy missile, he pulls out a tiny bottle of amaretto.

"Perfect," I say, flicking off my flip-flops and falling to the end of one bed. Because of a breakup during our sophomore year of college, Jill once tried to get wasted on amaretto while watching sappy movies. There wasn't enough alcohol content in the stuff to put her out of her misery, so I know it's not too potent.

After handing me the amaretto, Sam pours a whiskey in a glass, then sits down next to me.

"I had a great time today, Peyton," he says, before taking a sip of booze.

"It wasn't too bad."

His head snaps toward me. "What? It was great and you know it."

"I didn't get to go in the miniature store," I say in a sad tone.

"Well, I didn't get to see strippers."

"You made me sing karaoke."

"You were awesome."

"Yeah, I'm a virtuoso."

"Maybe not that good but better than I thought you were going to be."

"Your song choice was awful."

"That song is a classic. And I know your taste in music is as eclectic as mine. So I'm sure you liked it. You just don't have the balls to admit it."

I give him a narrowed glare. "The jazz band was totally commercial. Kind of lame."

"Who cares? They did 'Fever.'"

"It was hot and muggy all day."

"We partied from noon until now."

"It was exhausting."

Bending over, he sets his drink down on the floor. "Admit you had a good time."

I shake my head slightly, taking another sip. When I'm done, he snatches the glass from my hand. "Admit it was great hanging out with me all day."

I shrug. "It was okay."

"Okay? What about my dancing?"

"You dance . . . all right."

"All right?" he screeches.

I blink at him innocently. My lashes flutter like an idiot's.

He stares at me with hooded eyes, then lunges. We slide across the bed, and he lands on top of me. His hands find my stomach, and he begins to viciously tickle me.

"Admit I can dance."

I can't admit anything. I'm too busy laughing.

"Admit it!" he hollers, his fingers pausing for the slightest moment.

I gasp out, "You can dance!"

He attacks again.

"Admit you liked singing."

I try not to give in to this demand, but his fingers on my ribs soon have me shouting, "Loved the singing!"

"Admit you had a good time."

"Good," I gasp, then laugh loudly. "Good time!"

His fingers dig into my sides more furiously. "The best time?"

"Best time ever!" I yell.

Sam finally stops tickling me, and I can breathe. He's hovering above me, his knees on either side of my hips. Very little of his weight rests on me. He stares down at me with those pretty blue eyes. I try to catch my breath and contain the mixed emotions stirring inside of me. He leans the tiniest bit forward, his lips slightly parted, desire etched on his face. And lust hits me like a tsunami, crashing into me and fucking up everything.

The space between our locked gazes crackles with longing. He leans closer to me, brushing my waist with his thumbs, as if slowly asking . . . I don't move. Want courses through me. I should move. Put a hand up for him to stop. Something. But I'm rendered immobile by the desire for his lips to meet mine. The promise of his muscled weight pressing against me causes those lush bottled-up memories to surface. The hot touch of fingers on my skin. A soft sigh above me. A harsh pant in my ear. The quick flashes of recollection nearly have me reaching for him.

We stare at each other, the desire between us obvious.

The swish of someone slipping a key card into the lock on the other side of the door breaks the silence, and our glued gazes jerk apart. At the turn of the handle, I frantically buck Sam off me. He moves away, his expression a mix of confusion and hurt. Ignoring his expression, I roll off the bed and reach for my bag—which, luckily, is on the chair next to the bed—then disappear into the bathroom as Gabe strolls into the room.

The hot shower washes away my guilty tears—it feels like history is repeating itself. I take my time brushing my teeth, flossing, applying moisturizer, brushing my hair, and waiting for the redness to subside from my eyes. Fortunately, when I step out of the bathroom, the hotel room is empty. Sam and Gabe must have gone out.

I turn off the lights and crawl into the smallest damn rollaway on earth. It seems the more expensive the hotel, the tinier the rollaway. My fingers grip the edge of the sheet. I feel awful. I almost kissed Sam and cheated on Bryce. Maybe I would have stopped. I hope I would have stopped it. Or did I just get lucky that Gabe walked in when he did? I'm guessing the latter.

Ugh.

What the hell is wrong with me?

Too much booze? Away from my boyfriend too long? Sam is too appealing?

No. No. Sorta.

I've never once thought about cheating on Bryce. Drunk or not. Apart for a while or not.

Apparently, I need to stay away from Sam. Being with him brings up too many old memories and confusing feelings. Because that has to be what's screwing with me. It's like reliving memories that I should have never let loose.

I tug the sheet up and roll over toward the wall. I've always hated recalling the heartache of my memories with Seth. But recalling the scorching heat of Sam is starting to feel even more painful.

It feels like he can still burn me.

Chapter 12

The morning after my night out with Sam in New Orleans, my head is pounding like a package of lit firecrackers. As usual, I slipped from our room quietly, but it had more to do with not wanting to face Sam instead of waking him and Gabe up. Tired and hungover, I don't have the energy to cope with my guilt. In desperate need of coffee, I head to a café down the block. I don't even want to know how much coffee might cost in a hotel as fancy as this one.

At the counter, I order a beignet and an egg-croissant sandwich too. My head is dealing with an artillery attack, but my stomach is grumbling in need. I find a little table to the side of the café, in the shade of a small tree, and start sucking down coffee. I ordered the biggest one they offered.

I'm lifting the egg sandwich when someone plops down next to me.

"Hello. Peyton, right?" Allie asks, peeling back the tab of her coffee cup. Dressed in a blue tank top that matches her tattoo sleeve, she's a bit too bright for my pounding head.

"Hi," I murmur, my sandwich pausing between my lips.

"Mornin'," Riley says, plopping her food, then herself, down on the other side of me. She is in all black, but sporting a grin, and with her ponytail swinging behind her, she's also too bright and chipper.

I nod hello and then take a bite of fortifying, flaky croissant goodness.

Allie pours sugar into her coffee and grins at me. "So, who are you ready to murder? Justin? Romeo? Gabe? All of them?"

"Dang, Al," Riley says with a laugh, "let the girl finish chewing before bombarding her with questions."

Allie stirs her coffee and peers at Riley with a level look. "It was really just one question."

"Well, I'm sure it's Romeo." Riley breaks open a cala, a dough-nut or rice fritter–type breakfast thing that I almost ordered, and slathers half of it with raspberry jam. "He can be such a bossy jerk when it comes to the band. When I was in it, I wanted to drum on his head during every practice."

I'm about to say he keeps everyone in line as Allie shakes her head. "I don't know. I'd rather deal with him than Justin and Gabe at each other's throats." She laughs lightly and leans toward me in a conspiratorial manner. "They're better now. A couple months ago they hated each other like two bratty boys on the playground." She shakes her head and takes a sip of coffee.

They haven't been too bad but before I can explain, Riley says, "True. Sam's probably the only one who you don't want to head-butt. Other than smartass comments, he's the least annoying."

I smile weakly and reach for my coffee.

Both women stare at me in bewilderment, then say together, "Sam?" They both draw his name out in a long questioning tone.

Since I told Sam I wouldn't say anything, I shrug. "We kind of started off on the wrong foot. But he's a, um, good guy, I guess."

They both continue to stare at me in confusion.

Allie's brows knit together. "Thought you two hung out yester-day . . ."

Knowing I suddenly look obvious as all fuck, I stuff a huge bite of sandwich in my mouth. I may look like an idiot, *but* I will keep my promise.

Their confused gazes turn skeptical before they both look away—Riley at her plate of calas as she spreads more jam; Allie across the street, as if Justin stands naked on the other side. The artillery in my head had subsided a bit after I'd eaten, but now the cannons are back and roaring full tilt. Forcing myself not to go into the long explanation of the past that wants to escape my lips, I take a big swig of coffee.

"So-o-o," Allie says. "How has everything else been going?"

I pull off a fluffy piece of sugarcoated beignet and savor the rare indulgence. "Good."

Riley taps a plastic knife on the edge of her plate. "How are they doing onstage?"

"Great. Awesome. I'm more impressed each time."

Allie uses her stirrer to spear a chunk of cala swathed in jam from Riley's plate. "Was the radio-sponsored meet and greet in Austin a madhouse?"

"Yeah, pretty much, and I think they gained quite a few fans," I say, waiting for questions about groupies chasing after their boyfriends. Yet after several more inquiries that relate only to the tour, I realize these two aren't going to ask. Maybe Riley and Allie, who are both beautiful *and* incredibly down-to-earth, trust their men. From what I've seen, they should. Neither Justin nor Romeo seems interested in any of the women constantly hanging around backstage.

After explaining the past ten days in detail while nibbling on my beignet, I absently ask, "Where are the guys?"

"Wardrobe and makeup prior to their photo shoot," Allie answers.

"Oh crap," I say, standing up awkwardly and scraping my chair across the cement loudly in the process. How could I have forgotten that the tour manager asked me to take backup pictures? He'd even offered to pay me if any of my snapshots ended up on the cards he's having made for signings. Apparently, he charges ten bucks a pop for them at the autograph tables after concerts.

Chewing on a fritter, Riley frowns at me with confusion.

I wrap up my trash in a rush. "I'm supposed to be there."

"Go to ballroom C." Allie glances at her phone. "You have about ten minutes.

"Thanks," I say with a quick wave. I rush down the block toward the hotel. In our empty room, I grab my camera, change the lens, and then head to the ballroom. I stand at the edge of the room as the photographer directs the band in front of a white screen. He has Romeo and Justin standing in the center, Gabe and Sam a foot back. They're all dressed in stage clothes: dark jeans, boots, black shirts, and silver-studded belts. When a woman with a comb steps up to Gabe and tries to rearrange his hair, he gives her a look of death. I can tell they haven't allowed the makeup people and hairstylists to do much. All four of them look exactly like they do onstage every night.

I lean against the wall next to the door and wait for everyone to take their places. A warm rush of embarrassment flows through me along with memories when Sam looks up and notices me. I shove my feelings of awkwardness aside and force a slight smile.

He smirks at me.

I push away from the wall. Okay, I can do this even with a pounding head and confused feelings. I step farther into the room and the tour manager spots me. He quickly introduces me to the photographer, who looks irritated at us but doesn't comment.

The hour passes with the photographer taking pictures and rearranging the band members in various poses, with his assistants rearranging the lights. I take pictures of the actual shoot, a documentary sort of thing, but also squeeze in shots of the band each time the photographer pauses to look at his screen or rearrange lighting. I don't want him to have to wait for me. Obviously, the photographer is costing a pretty penny, but I can't say the guys look in awe of him. If anything, they look irritated. Sexy but a little angry. Luckily for them, their expressions kind of go with the whole rocker thing.

During the individual photo sessions, Sam's actually, the bass line from "Higher Ground" rings over the murmured conversations in the room. Sam stands up and whips his phone out. Frowning, Romeo shakes his head at him. Ignoring him, Sam stalks out of the room, the low growl of his murmur fading as he exits.

Ugh. It has to be his girlfriend.

The photographer, clearly irritated, calls Gabe over to pose. I step back as the guilt I've kept contained washes over me. *Sam has a girlfriend.*

And, of course, I have a boyfriend. Bryce and I might not be the most committed couple ever, but we are in a relationship. Not that I was thinking about Bryce last night. Obviously, there is a strong physical connection between Sam and me—one that would have taken us down a very wrong path if Gabe hadn't walked into the room and interrupted the moment.

I take another deep breath, lift my camera, and take several pictures of Gabe, his hazel eyes intense under the flash of the lights. Then Sam is back in the chair. The photographer has him lean forward with his elbows on his thighs and his hands slightly crossed. He looks forward, his lids lowered, his eyes pools of anger. After the photographer takes several shots, he moves over and lets me get some.

With Sam staring at me, taking the pictures is very uncomfortable. I'm guessing his current mood is because of the call from his girlfriend. For some reason his indignant expression reminds me of the text he sent me a week after we'd slept together all those years ago. It simply said, *You need to call me if you're pregnant.* I'd been shocked because I hadn't thought of the possibility—I'd been too consumed by my heartbreak over Seth. At the time, I'd texted him back that I wanted to talk. His reply was *I'm not interested in anything else you have to say.* That line had caused me to spend the rest of the day hiding in my room with eyes red from crying.

A few days later, I texted him a negative on the possibility of pregnancy—I'd never been so happy to have a period. Though that particular worry was over, the fallout from that night was just beginning. Rumors followed me the rest of my senior year. From Facebook to the old-fashioned rumor mill, it seemed like practically every teenager in the thumb of Michigan had heard something nasty about me. I saw one post about a sex tape with twin brothers; another one claimed that I'd slept with every member of the Bottle Rockets. All the rumors painted me as a desperate, lying slut. People who didn't even know me that well treated me like a pariah. Within months, my self-esteem was lower than it had ever been, even when I'd been at my heaviest. I tried to turn to Sam, who knew the truth, with a text. He ignored me.

Now as he stares at me with icy eyes, I'm reminded of how ruthless he can be. I'm reminded that I never want to be in that vulnerable position again. I'm reminded of the silent anger we've shared over the past three years when we've crossed paths at school. And I'm thinking maybe Sam was right. Maybe being around each other is too difficult.

The photo shoot wraps up, and the tour manager tells the band a town car is waiting outside to take the band to the venue for sound checks. I try to appear busy by looking at the pictures on my camera, but Sam comes over to me on his way out.

"Missed you this morning," he says, standing close to me.

My body is hyperaware of him, and the heat that flashes through me triggers a mixture of uncertainty and guilt and desire. I need to distance myself from him, physically *and* emotionally.

Not knowing what else to do, I shrug and do my best to edge away from him while feigning calm. I continue scrolling through pictures, and say, "I needed a coffee."

"I would have gone with you."

"I wanted to be alone."

He moves closer. "Is something wrong, Peyton?"

"Nope," I say without looking up. I detest being rude or mean, but I don't know how to deal with whatever's going on between us. All I know is that it shouldn't be going on.

"What's with the bitch mode?" he asks roughly.

Refusing to look up from the blur of pictures or argue with him, I shrug and say, "Just being me."

He leaves without saying anything more. I wait several long minutes until I'm sure he's gone, getting a few cold looks from the photographer and his crew in the process. Once it's safe, I hightail it up to the room.

I store my camera, then crawl into my tiny bed. I should call Bryce. It's been three days. Overcome with shame and confusion, I just stare at the wall.

Chapter 13

"Come on, Peyton," Riley says, handing me a beer from the fridge on the bus. "Quit picking up their mess and let's go. Geez, girl, you're not their maid."

Ignoring the bottle of beer in my face, I say, "I'm doing it for Gary, the bus driver, not the band."

Riley taps her foot, then sighs and sets the beer on the small counter. "Fine. Let's whip this out." She proceeds to help me straighten up the bus, moving much faster than me.

Because the major arena in New Orleans is under construction, the tour has two dates at a smaller venue. And because the backstage area is small, the tour buses are functioning as the bands' dressing rooms. The downsized situation also means that everyone is meeting at a local bar to party, since there isn't a place to hang out at the venue after the show. But I don't want to party, so I'm picking up clothes, shoes, and tubes of hair gel, prolonging our departure for the bar.

Beyond trying to stay away from Sam, I'm also buttass tired. The T-shirts, hats, and CDs arrived early this afternoon, which meant that I ran a booth before and after Luminescent Juliet went onstage. Romeo paid Mike from the stage crew to help me set up and tear down the booth, which was nice. But it was impossible not to notice that the other bands' booths were way busier *and* had about four times the amount of staff ours did. After hours of sales,

Mike helped me pack up the remaining gear in big plastic totes. Then I watched the other bands with Riley and Allie while the guys were busy backstage with local media interviews. Riley offered to come with me to the bus so I could change. After changing out of my Luminescent Juliet T-shirt and into a beaded tank, and slipping on high-heeled sandals, I started cleaning.

Truly, Gary shouldn't have to pick up this mess.

We finish straightening up the bus, pour beers into plastic cups, and go. Riley goes on and on about how awesome the band sounded, especially Romeo and Gabe, for the entire walk to the bar. Since I caught only about fifteen minutes of the show, and was taking pictures that entire time, all I can do is nod. From what I heard, yeah, they were good as usual.

When we arrive at the bar, it's packed. Framed pictures of historical New Orleans cover every inch of the walls. The ceiling is tin, and it has an antique feel. There are old wooden booths around the edges of the space and a huge ancient bar in the middle. Bob Marley's "Stir It Up" blares over the talking and shouting. We shove through the throng and spot our people behind a row of bouncers who don't let us in until Riley catches Romeo's eye. He leads us past the other bands' tables—the guys from Griff are loud and rambunctious while the Brookfield guys are much more subdued—to a table in the far corner, where I see Allie, the band members, and, naturally, a handful of scantily dressed women I don't know.

Without success, I try to keep my gaze from the far end of the table, where Sam sits with a dark-haired woman. His stage look is rocker sexy, and I can't help but notice how his fitted T-shirt shows off his muscular biceps. The cute disheveled college boy thing he usually pulls off with his shorts and flip-flops on the bus is totally different from this. He's a chameleon.

He's laughing with the girl next to him until he looks up and notices me staring. His laughter instantly dies. His eyes burn into me for a long, agonizing moment, until his attention returns to the woman next to him. She glances at me, then scoots closer to him. A spike of unwanted irritation shoots through me. It's merely irritation, I tell myself. Nothing else. I. Am. Not . . . Shit! The irritation flowing through me does feel a lot like jealousy. Now irritated with myself, I try to concentrate on anything but Sam and the girl across the table.

On one side of me, Riley and Romeo are nose to nose. On the other side of me, women surround Gabe. A server comes and I order a Diet Coke, wishing I were back at the hotel instead of here. However, walking across the French Quarter at midnight alone is a pretty stupid idea.

By the time my drink arrives, I'm coming close to dying of boredom and irritation. The brunette is now on Sam's lap. Her huge chest is inches from his chin. Ugh. I get up, seriously considering walking back by myself. Just as I'm about to pass the line of bouncers, Rick, the guitarist from Griff, is at my side.

"Hey, Peyton," he says loudly over the music. "I haven't seen you around lately. Missed you at dinner last night."

"Been busy." Over Rick's shoulder, I see the girl wrapping her hand around the back of Sam's neck.

Rick inches closer, his fingers brushing my shoulder where a strap usually is. "No camera tonight? Means you're off, right?"

The brunette's other hand disappears under the table and Sam grins. I force myself to look at Rick. "Yeah, I'm off."

"Buy you a drink?"

I pause, looking him over. Although not classically handsome like Sam, he has that lean, dark-haired rocker look that makes fan girls swoon. In my peripheral vision, I catch sight of Sam sliding his hand down the girl's bare back. "Sure."

Rick calls a waitress over and whispers something in her ear. He turns back to me. "How's the Big Easy been treating you?"

It's turning me into a confused piece of shit. "All right."

"All right? That's it?" He leans closer. "You should let me show you the town. Tonight. This town never sleeps."

It's pretty clear Rick would be showing me more than the town. "But *I* need to sleep."

He grins. "You've got the whole day to sleep away, baby."

Luckily, before I have time to comment, the waitress reappears and hands me an orange-colored cocktail in a tall glass. "What is this?"

"See if you can guess."

The girl in Sam's lap is now biting his earlobe. I take a long sip. It tastes like fruit juice and some kind of alcohol. "Mai tai?"

He cocks his head and an earring dangles. "Close. A zombie." He smiles. "Very similar, though."

I sip my drink and he keeps talking about different bars, about jazz bands, about taking me out, and about how this could be the best night of our life. Bored, I drain my drink. Rick orders me another amid his bragging about all his connections in this city. A half hour passes as I nod every now and then, not really listening, paying more attention to the scene to the left of us. Sam and his lady friend keep touching until their display has me feeling slightly sick.

The more they touch, the sicker I feel. My stomach starts to roll. It feels like I ate every dessert on Tony's Italian menu and then downed a thick cream soda. Sweat breaks out on my forehead. The loud bar is getting stuffier by the second. I stand up and immediately start to weave, my heels making my balance worse, and Rick catches me by the hip and wraps an arm around me. I set my second empty glass on the edge of the nearest table before it slips from my hand.

"You ready to go?" he whispers in my ear.

I shake my head. I'm ready to puke. I don't know if it's from the drinks or Sam's PDA, but I'm really, really woozy. I try to pull away. Rick yanks me closer. My stomach reels more at the sweaty smell of him.

His fingers dig into my waist. "Come on. You'll never have a hotter time."

Again, I shake my head and try to push away. His other arm wraps around me.

Suddenly, Sam is next to us. "Peyton? You okay?"

I shake my head. My stomach is seriously rolling now. "Need to go," I somehow get out.

"*We* were just leaving," Rick sneers at Sam.

My stomach heaves as Sam studies me, brows lowering. "Bathroom," I murmur.

Rick tries to snatch me away. Sam pushes his arm. I'm a human wishbone between them.

Sam now shoves at Rick. "I should let her puke on you, you stupid fuck," he snarls.

While Sam wraps his arm around me, Rick glances down at me with wide, horrified eyes and practically jumps away. Sam drags me beyond the maze of tables and out a side door. I make it to the curb as my insides eject a gush of acidic liquid fruit and alcohol. Sam holds both my waist, so I don't fall onto the street, and my hair, so it doesn't get puked on.

When there's nothing left but dry heaves, he gently lifts me up. "How much did you drink?" he asks with an edge of anger in his tone.

"Just a beer and two drinks," I say weakly, leaning on him. I'm beyond embarrassed, and so weak I can barely stand.

"Two drinks?" he asks in a tone of disbelief.

"Rick bought me two . . . zombies," I say, finally recalling the name of the drink.

"Zombies? That shit has like, more than four shots in it, Peyton."

"Well, now those shots are in the street," I mumble against his shirt, then add a self-deprecating laugh. "They weren't in me long enough to get me *that* drunk."

"I'm going kill that fucker," he says, his hands at my waist. "Shove that stupid flaming guitar right up his taking-advantage ass."

"His guitar is stupid," I say in agreement, weaving more as a hot flash hits me.

"Come on." He tugs me by the waist across the sidewalk. "There are cars waiting out front."

Forcing my feet forward, I groan. "So I could have left earlier instead of watching . . ."

"Watching what?" he asks, rounding the corner.

"Nothing," I say, and simply concentrate on keeping up with him.

Sam tows me through the mass of people waiting outside to get into the bar. The guy standing next to one of the waiting town cars looks us over suspiciously.

"I'm in Luminescent Juliet," Sam says, reaching for the door handle because the guy doesn't open the door.

The driver moves as if to stop him.

"I'm not in the mood for this shit, dude. She's sick"—he gestures toward me—"and you're taking us back to the hotel." Sam whips the door open. "Now."

I lean back against the leather seat and force myself to relax. The short car ride is quiet as my stomach slowly settles. When we pull into the roundabout in front of the hotel, the driver asks for Sam's name.

Gently helping me out, Sam says, "Samuel Fucking Carr." He slams the door shut and flips the guy off.

On the sidewalk, my continued weaving inspires me to tug off my high-heeled sandals. The cool concrete feels nice and solid under my feet. I take a few more steps toward the entrance but stop when Sam gently pulls my arm.

"You can't walk barefoot on this dirty-ass sidewalk."

"I can't walk in those shoes anymore," I say, taking several more slow steps forward.

Sam strides in front of me and turns. "Then get on my back."

His comment from yesterday instantly pops in my head. "No."

"No?" he asks over his shoulder.

"No boobs on your back."

Turning around, he rolls his eyes but as I step forward, he sweeps me off my feet and into his arms. My head swims for a moment from the quick movement as my body bounces in his arms, one under my knees and the other around my back with his hand wrapped around my ribs, just under my breast. I'm quickly mortified.

"You're not carrying me!" I hiss, embarrassed by being carried *and* because my breath is gross after puking.

He starts moving. "It appears that I am."

"Put. Me. Down!" I accentuate each word, with the sandals in my hand pointed at him.

"When we get in the room."

He steps into the foyer. Luckily, it's nearly empty, but the few people inside give us startled looks as Sam strolls past them with me in his arms. Unfortunately, the singer from Brookfield is at the reception counter. Watching us, he waves and grins.

I'm completely mortified as we pass him. "Put me down," I repeat.

"Soon." There's an open elevator waiting, and he moves into it and steps to the front corner. "Push nine."

"Okay." I don't push the button. "Just put me down."

Ignoring me, he shifts my weight and pushes the button himself.

I glare at his five-o'clock-shadowed chin all the way up, and then down the hall. Even at the door to our room, he doesn't put me down.

Shifting my weight, he says, "Get the key from my back pocket."

"Sam," I say in warning, not reaching for the key.

"I can stand here holding you all night."

"Fine," I growl, and jerk the key from his pocket, trying to ignore the appealingly tight muscle of his butt under his jeans.

I slide the card in and he pushes the door open with one foot. Once inside, he deposits me in a chair. The sandals drop from my hand and I push myself up to stand. Even without heels, I still weave. I put a hand to my forehead. "Whoa."

"Sit down," Sam snaps.

I follow orders and fall back against the cushions of the chair.

Sam kneels in front of me and grasps my chin gently. "Do you think that asshole slipped something in your drink?"

I recall Rick whispering to the waitress, yet she brought me the drinks. "No, I—I don't think so." Why would I be so woozy? My hand comes up this time to slap my forehead. "I haven't eaten since breakfast. Between the heat and working and then those crazy drinks . . ."

"Why the hell would you do that?" Sam growls, standing.

I rub the skin of my forehead, which I'd just slapped. "I just forgot."

He goes to the minibar and starts pulling items out, then dumps juice, peanuts, and a candy bar onto my lap. "Eat," he orders, then sits down on the bed across from the chair and stares at me.

Obviously, he's going to give me the cool stare until I eat. I open the juice and reach for the peanuts. As I pop a few nuts in, his mouth twists into a slight satisfied smile, and he gets up and goes to the bathroom.

I stare into space and follow his orders, eating slowly. I've finished half of the small bag of peanuts when he comes out, holding wet washcloths and a towel. As he kneels and reaches for one foot, I try to jump out of the chair.

"What are you doing?"

He gently pushes me down. "Washing your feet," he says in a simple tone. "They're grossing me out."

I tuck my feet under the chair. "Ah, no. Gross or not."

His expression turns stern. "Are you going to take a shower? Or just pass out?"

The thought of undressing, of simply turning on the shower, of the energy it will take, has me untucking my feet. "Pass out."

He gently washes both feet with one washcloth, then wipes the soap off with another. Staring at his dark curly hair, I'm completely mortified and extremely touched by his care of me.

He sits back on his heels and grins warmly. "No more gross."

"Thanks," I say, knowing my cheeks must be flushed.

He glances at the peanut bag, then raises a brow.

I dump the rest of peanuts into my mouth. "Happy?" I ask from a mouthful of peanuts.

"Almost." He stands and gestures to the candy bar on my lap.

I swallow the last of the nuts and tear open the candy wrapper. "Geez, I'm getting to it."

I'm munching on the chocolate peacefully but almost spit it out when I notice Sam going through my suitcase. He's holding up a lacy pair of pink panties in one hand and the matching bra in the other.

"What are you doing?" I screech.

"Looking for pajamas."

I wash down the candy with a huge gulp of juice. "Those are obviously not them."

He grins over his shoulder. "I know. I got distracted."

"Put those down! My sleep shorts and tanks are in the front."

His thumb brushes over a lacy cup, and I instantly imagine him touching me instead. He shoots me a smile like he knows what I'm thinking before carefully folding—folding!—both items and setting them down.

I glare at him as he comes over to me with shorts and a tank top bunched in his hand.

"Need any help getting dressed?" he asks innocently.

"No," I hiss. I stand slowly, then snatch the clothes from his hand. "Don't touch my underwear ever again."

He steps back with a smirk. "I'll let you touch mine if it makes you feel better."

"Better? It would reduce me to vomiting again."

"Right," he says, reaching for the other half of the candy bar on the table next to me. "Doubt that."

Ignoring him, I wobble to the bathroom. I find my cosmetic bag on the counter. Moisturizer, a brush, and my already loaded toothbrush are beside it. Again, despite all the innuendo, Sam's attentiveness is touching.

Sam always was the nice guy, and Seth the bad boy. Like almost every other girl, I fell for the bad boy. My ego wanted what seemed like the biggest prize, but in the end, I got burned.

Except for the light near the door, the room is dark when I emerge from the bathroom. Sam is lying motionless on the end of his bed, his hands splayed over his pretty face. I'm assuming he must have dozed off until I slip under the covers of the rollaway and he gets up.

"Hey," he says, leaning over me. "You feel better?"

"I'm good."

He stands.

"Thanks for everything," I say, then blurt out, "and I'm sorry."

He rears back a bit. "For what?"

I swallow. "You were right to get mad at me after the first concert of the tour. Everything you said was true. I used you. I didn't mean to, but I did."

It feels good to finally be honest after being in such denial about that night for so long. Sam offered me comfort and I took it without a thought. All while I was enamored with Seth.

"Oh, that . . ." He runs a hand over his curls. With the light at his back, I can't see his expression, yet from the dipped slope of his shoulders, I'm imagining a frown. "I was fucked up that night. I thought you were flirting with that douche bag. It brought back memories—but I was being an asshole." He steps farther back and opens his suitcase lying open on the dresser I catch the shape of flannels and a T-shirt in the shadows. "I'm going to hit the shower, so get some sleep." Moving toward the bathroom, he runs a hand over his curls again. "You need it."

Though I still can't see his expression, the tone of his voice and the tight angle of his body tell me I've hit a soft spot. Sam must have had feelings for me back then, I finally realize. It was probably nothing close to my obsession with Seth. However, my total indif-ference, my obsession with Seth that had me ignoring Sam right after having sex, must have been a bitch-slap to his ego. Truly deliv-ered by a thoughtless bitch.

I push up on an elbow. "Sam—"

"Thanks for the apology, but it wasn't needed. Like you said, it's been over three years." Light spills across my bed as he opens the bathroom door. "Just go to sleep. I'll see you in the morning."

He shuts the door and I fall back on the bed.

I'm such an idiot, and completely self-absorbed. How was it possible that I had never contemplated anyone's feelings except mine about that night?

I roll on my side carefully, so I don't fall out of the tiny bed, yanking the covers over my head. I'm not delusional enough to think Sam still carries a torch for me—he practically has women up his ass 24/7—but I'm starting to understand why he didn't give me the time of day after what I did. I deserved to be ignored by him.

Chapter 14

The next day, on our way to North Carolina, Romeo looks through the pictures on my camera. "Don't post any with Riley or Allie," he says curtly. "Besides infringing their privacy, it feels a little too personal."

"Okay." I start deleting some pictures in the current post I'm working on.

"The ones of the concerts in New Orleans are great. Put up as many of those as you want."

I'm about to say "okay" again but loud shouting comes from the front of the bus. The rest of the guys are watching a Tigers baseball game while Romeo and I are going over media-related items.

He scowls at their yelling, then asks, "Are we up on Twitter followers and Facebook likes?"

I nod. "More than double what we had two weeks ago."

"Good. I hope the sales numbers on downloads reflect that." He crosses his legs, stretching them onto the table, and keeps looking at pictures. "I like your idea of putting up a biography for each of us, and these pictures from the photo shoot are perfect. Just keep it simple."

Even though I'll remember his request, I jot down a note in my small notepad. He worships note taking, so I've learned to appease him.

We go over a few more things before he's off to watch the game too.

The bus rolling along is strangely comforting. Though yesterday was quite calm—Allie, Riley, and I went shopping and sightseeing during the afternoon sound checks, then I went back to the hotel right after the concert—it wasn't quite enough to overcome the clusterfuck of emotion and weirdness I'd experienced in the two days prior. The boredom of being on the bus feels like a return to normalcy.

Both Sam and I have been polite, but he has seemed aloof since he helped me back to the hotel. I'm thinking he's uncomfortable that the past still bothers him, and he's not the only one.

Talking to Bryce yesterday was a good distraction. While the itch of guilt at the back of my throat didn't go away, hearing his voice drew me back to the present. Bryce and I fit. There's no drama. No issues. And though I can admit I'm not head over heels in love with him, I really, really like him. We have fun going out, and neither of us is in any rush to dive into a deeper relationship. We're both serious about college and our future careers. We're both stable.

I like stable. A lot.

The day passes as we make the ten-hour drive to Charlotte. I work on loading pictures onto Facebook and writing a couple of new blog posts. One I'm hoping to post today; the other will be for tomorrow. I try to catch the excitement of the show in descriptive words, wanting to convey how incredible Luminescent Juliet sounded. I pull Romeo away from the TV to get approval on the first one, and once he nods, I load the day's post.

At around seven, I make what passes for dinner on the tour bus—microwaved hot dogs, a bag of chips, and a veggie tray. While he works on business figures at the small table, Romeo tries to get one of the guys to help me. I wave away his bitching. It's not a big deal to heat hot dogs, but I do almost laugh when I imagine the disapproving comments Riley would make if she saw me taking care of the guys. The game is over but ESPN stays on while the guys eat sprawled out on couches. After dinner, I watch TV in the back room, call both Jill and Bryce, and then decide to get ready for bed, so I can quickly crawl into my rollaway when we get to the hotel later tonight.

I'm brushing my teeth in the minuscule bathroom as the bus slows and then comes to a complete stop. I pause, recalling that we'd entered Georgia just over an hour ago. There's no way we could be in North Carolina yet.

Someone pounds on the bathroom door.

Confused why we've stopped, I slowly open it.

Sam rushes in, whips the door closed, locks it, and opens the toilet. Because the bathroom is tiny, I'm behind him, pressed in shock to the outer shower wall. He furiously begins digging through the backpack in his hands, throwing a myriad of novels onto the floor. Lastly, he hauls out several baggies and begins dumping the contents into the toilet. First, it's dry, green leafy stems, then a lot of fine white powder.

My eyes bug out at the sight of the drugs floating in the toilet.

"Turn on the pump," he says over his shoulder.

Shocked, I stand there immobile.

"Turn on the pump!" he hisses.

"It's already on," I say in a rush of air, gesturing to the switch on the wall. To get water, the pump has to be on in the bus, and I had it on to brush my teeth.

Sam begins filling the bowl with water and flushing, then repeating.

"What the hell is going on?" I ask loudly.

"Be quiet!" he whispers. "We got pulled over."

"Why?" I whisper back.

He shrugs and flushes one last time, then begins throwing the books back into his backpack.

Watching him, I cross my arms and say in a low tone, "Your stash is still going to be in the tank."

"I'm betting they don't want to search in a tank of chemicals, piss, and shit for it."

I wrinkle my nose at him. "That was quite a lot of drugs, Sam," I grumble.

He tugs his bag on his shoulder. "Do not say anything. To anyone."

I shake my head at him. "Sam—"

"I mean it, Peyton," he says, grabbing the door handle. "It's none of your business," he adds over his shoulder. Then I'm alone again in the tiny bathroom.

I absentmindedly pack my cosmetic bag back up. I'm shocked. I obviously knew he did drugs, but I didn't imagine the extent. Although I'm ignorant of the actual cost, he must have flushed hundreds of dollars down the toilet.

I take a deep breath and exit the bathroom.

Justin, Gabe, and Sam sit on the front couches, playing video games. I quickly assume Romeo's outside with Gary and the policeman. Or *men*?

Leaning on the small kitchen counter, I ask no one in particular, "What's going on?"

Justin shrugs. "No idea. Cop pulled us over. Couldn't be speeding. Gary never drives over sixty in this beast."

"Beast is right." Sam's gaze stays glued to the screen.

Gabe glances at Sam, then me. "Better hide your pot, Peyton."

I snort, "Yeah, I'll go do that."

Gabe laughs. Sam's appearance remains smooth and calm. Justin yawns.

I head to the back room and put my stuff away. Nervous and fidgety, I sit on the couch and peer out the little window. All I can see out there in the dark are the lights of passing cars and the faint blue swirling lights of the police car, which must be parked ahead of us.

A rush of nervous air escapes me as I fall back against the couch. Sam is sitting up front like a calm zombie and I'm the one freaking out, thinking of all the horrible outcomes if he gets caught. Sam sitting in jail. Sam ruining the tour. Sam getting kicked out of school. I sit up. Can they do that? Is his entire future at stake at the moment?

Finally, the bus lurches back onto the road. I head to the front. Except for Romeo hunched over a notebook at the small table, the guys are still playing video games.

"What happened?" I ask Romeo.

He looks up from whatever he is writing. "The bus has a taillight out. Gary's going to get it fixed in Charlotte, and the tour will take care of the ticket."

"Oh," I say, as the thudding of my heart at last slows. Sam glances at me with a smirk before his attention goes back to the onscreen fighting—and suddenly I'm angry. The dumbass is acting like he doesn't have a care in the world while I'm stressing out. Over his future. Over his stupidity.

I stomp back past the bunk beds, grab a blanket, and fall onto the couch.

Sam a nice guy?

Yeah, right.

I smack my pillow.

More like a major asshole. Grass-smoking, coke-snorting asshole.

Chapter 15

I sleep in the next morning and wake up to an empty hotel room. I should do some laundry, but I decide to hit the treadmill and maybe lift some weights. Though the guys seem to find time to work out in the hotel gyms whenever we stop, I've found time for the treadmill only once since we left. But when I push open the door of the hotel's exercise room, I almost close it and run away. Sam's in the far corner lifting weights. I'm still angry with him about his toilet-pouring drug spree, and still shocked that he's so much more of a druggie than I realized. But as I take the slightest step back, he looks up and smirks.

That smirk hits me in the gut.

Screw leaving. I'm not letting that loser control any aspect of my life. I ignored him last night when we got into the room. I ignored him at breakfast. And I'll ignore him now. Yet I do decide to skip weights and just do cardio. It's a little harder to ignore him since he's only wearing running shorts, and pumping iron with his muscles flexing every-fucking-where.

I go to the treadmill on the other side of the room and turn it on. I do stretches against the machine, pop my earbuds in and find a loud, angry, punk rock playlist, then start running.

About ten minutes later, when I've got him pushed from my mind, a sweaty Sam stands in front of the treadmill, his eyes purposely roaming my body. I'm too shocked to be self-conscious. Holy hell, Sam's body is as rocking as his music.

Loud lyrics, sharp guitar chords, and fast drums pound in my ears as I take in his killer physique. He is all rippling muscle. A fine sheen covers his sculpted chest. His eight-pack gleams under the florescent light. His abs look like they belong to a frickin' comic book character. Seriously, he's like six weeks and twenty protein shakes away from being a bodybuilder. But bodybuilders are usually on the side of too muscular. Sam, on the other hand, is perfection. The way I'm gulping for air has nothing to do with jogging, and everything to do with the sight of him.

I force myself to look away, above his head.

"Still not talking to me?" he says loud enough for me to hear over the music in my ears.

I continue running and looking above his head.

The treadmill slows and then stops. His finger hovers over the controls.

I glare at him and keep running on the motionless treadmill.

"Come on, Peyton. You've seen me toking before."

I turn around and run facing the other way.

"Nice view."

"Perv," I say. I jump off the treadmill, and he catches my hand, drawing me around toward him until we're inches apart.

"I only use when I party. It's not like a daily thing."

I finally lose it, ripping my earbuds out and hitting stop on the phone attached to my hip. "What about the illegal part? You could have gotten in serious trouble! You could have gotten any one of us on the bus in trouble! Do you think about anyone except yourself? And why the hell would you have that much coke?"

He lets my hand go and runs his own through his curls. "I'm sorry, okay. I just . . . Sometimes it's hard to get into a party mood."

"Party mood? In the middle of a tour that your indie band somehow landed, *that's* important to you?"

He shrugs. "Sometimes I need to unwind."

My eyes narrow on him. "If you can't unwind without drugs, you've got a problem, Sam."

He shakes his head. "It's not like that. I'm not depressed or anything. I—things in my life just feel a little too deep sometimes."

"I don't want to hear your denial." Unbelievable. I turn around to leave, and suddenly I'm surrounded by his warm, muscled arms. His hard chest presses against my back. He rubs his sweaty face on the side of mine.

"Come on. I'm sorry. That shit was supposed to last all tour. Six weeks. I'm not an addict or anything."

"Get off me! You're all sweaty!" But the truth is, he feels divine, even with the sheen of sweat. He is all hard, slippery muscle.

His arms tighten around me. "You're right. I should have thought about all the ramifications, especially for everyone else. I was, am, an ass. Forgive me?"

I can feel every inch of his sculpted form against my back. "Let me go! You sweaty pig!"

"Then forgive me?" he whispers in my ear, somehow pulling me closer.

Damn. In addition to the awesome texture of him, beyond the clean scent of soap and his fresh-scented deodorant, I can smell his sweat and it's making me imagine hot, sweaty sex. With him. Who's the pig here? My reaction to him overwhelms me to the point that I just give up. "You're forgiven. Now let me go."

Releasing me, he reaches for his T-shirt hanging from a stationary bike and grins before tugging the shirt on. "Want to go do something after sound checks?"

His grin has me thinking he's aware of my response to him, which is so not good. "I'm busy," I say in a snotty tone.

"Really?" He leans on the bike, his thigh muscles flexing from his weight. "Doing what?"

I tear my gaze from his leg. "Laundry, calling Bryce, and stuff."

He rolls his eyes, essentially dismissing the reference to my boyfriend. "How about I help you do laundry again, and we can do lunch while we're at it."

They won't be back from sound checks until after two. "It will be too late to eat."

"Grab a snack. I'll get lunch. My treat."

He's making a refusal extremely difficult, as in having to admit he's starting to do weird, hot things to my insides difficult. Hell will freeze over before I admit that to him.

"Fine." I glance at the clock on the wall. "You'd better get going or you're going to miss sound checks."

Those baby blues roam slowly over my shorts and tank top. "See you later," he says wistfully, then exits the exercise room.

I move toward the weight station. What the heck was that? I'm not sure what's worse. Sam coming on to me. Or Sam being nice to me. Either way I'm in trouble.

The hotel in Charlotte is nothing like the one we stayed at in New Orleans. It's not a dive or anything, just a normal hotel, with no chandeliers dripping crystals in the lobby or limos pulling up under a canopy out front. But at least the rollaway is much bigger, which confirms my suspicion that luxury hotels like to torment the extra person.

Hours after exercising, I'm in our small room, rearranging stuff in my suitcase because I already did the laundry—I'm *not* hanging out with Sam any more than I have to—and seriously contemplating taking off before the band returns, when a knock booms on the door. Dang. I contemplated too long. They must be back. Thinking Sam or Justin forgot his room key, I march over to the door and whip it open.

My eyes widen at the sight of the person standing in the hall. It can't be him but it is. Shock like the sizzle of lightning courses through my veins. Seriously, I'm about to faint like a Southern belle in an old movie.

His shocked expression, which I'm sure mirrors mine, becomes tighter and more confused with each passing second. "Peyton?"

I grip the edge of the door for support. He is thinner than I remember, more lanky than muscular, and his once shoulder-length dark hair is cut super short, but there's no mistaking that blade of a nose and his angular face, even drawn out and fatigued-looking as it is now. His dark blue eyes look as vivid as ever.

"Seth," I say.

Hands deep in the pockets of his long shorts, he glances at the number on the door as his beat-up checkered Vans shuffle on the hallway carpet. "What are *you* doing here?"

"I . . ." *Holy hell, breathe, Peyton!* The sight of him still brings on hurt and guilt.

"Seth?" I hear the incredulous tone in Sam's voice from down the hallway.

Seth turns and I draw in much-needed air. He looks back to me, then down the hall again to Sam, whom I can hear almost stomping toward us. "Sam, what the fuck is this?" Seth pulls a hand from his pocket and points at me. His lips twist into a snarl.

Sam steps into the doorway. Drawing in a deep breath, he wears a shocked expression too. "What are you doing here?" he asks his brother, obviously ignoring the reference to me.

Crossing his arms over his white beater tank, Seth glances at me. "Caught a bus. What is *she* doing in your room? What the hell is going on?"

Sam doesn't look at me. Staring at his brother he says, "Peyton, can you give us a few?"

"Sure," I say weakly, spinning around to grab my purse from the dresser.

Pushing a pissed off–looking Seth into our room, Sam says to me, "Wait in the lobby."

I reach for the door handle. I'm not going to lunch with these two. There is absolutely no way. Other than the fact that Seth destroyed my reputation with wild rumors and my teenage heart, it would be very, very weird. "Um . . ."

Sam's eyes bore into mine. "Please, Peyton."

I'm not sure if it's the plea in his eyes or the desperate tone of his voice, but I find myself stupidly nodding.

After shutting the door behind me, I move toward the elevator in a haze of confusion. The doors of the elevator open and Justin steps out.

"Hey, Peyton," he says casually.

Still in shock, I drag him back into the elevator with me. "Don't go to our room right now."

He gives me an odd look. "Why?"

"Sam's brother showed up unannounced." With a shaky finger, I push the button for the ground floor.

Justin's expression grows more confused. "Sam has a brother?"

I blink at Justin. How does he not know about Seth? He and Sam have been in a band for years together. "A twin brother."

Justin gapes as the elevator doors open to the lobby. "Like identical?"

I shake my head. "No, not identical. They're . . ." I was about to say "fraternal" and "eleven minutes apart, with Seth being the 'older' one." But luckily, I catch myself. In my shock, I almost blew our cover. This is definitely not the time to reveal to Justin and the others that Sam and I have only been acting like we didn't know each other before the tour. I really, really don't want to open that can of craziness with Seth here. I don't want to open it at all. "They must be fraternal." I step out of the elevator and Justin follows. "I mean, they do look like they could be brothers, but they're not identical."

"Strange, he never said anything about having a brother," Justin says, shoving his hands into his pockets as we enter the lobby. "Why shouldn't we go up?"

"Well . . ." I desperately search for a plausible reason, but I don't know what the hell is going on and decide to stick with the truth as much as possible. "Sam looked shocked and a little pissed that his brother was here. He asked me to leave," I say, adding a shrug for good measure.

"Huh," Justin says. "I can't believe he has a twin brother." He shakes his head. "Sam sometimes is closemouthed, but this takes it to a new level."

I'm a little freaked out too that Sam never said anything to Justin about Seth. Is there still a huge rift between the brothers? If so, there's no way I can still be the cause. That would be insane.

Justin glances around the lobby. "I'm supposed to meet Romeo for a workout."

Guess today is workout day. "Sam told me he'd be down in a few."

Justin digs out his phone, shaking his head. "I'll give Sam ten, then I'm going up." He puts the phone to his ear and says, "Hey, baby."

While he talks to Allie, I go to one of the couches in the lobby and send a *What's up?* text to Jill. While I wait to hear back from her, I have to force myself to stay seated, because I feel so agitated after seeing Seth. The guy annihilated my reputation *and* my heart.

It's really, really not fair for Sam to ask me to wait for them. I'm about to leave when Sam and Seth step out of the elevator. Both appear tense, and my instinct to take off goes into overdrive. But when Sam's pleading gaze finds me, I feel stuck in the corner of the couch.

Sam comes over with Seth slowly following. "I noticed you got the laundry done, so how about that lunch?"

I glance at Seth, who is studying me with a suspicious gaze. "I . . ."

"Come on, Peyton," Sam says. "Like I said, my treat, especially for doing the laundry."

My eyes implore Sam to go without me as I say, "I already ate."

His eyes beg me to come. "We're going to grab something quick, then we're walking to the bus terminal."

"Bus terminal?" I repeat.

"Yeah, Seth needs to get home," he says in a tight tone, though Seth shakes his head behind him. "He'll miss work. We're heading to the bus station so he doesn't lose his job. Please come?"

"Okay," I say, standing. None of this makes sense, yet I can't seem to refuse Sam's pleading.

Sam gives me a pained smile before we all start walking toward the entrance.

"You're aware," Seth says as we step outside, "there might not be a bus back home today."

"Detroit has to be a main hub. There'll be a bus there today," Sam says through gritted teeth.

"We'll see," Seth says, and I notice Sam's entire posture visibly tightening.

Sam stalks a bit ahead of us in obvious anger, but over his shoulder he says, "Just ask her your questions."

Watching him, I'm completely confused by whatever is going on between them.

"So," Seth says, bringing my attention to him, "you and Sam haven't talked since—well, in years?"

No. No. No. This weird tense crap between them can't be because of me. I draw in a breath and force myself to remain calm. "Nope. And he wasn't too excited—was actually quite upset—when Romeo asked me to come on tour."

"And you came because—because you're on the school newspaper, right?"

Obviously, Seth didn't believe Sam's explanation and now I'm being interrogated. "Yes, Romeo asked me because this fall I'll be on the editing team for the university paper."

Seth looks at me blankly, lost in thought and pulling at the unkempt scruff on his chin. "Huh? I don't recall you wanting to write."

He wouldn't. We never used to talk about serious stuff. "I'm getting a degree in journalism and hoping to make it as a music journalist."

His head tilts toward me, and he rubs the back of his neck with a palm while the lines of his face scrunch in confusion. "Well, I guess that makes sense."

I stare at Seth. He's not just thinner but kind of disoriented, in complete contrast to the cocksure attitude I remember him having.

"Actually, things don't make total sense," Seth says, tapping on his chin as we stop at a corner. Sam has his back to us. Seth looks down at me, studying me again with a suspicious glare. "I have to admit, Peyton, when I saw you standing in Sam's room, I thought you guys were still going behind my back."

Behind his back? After so many years, I don't know what to say. Sam apparently does, because he whips around. "Dammit, Seth! I told you to quit. I told you that shit wasn't happening."

Seth crosses his arms, tucks in his bottom lip, and glares at his brother. "Then why didn't you tell me she was with you?"

Sam runs a hand through his curls and tugs on them before lowering his hand. "I didn't want to upset you, okay?" he says in a pleading tone. "Nothing is going on. It wasn't worth you worrying about it."

Frowning, Seth looks from Sam to me. I fight the urge to run away from both of them. I'm feeling super weirded out.

"Tell him, Peyton," Sam says roughly. "Tell him we're just friends."

"Um," I say, my hands twisting the strap of the purse hanging across my chest. "Sometimes we are, I guess, but usually we're not even really friends, to be honest."

Seth looks confused by the statement, while Sam throws his head back and lets out a roaring laugh.

Chapter 16

The swipe of a card sliding in the lock has me hitting the power button on the TV remote, which engulfs the hotel room in darkness. And for a quick instant, I consider jumping across the room into my rollaway. But I'd never make it in time. I slip into the dark bathroom instead.

After Seth had refused to get on a bus, Sam reluctantly agreed to let him come to the concert. Seth had hounded me all day with questions. He'd been by my side while I ran the booth, before and after I took pictures of Luminescent Juliet onstage, while I packed up the booth, and then backstage. No matter how many times I'd refuted the notion, Seth had come up with more ways to insinuate that Sam and I are together. He's obsessed with proving it. The harassment got so bad that I snuck away, paid for a cab myself, and came back to the hotel alone. As the door starts to open, I'm practically praying Justin is on the other side of it because I *can't* deal with Seth anymore.

Unfortunately for me, it's not Justin. I hear Sam's voice blare angrily, "No, no, no. Gabe doesn't give a shit about you."

"Wrong!" Seth's voice sounds wild. "He's after me. Wants to take me down! Of course he'd slip something in my drink! He tried to poison me!"

What? Seth has to be wasted or something. I stand quietly in the bathroom, debating whether to turn on a light or say something to make them aware of my presence.

"Enough of this bullshit! No more of your bullshit!" Sam yells angrily. I freeze at the tone and volume of his voice.

"It's the truth," Seth says in a tone that borders on a whimper. I can sense that he's cowering and refusing to back down at the same time. "It's the truth," he repeats.

Someone hits or kicks the bathroom door, then Sam says, "Okay. Okay. Why is he after you?"

"I don't know. Ask him." Someone, most likely Seth, stomps on the floor. "But I could tell he was planning something."

I hear the frown in Sam's voice as he says, "He was making out with a groupie. How or why the fuck would he be worried about you?"

Seth's voice drops to a conspiratorial tone. "He wants to get rid of me," he says. "Do me in. He might be one of the bad guys or even an alien for all we know. "

At those words, I want desperately to disappear, melt down the drain or something, and avoid hearing all this craziness. But there's only one way out, and it involves leaving the bathroom and passing the brothers. So I stay put.

"Alien? Do you in? Do you in?" Sam repeats incredulously. "A drummer for an up-and-coming band has plans to murder the bass-ist's twin brother because . . . ?"

"He's evil," Seth says in a wild tone. "You refuse to see it. Like always, you refuse to *listen*."

Sam groans. "How long have you been off your fucking meds?"

I hold a gasp in. Somehow, I stay frozen, probably because of the shock hammering my brain.

"I told you, the pills were poisoning me!" Seth takes a deep breath. "The pills are bad. I can't think with them, and they slowly kill a person, like arsenic. Everyone in my therapy group knows that."

I'm still wishing I could dissolve into thin air when everything clicks into place: Seth *is* certifiably insane.

Sam's next words come out sounding dull and cold. "You are getting on that bus tomorrow if I have to tie you to a fucking seat. Then you're going back to your doctor and taking your fucking meds."

"No," says Seth, sounding stubborn. "I want to stay on tour with you."

"What about the guy who wants to do you in?"

"He—"

"No!" Sam shouts. "Forget I asked. We're going to bed, then getting up early so you can catch that six o'clock bus."

The door to the bathroom opens and the light flicks on.

I stand frozen, staring at Sam.

"Peyton?" he asks, horror in his tone.

Seth is instantly by his side.

Oh crap. They both stare at me wide-eyed and openmouthed.

Seth takes a step past Sam, pointing at me. "She was listening!" He turns to his brother. "She's spying on me," he says angrily. "You brought her to spy on me!"

I back away from him and almost run into the tub. "I—"

"She's not spying on you, Seth." Sam draws in a deep breath, looking at me angrily. "She should have made her presence known, but no one is spying on you."

"I'm really sorry," I say, more to Sam than to Seth. "I was going to say something, but you started yelling and I didn't want to come out and interrupt you. I kind of froze. I didn't mean to listen," I add when I see Sam's jaw harden.

Seth's fists bunch at his sides. "Stay out of my business, Peyton."

"Okay," I say simply. I step past Seth and then Sam, wanting to get the heck away from the drama. In the room, I reach for my purse.

"Just a minute," Sam says, looking at my bag. "I need to make a call home. Can you wait with him? I'll just be a few minutes." Before I can answer, he points a finger at Seth. "You stay put." With his phone in hand, he disappears into the bathroom.

Not wanting to hear anything Seth has to say, I flick on the TV and fall into a chair.

But of course Seth comes and stands in front of the TV. He pulls at the edge of his white tank until it's stretched past his hips. "So why were you listening, Peyton?"

Not sure how to deal with him, I decide to be honest and say, "With you two barging in, it was kind of hard not to."

His mouth twists as he glances toward the door. "Sam thinks I'm crazy. I'm not. I know things. See things. Lots of things. Things that others can't see."

Very uncomfortable, I stare at the TV. "Okay." I'm not going to argue with him. From everything I've just heard, arguing fuels his paranoia.

"This isn't good." His hands twist in his tank now, causing his white stomach and protruding ribs to show. "Sam is calling my mother. They're plotting right now. I'm not going to let them work against me," he snarls. Then he releases his twisted shirt and moves lightning fast toward the door of the room.

"Wait!" I yell, stumbling after him. But before I can stand straight, he's gone down the hallway. This can't be good. I pound on the bathroom door. "Sam! Seth took off! Sam!" I shout and pound harder.

The door whips open. Holding the phone to his ear, Sam says, "He took off. I gotta go." Racing past me, he goes to the door and looks down the hall. "Fuck!" he yells, then over his shoulder adds, "Peyton, I'm going to check the stairwell. You take the elevator. Meet me out front."

I grab my purse, slip on my flip-flops, and head toward the lobby. I rush around the hall corner, but no one's in front of the elevators. I tap my foot in irritation as I wait for an elevator. Once in the lobby, I don't spot Seth anywhere. Outside, Sam stands at the far end of the sidewalk, his gaze sweeping the area.

I run over to him. "Where would he go?"

He shakes his head furiously. "I don't know and he won't answer his phone."

"Would he try to confront Gabe?"

As he considers the idea, he winces. "Maybe."

I haul Sam by the hand toward the hotel entrance, where cabs always wait. "Let's go to the arena."

He follows slowly at first, but within a few seconds, he's dragging me. Luckily for us, there *is* a cab waiting. We slide into the backseat as Sam barks at the driver to go to the arena, which is about five blocks away.

Once we're on the road, I ask, "What exactly is going on?"

He shrugs. "I don't know. He wasn't supposed to know about the tour, but he clearly found out somehow. I never know what the hell Seth's going to do. It's just like him to get on a bus and come to Charlotte. Why fucking come to Charlotte?" he asks in a frustrated tone, staring out the window.

Aware he's not looking for a response and forced to acknowledge that he's not answering my question, I keep my mouth shut while many, many other unasked questions burn in my mind. Now is not the time, especially with Sam obviously dealing with so much.

The driver drops us off in front of the arena. We rush past masses of people leaving. But when we get to the front gate, they won't let us back inside because the concert is letting out. Local people work the entrances, and Luminescent Juliet is not that well-known. Which is why the two guys at the gate don't believe that Sam is in the band. At the point Sam is about to blow up, one of the roadies comes by pushing a flat cart full of boxes. Even when the roadie tells the gate guys Sam is in the opening band, they are reluctant but finally let us in.

We rush backstage and find the party in full swing, stereo blasting Pong. The large cement-walled room is packed with people, and a few band members. Gabe should be in here somewhere. Although the guys from Brookfield are usually tired and hang around only for a bit before heading to their hotel, Gabe always hangs out to party—usually with Sam.

After shoving through the mass, we find Gabe at the back. Girls hang on him, but he steps out of their embrace as we come at him.

Before either of us can ask about Seth, he yanks Sam by the collar and shouts in his face, "What the fuck is wrong with your brother?"

"Is he here?" Sam asks wide-eyed, obviously not caring Gabe is manhandling him.

Gabe jerks him closer. "The fucktard got in my face screaming weird shit. I almost punched his lights out. Luckily, I'm on probation. I settled for a bitch-slap," he says, releasing Sam's collar.

I tuck away the little nugget about probation.

"So he left?" Sam asks.

Gabe shrugs and wraps his arms around one of the girls. "Fucking hope so."

"Fuck! Fuck! Fuck!" Sam says, then starts pushing through the crowd.

I stay close, a shadow in the swath he cuts through people.

Near the back entrance, he interrogates several bouncers. The third one thinks he saw someone fitting Seth's description leave a few minutes ago through the parking lot. Out near the buses, Sam starts tearing at his hair and swearing under his breath, pacing back and forth across the cement.

After a few minutes of letting him vent, I ask, "Would he go back to the hotel?"

He stops and releases the tight hold on his hair. "I don't have a clue!"

Knowing he's frustrated, I choose to ignore his anger and think of possible solutions. "I could go back to the hotel while you look . . . somewhere else."

He's staring at me, breathing heavy, when the bass line of his phone rings and he takes it out of his pocket.

"Mom," he answers curtly, then turns away. Staring at the back of him, I see him shake his head several times but can hear only the low murmur of his voice as he continues walking away. Minutes later, done with the call, he comes toward me, searching on his phone. He stops a few feet from me without looking up.

"He's at the bus stop."

"Really?" I ask incredulously. He didn't want to go home this afternoon. He'd told me repeatedly he was staying on tour with his brother.

Sam continues studying the screen on his phone. "According to what he told my mother."

"If we go back out front, we could probably catch another taxi."

He shakes his head and turns. "We're about two blocks away." He shoves the phone back into his pocket and takes off past the bus. "It should take less than five minutes to walk," he says over his shoulder.

Jogging in flip-flops is a bitch.

Sam was right. About five minutes later, we come up to the bus station. A bus slowly passes us and we both stop running at the sight of the person giving us a middle-finger wave from the back.

Actually, Seth's twisted grin pairs rather well with his one-finger wave.

Chapter 17

I sit on a bench while Sam talks to his mother. He paces back and forth across the sidewalk. To say he looks frazzled is an understatement. When the woman at the outside ticket counter told us the bus was heading to Kansas City, Missouri, Sam about hit the roof, hearing his brother was traveling across half the country.

I pull my gaze away from Sam, unwilling to watch him wear a path into the cement. The man on the bench across from me tips his brown paper–bagged bottle to his mouth, staring at me with blurry eyes. A woman nearby talks into her phone loud enough for people two blocks over to hear. Along the far wall, another man sleeps on a bench, drooling on the wood. The open-air pavilion is nearly vacant in the middle of the night. I'm guessing the inside of the terminal is as quiet.

Sam finally comes over and plops down next to me. He runs a hand down his face. "Supposedly, he's catching a connection to Detroit tomorrow."

"That's good, then."

"If he does it," Sam says with a sigh. "If there was another bus going out tonight, I'd be able to follow him."

I'm shocked at that. Apparently, Sam would be willing to abandon the tour to chase his brother down. I suppose, from what I've witnessed, that makes sense. Seth out in the big world by himself could be dangerous, mainly to himself, possibly to others.

Sam glances at his phone and sighs. "It's past two o'clock. We should head back."

We start walking to the hotel. From what I can gather, the bus terminal is somewhere between the arena and the hotel. Though the area is rough, the streets are empty this late at night. Sam is silent as we make our way back. His shoulders slump, as if he carries the weight of the world on them.

After the first block, I say, "The person who calls you all the time isn't a girlfriend. It's Seth, right?" Sam silently nods. On the third block, the main question that's been screaming in my head all night comes out in a light tone. "What's wrong with Seth?"

Sam glances at me, then stuffs his hands into his pockets. After a few minutes, I assume he is never going to answer, but then he says tightly, "He—he's schizophrenic."

"Oh, that's . . . that's too bad," I say, trying to grasp that news. The little I know about the disease is what I learned in general psychology. Even with that limited knowledge, Seth's erratic behavior starts clicking into place for me. I even recall how bizarre and unpredictable he started acting during the last two months of our relationship.

"How long has he been?"

Sam doesn't look at me, just keeps walking. "Since senior year of high school."

I stop in the middle of the sidewalk. "Why didn't you tell me?"

Sam keeps going. "He wasn't diagnosed until after Christmas," he says roughly.

"Still," I say, running to catch up with him. "Everything"—from the heartbreak to the rumors to Seth's gradual change—"would have been easier to deal with if I'd known."

Without looking down at me, Sam's features twist into a mocking expression. "So while my parents and I were trying to understand Seth's diagnosis, and putting him in and out of the mental ward, and doing everything in our power to make sure he'd graduate from high school, I was supposed to contact you, the ex-girlfriend who most likely hated him, to make things easier for you to *deal with*?"

His words have me feeling small and selfish. I look down at my feet moving over the cement. "No. I guess not," I mumble. Throughout the entire day, my perspective on the past has been changing so dramatically that I'm having a hard time keeping up. The knowledge of Seth's disease makes the guilt and hurt I've dealt with for years go away almost entirely as I realize he wasn't in total control of his actions—and as I kind of understand why he had the demented need to fuel the rumor mill.

Sam shrugs. "Besides, we didn't want anyone to know at first. We didn't know how to handle it." His mouth turns down. "We hoped treatment would turn things around and get him back to something like normal."

"Is that why don't you tell people about him, because you wish he would be normal? Are you embarrassed by him?" My tone has an edge of incredulity.

"That he has a disease? No. That he acts like a frickin' idiot most of the time? A bit."

"Well, he can't help it." Suddenly, I'm overwhelmed with sorrow for Seth. Knowing him before and seeing him now is sad.

"He could take his fucking meds," Sam says, his tone exasperated. "That would help."

"Isn't it normal—I mean, isn't it part of the disease for him to not trust the meds?"

"Yeah, but as you've witnessed he's off his rocker without them."

My mind whirls, and questions come tumbling out of my mouth. "Is this why he didn't continue at the University of Michigan? It that why you didn't go to Michigan?"

"Yes. And yes."

As we enter the empty hotel lobby, resentment starts boiling inside of me. "Why would you do that to him? Why wouldn't you go with him to college to help him succeed?"

I don't say it out loud, but I know in my heart that if Jill needed support like Seth clearly does, I'd stay by her side. I would do whatever possible to help her succeed.

Sam stares at me.

Maybe it's because I'm tired from the long day or shocked by Seth's condition—or maybe it's because I'm imagining Jill, who is like a sister to me, in a similar situation—but I'm truly angry. "I can't believe you'd be such an asshole. To your twin brother, no less."

Sam opens his mouth, then snaps it shut. He grabs my arm and drags me to the inner court of the hotel, plops me onto a chair next to an aluminum table, steps away, and lights a cigarette.

Still angry, I'm about to stand and walk away, until Sam says, "Give me a minute to explain."

His tone, sad and guilty, glues me in the patio chair.

He takes a long drag before crushing the half-smoked cigarette under his boot. "Trying to quit," he says absently, tossing the butt into the trash.

Really, I haven't seen him light up that much, except for a few times and the illegal stuff.

He plops down onto the chair next to me, lowers his elbows to the table, takes a deep breath, and stares at me. "Do you know what I want?"

Thoroughly confused by the question, it takes me a few seconds to respond with a shake of my head.

"I want my brother back. We're twins, for fuck's sake." He slaps a hand on the table and the ping of the aluminum reverberates across the darkness of the patio. "We shared a room until we were fifteen. We were in every class together up to the age of eleven, several after that too. Played Little League on the same team for five years. Played in a band together. Sure, we'd argue and fight, but nothing"—he glances at me—"nothing could separate us. It was like having a best friend from birth."

He stares out over the patio as I try to keep my expression neutral, so I won't interrupt his explanation with the growing sadness building in my chest. This isn't about me.

"The brother I grew up with is gone. He's not the same. I'm never getting him back." The hum of the huge hotel air conditioners fills the silence. Sam turns to me. Even in the shadowy darkness, I can see the anguish lining his face.

He gestures to the tattoo on his arm. "I wanted to remember the real Seth with a line from a song he wrote for the Bottle Rockets." Shaking his head, he sighs sadly. "I got wasted so I could deal with the needle, but I wanted to freeze him in my memory with the permanence of a tattoo."

Though I've tried, I can never make out the black swirly writing on his arm. "What does it say?"

"Can rule the world with my twin at my side," he says.

"It's about you?"

"It was about both of us. From some crap song he wrote."

"Oh," I say softly, recalling the old Seth. The Seth who believed he did rule the world.

"I couldn't deal with it, Peyton. I couldn't go to college with him." His hands grip the edge of the aluminum table. "It was as if my brother had died and a stranger had taken his place. It had always been us, yet suddenly I was alone. I had to get away from the loss. The loss that stared me in the face every day," he says hoarsely. "From the heartbreak of losing my brother and best friend."

For one long moment, I stare at his sad face, taking in the glare of tears in his eyes, and imagine losing Jill like he lost Seth. It would be devastating. Then, without thinking, I'm across the flagstones and in his lap, hugging him to me and trying to absorb the raw pain pouring out of him. His hands grip my back and he shudders underneath me as he buries his head against my neck and shakes with sobs.

Feeling wetness on my neck, I mumble, "I get it. I really get it. You're not an asshole."

His fingers dig into my back and we hold each other, rocking and gripping and mourning what can't be changed. It's an embrace filled with sorrow and desolation. I'm not surprised to find I'm crying too. For him, for Seth, for the loss of what they had. Gone now. Forever lost. The sadness of it is overwhelming.

The resonance of a throat clearing loosens my grip on Sam. When the beam of a flashlight hits us, I almost fall out of his lap.

"It may be the middle of the night," the person holding the flashlight behind us says, "but this is still a public place, not a bedroom."

He lowers the blinding light a bit and I can make out a guard uniform.

Sam whips his head around. "Fu—"

I slap my hand over his mouth. "It's not what you think," I say, mortified at the guard's insinuation. I start untangling myself from Sam's lap. "We were—his brother . . ." I stand and pull my hand from Sam's mouth. "We were just hugging."

The guard makes a *harrumph* sound, and Sam shoots up to standing. "Are you blind, old man?" The guard lifts the light again and Sam puts up a hand over his face. "Get that shit out of my eyes!"

The guard lowers the light a bit.

"Seriously?" Sam wipes an arm over his wet cheeks. "The one time I let myself cry like a baby, some asswipe thinks I'm fu—"

"Okay," I say loudly, cutting Sam off and reaching for his arm. "We're going to go." I drag Sam by the arm toward the door leading to the lobby. "Sorry for hugging on your patio," I say in a tone laced with sarcasm.

The guard doesn't respond, and I don't wait, just drag Sam into the lobby and then to the elevator.

Inside the elevator, Sam leans his forehead against mine. "Now, *that* guy is an asshole." A giggle escapes me, and Sam reaches up and wipes the wetness from my cheeks with his thumbs. "Thanks for listening to my shit, Peyton."

The elevator doors open. We don't move.

Troubled by his despondent tone, I catch his wrists. "It wasn't shit, Sam."

He shakes his head against mine. "It's never-ending shit."

My grip tightens on his wrists. I want to fix this and help him, but it's unfixable.

He pulls our entwined hands to his mouth and lowers his head to give my knuckles a whisper-light kiss. "Thanks again," he murmurs, lifting his head back up and looking at me with his warm sky-blue eyes.

The touch of his mouth lingers on my skin, brings memories of the caress of his mouth on other parts of my body, and my breath catches at the tenderness of his gaze.

"Come on." He gently pulls his wrists from my grasp and turns me toward the hall with a hand on my shoulder. "We're going to be dragging ass tomorrow."

As we tread down the hall toward our room, I wish for the millionth time that I'd never fallen for Seth. Now I wish I had fallen for Sam instead.

Chapter 18

S tanding inside the U-shaped configuration of foldout tables that make up our booth, I slide another card through the credit device attached to Romeo's phone. Selling T-shirts, hats, and CDs is a mind-numbing experience. I've come to hate running the booth. But the band has no one else, and the earnings at the end of a night total from about three hundred to a thousand dollars. Not too shabby for an up-and-coming band. I can't imagine what the other bands pull in. They have multiple booths, with long, long lines.

The next few hours will drag. We just got to Richmond this morning, but right after the show, once the crew packs everything up, we're hitting the road again around two a.m. to drive to Philly. And we won't arrive until early morning. I'm not looking forward to the next run of concerts and bus trips we have lined up.

The muffled first riffs of Luminescent Juliet's "Midnight" echo through the venue as I fold up a T-shirt, slide it into a bag, and hand it over to a guy with a pink Mohawk. He purposely brushes his hand along mine in the process, smiling slowly. "When you're done, I'd love to buy you a drink."

My standard concert outfit has become a pair of denim cutoffs, cowboy boots—my dumb ass didn't bring fashionable yet comfy shoes—and a Luminescent Juliet T-shirt. Of course I have one of each of the three designs, which put the band's name and logo across my chest. Not the most flattering outfit, yet male rockers seem to like it. I've gotten a few compliments on it, and a few propositions like the current one.

I force a smile. I don't have anything against pink Mohawks, and of course this guy doesn't know I have a boyfriend. But hello, dude, you could be a serial killer for all I know. "Tempting, but I have to work all night."

At that moment Mike, the roadie whom Romeo pays to cover the booth so I can take pictures, slips in to take my place. "Hey, Peyton." He reaches for Romeo's phone in my hand. "Go on. They just went onstage. I'll take care of this."

Mohawk guy frowns.

Ignoring him, I go snatch my camera from behind a bin of T-shirts and then slip out of the booth. Getting backstage is not an easy feat. First, I have to get through the masses in the hallways around the arena. Then I have to take a tunnel that goes under the bleachers and around half the arena. Next come the checkpoints where I hold out the pass around my neck for inspection. Once out of the tunnel, I pass the green room and spot the Brookfield guys being interviewed by the local media.

I pass an area where backstage ticket holders are getting pictures taken with members of Griff.

The excitement on the fans' faces always gives me a little surge of exhilaration. I'd never been backstage until this tour, but I have been to several concerts. My first was the most exciting. When I was fifteen, my grandpa took me to see the Red Hot Chili Peppers when they were on their *Stadium Arcadium* Tour. Each time I see backstage pass holders looking giddy and wide-eyed as they meet the bands, I remember how I nearly pissed my pants with excitement during the hour-and-fifteen-minute ride to the Palace of Auburn

Hills. My grandfather and I had nosebleed seats, yet we both had an awesome time.

The music from the stage gets louder as I continue my journey, and I hear the guys break into "At the End of the Universe," an energetic song that I've loved from the first time I heard it. Some songs need to grow on you. Not this sucker. Fast and rocking—I immediately liked it.

The area directly behind the stage was a bitch to get into until the roadies got to know me. This is the place where the instruments are tuned and shined up, and where costume changes are stashed. Fans are never allowed here. A few roadies wave to me as I pass but most are busy.

Heading around the back of the stage, I go out onto the floor past the bouncers instead of my usual spot in front of the stage, and I use my concert ID to make my way backward through the crowd on the floor to the sound booth. The perfect place to get pictures of the Luminescent Juliet guys all together, playing onstage. Earlier this afternoon, wearing a smile and a low-cut shirt—a girl's gotta do what a girl's gotta do—I'd stopped by with a large pepperoni pizza to ask the engineers if I could get a few pictures during the concert. Between the pie and the cleavage, it didn't take them too long to agree to let me into the most off-limits area of all.

Now, here I am, and the engineers at the sound and light boards don't look too happy to see me. Still, they let me in. I quickly take some pictures of the entire stage. Some zoomed in and others from far away. I get some of the guys on their instruments, others of the silhouettes of the crowd's heads and arms.

Then I bolt from the sound booth before one of the guys decides to kick me out. I pause at the booth, watching the band. For once, smashed in the crowd, it's like I'm really at a concert. It's not a business out here. It's not a production. It's music blaring with the crowd swaying and screaming. It's a different type of energy. And though I know they're a talented rock band, out here in the mass, Luminescent Juliet seems more real to me. They seem like actual stars. A tattooed shirtless singer belts out lyrics, moving across the stage. A dark guitar player intricately fingers out a riff. A lean drummer moves gracefully around the drum set. And a gorgeous bass player plucks at his strings and bounces while his curls tumble over his forehead.

Sam stands facing the crowd, bouncing to the rhythm as usual. Dressed in gray cargo pants, black boots, and a black tank, he's looking sexy. His smooth arm muscles bunch as he plucks at his orange bass. During the past three weeks, his curls have grown longer. They bounce with him, falling over his forehead at each beat from the drums.

He's rock star perfection. Slightly elusive, bigger than life, and totally hot.

Damn. I have to stop thinking about him as so attractive.

But it's good to see him having fun after last night. He'd moped through the day, appearing depressed and spending most of it dozing in his bunk, except when he'd come to the back of the bus to tell me his mother had picked up Seth in Detroit. But onstage, he's energy and grins, his gorgeous body always in motion to the music.

With a shake of my head, I turn to go, but as the band starts the next song, "Trace," I'm frozen by the sudden, obvious change in Sam. Once energetic and bouncy, he's suddenly wooden and robotic. Without thinking, I start moving through the crush of people toward the stage. When a girl elbows me, I hold up my pass. Keeping my pass in the air, I move far enough forward that I can see the bleakness on Sam's face.

His lips are thin and angry-looking. Lines groove his cheeks. And his jaw is clenched tight. He sings the chorus, and the words come from his mouth as if he's forcing them out. Something is very wrong. I've never seen Sam onstage like this. He's always happy energy, as if there's nothing better in the world than playing for a crowd. At the moment, he's dark anger.

As if the song flipped his switch.

I try to recall the lyrics as Romeo plays the guitar solo. Something about traces of a girl being left. A song about the heartbreak of love? Why has it got Sam all tense? Does it remind him of someone breaking his heart? Surely not me. Though he may have been attracted to me, we were never close enough for the kind of heartbreak to show up in a song.

They sing the chorus again: "Gone, gone, gone / nothing left but traces of you. / Gone, gone, gone / But still holding on to these traces of you." Again, Sam spits out the words.

The song ends, and then—after Justin yells out "Thank you!" and "I hope you like this one!"—they start "Inked My Heart," their biggest hit, which always gets the crowd going. Sam instantly looks more relaxed. Since the song is slower, he doesn't bounce, but he's back near the edge of the stage and flirting again.

Totally confused, I make my way back to the booth. And just in time too. Mike stays and helps me with the fans wanting T-shirts during the lull. Once Griff gets onstage, business dies down immediately. Mike takes off but says he'll be back in about an hour to help me pack up. I text back and forth with Jill. This being Friday night, she's out with the girls, so she keeps sending me pictures of drinks and shots. In between reading her incoherent texts, I try to look up the lyrics for "Trace." Unfortunately, Luminescent Juliet isn't popular enough for their lyrics to be listed on any websites. Yet.

So I pop in one earbud and listen to the song while waiting on customers. I've figured out half the lyrics and typed them into my phone when Mike shows up to help me pack the stuff in bins. Once we get everything on a flat cart, Mike waves at me and rolls the cart away.

Brookfield is playing now and the green room is party central. More band members are hanging out than usual because there's no hotel to go to, just the buses. I snag a beer and head over to the area where Luminescent is hanging out.

I instantly realize Sam isn't in the room, which is strange. He always parties after a concert. I inch closer to Justin. When he's done nodding and smiling at whatever the girl next to him is saying, I loudly ask, "Where's Sam?"

Justin shrugs. "He took off. Maybe the bus?"

Recalling the weird way Sam acted onstage, I step back and take a sip of my beer. Is Sam depressed about his brother? Or did he leave with someone? When it comes to Sam and groupies, speculation leaves me slightly jealous. An emotion that makes little sense, and that I should not be feeling.

One of the scantily clad women absently pushes me aside in her quest to get near Justin. I move back and let her at him. Though he smiles, I catch a look of irritation crossing his face.

I down the rest of my beer, trying to push the images of Sam and a groupie out of my mind. I shouldn't be thinking of him. I have a boyfriend. Sam is a rock star. My jealousy does not fit into any part of that equation.

By the time I'm on my second beer—on tour sometimes I feel like I'm on a liquid diet—the concert is over and the room is overflowing. I'm a content but bored spectator, leaning against the wall, until I notice Rick coming my way.

Constantly on the lookout for a piece of ass, some of the other band members in Griff and one from Brookfield have shown an interest in me. Since they hit on anything female younger than fifty, the attention isn't much of an ego booster—but everyone has left me alone when I showed disinterest and explained I have a boy-friend. *Everyone except Rick.* He's about ten feet and four people away, eyeing me.

I cannot deal with Rick tonight.

Screw giving Sam time to screw his groupie on the bus. I shove off the wall, then push my way through the mass and out the door, leaving Rick and his sultry looks in the dust. After tossing my almost-full beer into the trash, I go down a long hall and pass several roadies on my way outside and into the muggy Virginia night.

The hum of the buses' air conditioners fills the silence in the parking lot. Because the buses are gated off and security guards make rounds around the buses, they're usually open. I'm hoping that's the case with ours. Luckily for me, it is. I stand on the cement, holding the door open and debating how to make my presence known before going in. I do not want to walk in on something that will have me wanting to bleach my eyeballs, or cry my heart out. Stepping up, I decide on a door slam—*bang*—and then shout, "Hello?"

Hearing nothing but the hum of the air conditioner, I yell out another "Hello?"

Nothing again. I go up the stairs and enter the main cabin. It's super dark. "Sam?" I say as my hand brushes the wall, searching for the light switches. I hit the first one my fingers find. The light over the kitchen sink pops on, leaving the rest of the cabin shadowy, and I make out a motionless, shadowy figure on the couch.

The whole scene is a bit freaky.

"Sam?" I repeat. My fingers find the main switch, and when I flick it on, the cabin is bathed in light. So is Sam. So is the blood running from his nose, down his chin, and soaking into his shirt.

I'm at his side in seconds, shaking him. "Sam! Sam! Sam!"

His eyes open sluggishly. "Hey, Peyton," he says. He lifts his head slightly and more blood squirts from his nose.

"Holy shit, Sam!" I'm relieved he's awake but scared by the sight of all the blood as I jump up and grab a towel from the counter, then press it to his nose. With a shaky hand, I dig my phone out. "We need to call an ambulance."

"Ambulance? No ambulance," Sam says, trying to push himself up and touching under his nose. He frowns at the blood on his fingertips but repeats, "No ambulance."

My phone falls to the floor as I push him back down. "Stay down! You're bleeding all over!"

"Don't call anyone." The words come out muffled from under the towel. "Just get me some ice."

"Ice? Ice! You're bleeding like a stuck pig!"

After looking down at his blood-drenched shirt, he tears the towel from my hand and presses it to his nose. Laying his head back, he growls, "Just get me some ice!"

With shaky hands, I get another towel and fill it with ice. He has lost a lot of blood. He needs more than ice. He needs medical help whether his stupid ass realizes it or not. I hand him the ice-filled towel, then pick up my phone from the floor. I get only one number punched in before Sam kicks the phone out of my hand, and the device flies across the room onto the other couch.

Sam pushes himself up. "Do *not* call anyone."

I stand there breathing heavily as we stare at each other, trying not to go off on him. "What's going on?" I ask, though I'm starting to put two and two together.

He sits up fully, but leans his head back and shrugs. "My left sinus membrane may have broken open."

"Why the hell would your sinus break open?" I ask evenly.

"Maybe the coke was cut with something. Or maybe I snorted too much."

"I thought you dumped all your stuff," I say, my teeth clenching.

"Got it from a roadie. Needed a couple hits."

If he weren't a bloody mess, I'd smack the living crap out of him. "You said you weren't addicted."

He shrugs. "Sometimes I need the high. It's not daily or anything. Just when things get rough."

"Rough?" I ask, but the answer comes to me immediately. Seth. The never-ending shit with his brother. That is what drives Sam to this.

He stands, then weaves. "I need to get cleaned up before they get back. Romeo will kill me if he finds out. Or worse. He'll find a new bass player."

I reluctantly go to his side. "Do you have any more stashed away?"

He doesn't answer me.

I step away and cross my arms. "I'm not helping you unless you give it to me."

He weaves. I don't make a move to help.

My arms tighten across my chest. "There's no way in hell I'm helping you if you're going to turn around and pull this crap again."

Glaring at me, he jerks a baggie from his pocket and holds it out. I distastefully pluck the small bag from his hand with a finger and thumb.

After helping him to the bathroom, the first thing I do before he sits down on the toilet lid is flush the baggie. I help him remove his blood-soaked tank top. I wrap it in plastic grocery store bags, planning to toss it into a trash bin later. Using soapy paper towels and putting them in grocery store bags too, I wipe down his chest and neck as he leans his head back, still holding the ice to his nose.

This mess would be much easier in a real bathroom with unlimited water, because he could just take a long shower. But the limited amount of water in here would leave blood all over the shower stall. Or use up the water supply. Neither scenario would be good.

When Sam pulls the ice away from his nose so I can wash his face, a thin line of blood leaks out.

"Ugh," I say. "If you didn't have a bloody nose, I'd give you one."

He grins.

I don't grin back. Leaning over him, I begin cleaning the mess off his face. The scruff on his jaw tears at the paper towel, but he's at last cleaned up and no longer bleeding.

When I'm done, he grabs my hand and kisses my palm. "Thank you, Peyton."

We stare at each other for a long moment. His crystal-blue gaze is filled with soft warmth that is almost melting my anger. And it does, to a point.

I tug my hand from his. "This is the last time I'm covering for you. I'm not playing." I stand. "Got it?"

Jaw tightening, he nods.

"And if it keeps bleeding, you're going in," I say in a steely tone, wrapping the already-bagged shirt and the bloody paper towels into the last plastic bag from under the sink. No doubt Romeo will be asking where all the bags went.

Sam dumps the bloody ice towel into the trash too, then stands and flicks open the buttons of his jeans.

I jump back and crash into the plastic shower wall. "What are you doing?"

"Getting in the shower," he says, weaving and holding on to the counter for support, as he lifts one eyebrow that matches his cocky grin. "Care to join me?"

"Ah, no." I angrily snatch the bags from the floor, planning to dump them in a bin outside, as he pushes his pants down and reveals black boxers. "Well, I guess if you can still flirt like an ass, you don't need an ambulance after all," I say over my shoulder as I step out of the bathroom.

Chapter 19

Two concerts and two nights later, I wake up and realize the bus isn't moving. Artificial light shines through the window above the couch. Something clanks below, and I slowly comprehend we're at a truck stop. Gary must be draining the tanks. I reach down and dig my phone out of my purse on the floor. Five twenty-nine a.m. I check our location with the phone. We're only two hours out of Toronto. Damn. Still almost five more hours until we get to New York.

More clanking from below ensues and I sit up, burying my head in my hands. I'm exhausted and getting more irritated by the second. These past five days have been grueling. Concert after concert without hotels. Sleep, wake up in a new city, set up, deal with concert, help pack up, and then get back on the road. So I'm excited that when we reach New York City today, we're staying for three full days. Though I want to sightsee, I might use all the extra time to sleep.

I tiptoe through the bus and retrieve a bottle of water from the fridge. On my way back to my little room, a bunk curtain opens.

"Peyton?" Sam whispers.

I ignore him, but a minute after I'm back on the couch, the heavy plastic curtain between the two rooms quietly opens. The leather couch moans as Sam sits down next to me.

"I'm sorry, Peyton," he whispers.

The bottle of water twists in my hands. I've stayed away from him or ignored him and his swollen nose—he told the guys he ran into a wall in the darkened bus—for the past couple of days. Every time I'm near him, my blood about boils because he could have killed himself with his stupid-ass drugs. For him to come in here and ask for forgiveness in the middle of the night has me about to erupt with anger.

He sets his chin on my shoulder. "Please, Peyton," he begs.

My lip quivers as I set the bottle of water on the table. "So this is the right time for an apology?"

"I couldn't sleep either. Kept thinking about you being pissed."

That my anger kept him awake softens me a bit. "You scared the crap out of me," I whisper, and my voice nearly breaks.

His arms wrap around me, and I'm suddenly pressed to a warm naked chest. "I'm sorry, so sorry. I needed to get away from everything."

I try to ignore the smooth sensation of his skin. "But you're not escaping. It's called getting high."

"Those short moments of escape keep me going," he says in a soft whisper.

"Those short moments are going to kill you!" I hiss. "If I hadn't shown up—" My voice breaks on the last word.

He buries his head in my neck. "I know. I know. I'm trying to stay away from that stuff. It's just that when Seth came, and it was evident he's doing worse and not taking his meds . . ."

And there is the crux of the matter, the reason I have kept my mouth shut and my anger in. Because no matter how nuts it is to mess around with drugs like he is, I get it. I understand why he wants to escape. I'd probably want to escape too if I were him.

Giving in, I wrap an arm around him. "Don't simply try. Stay away from that stuff."

His hold tightens on me, his fingers dig into my waist, his nose slides against the skin of my collarbone. "I'll do it for you."

"No, Sam," I say in a sad tone, pushing away a bit and rubbing his scruffy jaw. "Do it for *you*."

"For me," he says miserably.

I wrap both of my arms around him, and my pulse quickens at the feel of his hard, muscular body. *This is not the time to get revved up, Peyton!* Sam is hurting so much, he can't see past the pain.

"You're in an up-and-coming band," I whisper. "Your album just went up three spots on several lists. You're talented. A new set of ladies are after you every night. You're on a major tour."

He sighs against the skin of my neck. "None of that shit is important."

"Stop. Tons of people would kill to be in your place. Don't waste what you have, what you've worked for, with drugs or depression, and never, ever stop valuing you."

He holds me super tight for several long moments, then sighs sadly as his hands slide along the bottom of my back. "You feel right."

"Sam," I warn, and try to pull away from the tingle his touch causes.

His hand spans my back. "I don't mean like that. I mean strong, someone to lean on."

"Oh," I say, letting him tug me close again.

"We both can't sleep," he says, gently pushing me back until we're lying on the couch, my pillow under our heads. "Can I just hold you?"

I should say no but his voice is so sad, so lost, I can't help but nod. He tows the blanket over us, then we both turn sideways with his arms wrapped around me. Though the press of his body is comforting, I feel awkward too. I'm far too aware of his breath in my ear, his muscled leg over mine, and the crisp, clean scent of him. The bus starts moving, and in minutes, his breathing evens. The awkwardness diminishes. I relax into his strong arms and let the warmth of him and the movement of the bus entice me into sleep.

Someone is shaking me. I open my eyes and the sight of Gabe above me has me rearing back into . . . Sam.

Oh shit.

Gabe grins, his long hair shaking with his laugh. "You two might want to separate before anyone else gets up," he whispers, then grabs my computer from the table and disappears out the curtained door.

He's using the computer for a good cause. Apparently, because Gabe's on probation for getting into several fights, he has to Skype with an anger management counselor every other week.

Sam pulls me close and tries to wrap a leg around me again. I crawl out of his arms and stand, hovering over him. Gabe thinking we're together is bad enough. The entire band thinking it would be mortifying.

"Get up, Sam," I say in a hushed tone.

His eyes stay closed, but he says, "Too early."

I shake him, much harder than Gabe shook me. "Get up!" I hiss.

One blue eye pops open. "Come cuddle."

I tug his arm. "Sam!"

"Okay, okay, I'm getting up." He sits up, stretches, and runs his hands through his messy curls. His pectorals lift, then bunch. "What time is it?"

I drag my gaze from his chest. "I don't know. Get back to your bunk."

Smirking, he stands next to me. "You really care what they think?"

My eyes shoot darts at him. "I'm not into drama."

He shrugs and gazes at me through his lashes. "You going out on the town with us tonight?"

I push him toward the door. He doesn't move. "I'm going to smack you!"

"Tell me you'll come out with Gabe and me."

When I don't answer, he crosses his arms, waiting. A freaking unmovable rock.

"Fine, I'll go." I point to the curtained door. "Now get out."

He laughs and gives me a quick peck on the lips.

My lips are tingling. Stunned for a moment, it takes me a few seconds to grab a pillow. It hits him on his way out, bouncing off his muscular back.

I take my time getting dressed. Then I take my time in the bathroom, brushing my teeth, washing my face, applying a little makeup, and brushing my hair until it's a crackling mess of static. After that, I take my time organizing and packing up my stuff. I'm a bit freaked out, and don't want to see Gabe's or Sam's knowing smirk. Because nothing happened.

By the time I'm ready to go, the bus is parked. I peek out the window. Perfect timing. We're at the hotel.

I ignore both Sam and Gabe, who are sitting at the table eating cereal as I pass by with my shoulders and hands loaded down with bags. Head held high, I step off the bus ready to start building a pile of bags outside the door. At the sight of the person standing on the sidewalk, the bags fall from my grasp.

Thunk. Thunk. Thunk.

Luckily, my camera bag is around my neck.

Chapter 20

"Whoa, baby," Bryce says, rushing over to help me. He bends to pick up bags while I stand there shell-shocked. Dressed in khaki shorts, a buttoned-up shirt, and slip-on boat shoes, he looks like a preppy catalog model as his thick blond hair blows in the breeze.

"Bryce," I say, staring at him with big eyes. "What are you doing here?"

Before he can answer, Sam says from behind me, "You okay, Pey—"

I glance back and see his stunned gaze resting on my boyfriend.

Now we're both staring at Bryce like he's a Martian.

"Hey, Sam," says Bryce, now loaded up with my bags. When Sam doesn't answer, he looks from me to Sam. "What's going on, Peyton?"

Knowing we both probably look guilty—though we shouldn't—I force myself to speak. "Nothing. Well, you're here, and I'm completely shocked." I step closer to him. "Shocked happy," I say, forcing a smile. "But very shocked." I wrap my now free hands around his waist and lift my face for a kiss.

His kiss doesn't have any of the heat of Sam's swift peck, and it is entirely too weird kissing Bryce while Sam is behind us, coughing like he suddenly has bronchitis. I pay no attention to Sam.

Bryce grins down at me. "Maybe I should have called, but I wanted it to be a surprise."

"Oh, it's a surprise. Very nice, though," I say, smiling again. The curve of my lips is starting to feel as rigid as plastic.

Sam comes down the stairs and holds his hand out. "Nice seeing you."

Bryce shakes his hand. "Good to be here."

At six one, Bryce is taller than Sam by almost three inches, yet somehow Sam generates a more masculine presence with his muscular build. Not that Bryce isn't muscular. He's just leaner, in contrast to Sam, who has a little more bulk.

"Come on," Bryce says, reaching for my hand. "I've already got us a room."

Sam frowns at that news as Bryce tugs me away.

"Great," I say, dumbfounded. The idea of sharing a room with him feels foreign. Bryce and I have never spent a night together. Sex, yes. Waking up together, no. After having just slept and cuddled with Sam, the idea of sleeping with Bryce seems . . . off.

When we're almost to the revolving door entrance, Sam yells from behind us, "Hey, Peyton!"

I turn halfway around, giving him a questioning glare.

"You're still coming out with us tonight, right?" His gaze is a mix of persuasive and threat.

Not wanting to know what he plans to do or say if I refuse, I nod curtly and then turn back around.

As we enter the hotel, Bryce says, "I wanted to take you to a romantic dinner." I detect a whine in his voice.

"We can go to dinner, but I already made plans for later." More like I was coerced into plans. "If I would have known you were coming, of course I wouldn't have made them."

I smile reassuringly while he takes a minute to pout. "Guess if we're together, that's all that matters."

"Keep that thought in mind. I do have to work tomorrow night," I say as we move through the huge lobby.

"Maybe the surprise thing wasn't the best idea," he murmurs as he hits the up button for the elevator.

We step onto an elevator—and standing across from him, I'm shocked all over again, but it's good to see him. He reminds me of home. "I still can't believe you're here. Did you fly in?"

"Yeah, got here at eight," he says, and pushes the button for the tenth floor. "Took the first morning flight."

I blink at him. "When did you decide this? When did you get a ticket? A room reservation?"

"About a week ago. I'd been thinking about it since you told me about the guys' girlfriends showing up in New Orleans. When our tournament got canceled for this weekend, I decided to do it."

"Huh, that's pretty amazing," I say, recalling all the times we texted over the past week and the few times we talked. "I can't believe you never slipped up."

He grins, and I'm reminded of how cute he is. "I wanted it to be a surprise."

The elevator doors open, and I step out into the hall saying, "A lovely thought, but being on the road so long has kind of worn me out."

He shrugs. "No biggie. I know how it is."

I suppose, because he's on a college baseball team, he does.

"Isn't this hotel a bit expensive?" I ask, taking in the hallway that screams swank, with its fancy textured wallpaper and lush carpet.

"Over three hundred dollars a night," he says, then smiles down at me. "But you're worth it."

I smile weakly. Bryce works off-season in the school store, and I know his parents send him money to help out each month, but for a college student this hotel is really expensive.

Once in our room, we set my bags down and Bryce glances toward the bed. "What do you want to do?"

I unzip my suitcase. "I need to take a shower."

He stares at me, his dark brown eyes gleaming. "Shower sounds good."

I can't help the irritated look that crosses my face. Really? I'm going to get off a bus, then fuck his brains out? We have never showered together, but suddenly we're a domesticated couple?

Obviously reading the look on my face, he reaches for the remote. "I'll watch TV while you shower."

I dig through my suitcase, trying to get a grip on my irritation. "Then maybe lunch?" I say lightly.

"Lunch would be good," he says flatly, settling onto the chair by the bed.

"After that I need to do laundry."

"Laundry?" he asks, his tone even more dull than before.

I keep digging for something clean to wear. "Yeah, we've been on the road for six days straight."

"Okay," he says, looking disappointed. "Lunch then laundry."

I grab my cosmetic bag and march to the bathroom. Why am I getting the feeling that Bryce made this trip to get laid? It's like he imagined coming for a three-day sexathon. It's as if my boyfriend thinks he has free rein with my body.

I turn on the shower and lean against the sink counter.

Bryce and I have always worked. Both of us are busy, but for the past year, I've thought going out once or twice a week with him was fun. He was patient with me when it came to the sex. At least he worked at helping me get more comfortable, and it's been getting good. I'm not sure if it's my body image issues, but when it comes to sex, I can be too self-conscious to enjoy it. Besides losing my virginity to Sam, and being with Bryce, the only other experience I've had was one short, fast, and awkward relationship sophomore year with a guy in my journalism classes. The one thing I will say is that since I've noticed how my body responds to Sam, I'm realizing that maybe the good between Bryce and me could be better.

Now that he's here visiting, acting like we have some deep, committed relationship, I'm realizing that what we have feels like convenience. At the moment, a three-hundred-dollars-a-night convenience. Am *I* worth the three hundred dollars a night? Or is the sex?

It's not even 10:00 p.m. and we're already at our third bar of the evening. I still can't believe I agreed to hit the town with Gabe and Sam—and Bryce.

"Six more shots of vodka," Sam tells the waitress. I give him a dirty look since one round of vodka is more than enough for me. "Make it four," he says, then glances at Bryce's beer. "And another Budweiser."

I sip my beer, trying to ignore the huge deer head on the wall above our tiny table. After a nice dinner in the hotel, Bryce and I had met Sam and Gabe in the lobby. Though this bar doesn't have loud, roaring music like the last one, where we couldn't talk, the brick walls are adorned with dead animals. Bears, raccoons, and owls stare at us. Very odd.

Bryce sits next to me with his hand on my cotton-clad thigh. We're a bit dressed up from dinner. Bryce is in khaki pants and a polo shirt, and I'm wearing white capris and a flowery top. Sam and Gabe are dressed sloppy in shorts, T-shirts, and flip-flops. We make an odd-looking group.

Curling his lip at Bryce's hand movement on my thigh, Sam tosses back a shot. I did one at the last bar. I'm not doing another. At least Gabe has moved to the bar to talk to a group of women. I want to throw my beer at him for the knowing smirk *he* has worn all night.

We entered the bar through a telephone booth in a hot dog place after Sam called the concert manager because, apparently, this tiny taxidermy haven of a bar requires reservations. When the phone booth magically opened after Sam's call, Bryce was impressed with Sam's connections. I rolled my eyes. The bar is kind of neat, but this entire night is annoying me. It's like I'm tagging along on a guys' night out.

"So, baseball, right?" Sam asks Bryce, who nods though we already covered this in the taxi ride over. Sam taps his full beer on the table. "You hoping to go professional?"

Bryce pulls his hand from my lap to twist the class ring around his finger. "Always hoping, but we're not a major college nor do we have the best record to attract scouts. Yet I might try out, even for a farm team."

Stunned, I stare at Bryce as he finishes off his beer. He has never told me this. He's getting a degree in physical therapy. I'd always assumed he'd pursue that career once he graduated. Not that I care what he does, but it seems odd that this is the first I've ever heard of his future plans, given that we've been together for the past seven months.

Sam leans over the table and gives Bryce a conspiratorial look. "You ever use steroids?"

"Um . . . no," Bryce says, pushing his empty beer bottle to the edge of the table.

"Never?" Sam says with raised eyebrows.

The waitress appears with the beer and shots. Sam shoves a shot and the Budweiser at Bryce, then pays. He's been paying all night, and unfortunately, I don't think it has anything to do with goodwill. To me it looks like he's out to get bombed and take Bryce along for the ride.

Once the waitress leaves, he raises his shot toward Bryce. His tone is sarcastic as he says, "To clean athletes."

I resist kicking Sam's shin under the table as they down the shots.

Sam shoves yet another shot of vodka at my boyfriend while I glare across the table. Ignoring me, he says to Bryce, "Dude, I wouldn't think less of you if you had. If your career's on the line, you gotta do what you gotta do."

Bryce twists the shot around, holding it by his fingertips. He stares intently at the short glass of clear liquid. "Yeah, we'll see how my hitting goes this fall. I need to bat above three hundred for scouts to come."

Sam makes a finger motion in his groin area that's clearly meant to insinuate shrinkage, and since we're sitting on high stools, the insult would be entirely visible to me *and* Bryce, if he were to look up.

I kick Sam in the shin.

He lets out an "oomph" and Bryce looks up. Sam smirks and lifts the second shot. "To batting over three hundred," he says.

Bryce downs his shot with a grimace and I place a hand on his shoulder. "Don't you think that's enough shots?"

He points to Sam, who is wearing a smirk. "Keeping up with the locals."

Really? Are we in fucking high school? "He's not local. He's in a rock band. He parties regularly." Tired of the little games he's playing, I glare at Sam again. "Trust me. You don't want to keep up with him. You don't want to be anything like him."

Sam's mouth goes from a frown of hurt to a lazy smile so fast, I question if I imagined the hurt.

Sam lifts his beer, the one he'd ordered in the first round and hasn't touched, before taking a drink, and says, "Yeah, who'd want to be a famous rich rocker?"

I snort but Sam grins.

Bryce asks, "Is it weird?"

Sam cocks his head in a question.

"Being famous, having people fawn over you, girls you've never met want . . ." Bryce doesn't finish his sentence. Nor does he look at me.

"Not there yet," Sam says, gesturing around the bar. "These people don't know me from dick, but yeah, the getting chicks part has always been a bonus of the gig." He glances at me. "Even when I was in a high school garage band."

Anger burns through me and I clench my jaw. Sam is related to Dr. Jekyll.

Bryce shakes his head. "Chicks come with the territory, then. I should have learned how to play an instrument," he says with a laugh, wrapping an arm around my waist. "But not my girl. She's smarter than that."

"Oh yeah, Peyton's definitely immune," Sam says sarcastically as his gaze pins me to my stool.

What the fuck? I'd like to kick him in the shin again *and* throw my beer in his face. The snide reference to our past is making me furious. I've never made a remark about it to anyone, even a veiled one.

Bryce's gaze snaps to Sam. "You saying she isn't?" His tone is somehow both threatening and horrified at the same time.

Sam shakes his head. "No, bro, I meant she was immune." He cuts a hand through the air and adds, "Like totally."

Bryce's fingers dig into my waist. "Peyton would never be a groupie."

Ugh. Hello? I'm right here. I can stand up for myself if needed. What is wrong with these idiots?

Suddenly, Gabe's back, standing at our table. "You guys ready to head out?"

I look around and notice the girls he was talking to are gone.

Sam jumps off his stool and tugs out his phone from a pocket. "There's a place I wanted to check out a few blocks from here."

I should talk Bryce into going back to the hotel, but that king-size bed has been looming in my thoughts all night. So we head into the muggy summer night and stroll several blocks in the direction of the hotel. We took a cab to the East Village, which means it's way too far to walk all the way back to the hotel, especially since it's obvious to me now that we're outside that Bryce is drunk. Though his arm is around my shoulders, he can't walk straight. He keeps veering left, then right. A few feet ahead of us, Sam and Gabe jokingly argue about who can kick more ass. My opinion? They're both jackasses.

The next bar is somewhat similar to the last. No dead animals, yet it has a dark, modern interior filled with eccentric antiques. The furniture reminds me of the antique shop below where the band practices when they're home—maybe that's why Sam likes these spots.

Only a few minutes pass before the real reason Sam wanted to come here is revealed: Jell-O shots. The bar serves them, and he buys each of us three. I cave in and do one, but refuse the rest. I'm more than aware that the sweet, fruity taste of a Jell-O shot can mistakenly cause people to consider them harmless. I know otherwise, since I once spent a night at the toilet bowl regurgitating a colorful array of Jell-O shots after a fraternity party. Besides, since Bryce seems to be on a tear, I'm trying to stay functional.

Unfortunately, when I emerge from the postcard-covered bathroom, I find my remaining two Jell-O shots empty and Bryce gone from the couch area where we're sitting.

Sam looks up from whatever he was saying to Gabe and laughs at my expression as I hold up the little plastic cups. "He got mine too," says Sam.

I look around. "Where is he?"

Sam points to the far end of the bar. "At the jukebox, socializing with the locals." He wiggles his eyebrows as if I should be jealous and pissed.

I glare at him before following the direction of his pointed finger. Hunched over the jukebox, Bryce stands in between two women. The women are bopping to the music. Bryce is swaying off beat. I mentally do alcohol math. In the past three hours, he has had at least five beers, five vodka shots, and now at least five Jell-O shots. If not wasted yet, any minute he's going to be blind drunk.

I'm not close to jealous, though I'm beyond irritated. I make my way over to the jukebox.

"Hey, Peyton," Bryce slurs, then points above one of the girl's heads. "Kimmy and—um, Braily."

"Bailey," the second girl says, correcting him with a laugh.

"Nice meeting you both," I say. "But Bryce here really needs to go sit down."

"I'm picking all your favorite songs, baby," Bryce slurs.

I almost laugh. As if Bryce would know my favorite songs. His music taste is whatever is popular at the moment. We've never connected over bands. In fact, so far as I know, he thinks my interest in music, especially punk rock, is peculiar.

"Great," I say, grabbing his arm. "Let's go sit down and listen."

Kimmy frowns at me. "He has five songs left to pick."

I yank Bryce toward the couches in the corner. "How about you pick them?" I say over my shoulder.

The girls give me sour looks, as if I'm being a bitch. Whatever. Fortunately, Bryce lets me lead him back to the little seating arrangement. He bumps into stools and people along the way. I murmur "Sorry" about ten times.

Once we get to our couch, which now has several girls sitting and keeping Sam and Gabe company, Bryce decides he needs another beer.

Grinning, Sam looks around for a waitress.

Standing, I decide it's time to go.

"We're leaving," I say loudly.

"What?" Gabe says, cutting off whatever the girl next to him was saying. He lifts up his phone. "It's only one thirty. The bars stay open until four here."

I hold out a hand for Bryce. There is no way in hell I'm babysitting Bryce for hours at the bar. "You can stay. We'll get a taxi."

Sam looks indecisive.

Bryce slobbers near my ear. "We should go dancing, baby."

If he says "baby" one more time, I *will* scream. "Sure," I say, knowing not to argue with the inebriated. "Let's go."

At last he allows me to drag him from the bar. Completely intent on getting Bryce out of there, I'm surprised when I find Sam is on the sidewalk next to us. "Go back inside, Sam," I snap as Bryce leans on me and murmurs incoherent babble that definitely involves saying "baby" repeatedly.

With a remorseful expression, Sam says, "Let me help you find a cab at least."

It takes Sam ten minutes to hail a cab. The entire time, Bryce slobbers on me and tries to grind on me as if dancing. After we get him into the backseat of the cab, Sam holds the door open. "You sure you don't want me to come along and help?"

"I'm sure," I say heatedly, tugging the door out of his grasp. "You've 'helped' enough already."

His expression turns contrite.

I resist giving him the finger.

Finally, the cab takes off, so I don't have to see his guilt-stricken face any longer.

Chapter 21

Y ou're sho seshey in these pantsh, baby," Bryce says, running his hands up my thighs and over my butt. He slobbers on the skin below my ear. "I want you sho mush."

Drunk off his ass, he's like a wasted, slurring Energizer Bunny who won't fucking run down. He mauled me in the taxi and groped me during the never-ending hike across the lobby and the ride up in the elevator. Getting him to stay focused enough to walk was a chore. Of course, as soon as we get into the room he goes in for the kill. But his drunken seduction ain't happening.

I rub my palms over his chest. "Why don't you lie down?"

Swaying, he grips my hips. "You too?"

"Yeah, give me a minute to slip into something sexier." Using my hands on his chest, I push him toward the bed. The back of his legs hit the end of the bed and he falls onto it with a plop.

With heavy-lidded eyes, he grins at me and grabs my butt again. "More seshy than these pantsh?"

"Way more," I say, stepping out of his embrace and pushing him back. I unbutton his dress khakis and his lopsided grin grows, causing me to tear them off with an irritated tug.

He keeps grinning. Almost drools.

Going to the side of the bed, I tug his arm. "Lay on the pillows. You'll be more comfortable while you wait for me."

"Wait for you," he says dreamily, scooting toward the headboard.

Once his blond head hits the pillow, I say, "I'll be a minute."

He looks up at me. "Thish ish going be sho good."

I resist the urge to smother him with a pillow and just about run to the bathroom. Inside, I take my time washing the makeup from my face and applying moisturizer. I even decide to file my nails, then paint them.

Blowing on my fingertips, I exit the bathroom and can't help but smile. As planned, Bryce is passed out on the bed in his boxers and shirt. After waving my hands around to dry my nails for a few minutes, I rummage in my suitcase, looking for a tank and sleep shorts.

The tank in my hand drops to the floor when a knock sounds at the door. I glance at Bryce but he keeps snoring. Another knock, louder this time, has me rushing to unhook the chain. If whoever is out there wakes up Bryce, there will be hell to pay. I open it a crack to see Sam standing in the hallway.

"I need to talk to you," he says loudly.

"Go away!" I hiss and shut the door.

He knocks again.

I crack the door open again. "Go away, Sam!" I vehemently whisper.

His brows lower. "Not until I talk to you," he says, louder than before.

About to blow up, I step into the hallway and quietly shut the door behind me, knowing my card key is in my back pocket.

Sam blinks at me, then smiles wide. "You're still dressed."

Ignoring whatever that is supposed to mean, I snap, "What is so damn important that you need to talk to me at three in the morning?"

The door across from us cracks open and a woman hisses, "Can you shut the hell up? We're trying to sleep."

The door slams shut. Tapping my foot, I gesture to the closed door and give an irritated shrug that says, *See?*

With a sigh, Sam grabs my arm and drags me to the end of the hall and through the door into the fire escape stairwell. He stands there holding my arm and staring at me.

I tug my arm out of his grasp. "Okay, spill it, because I've got about this"—my extended index finger and thumb signal the length of a centimeter in front of his nose—"much patience left."

He shuffles his feet, looking sort of nervous. "I'm sorry your boyfriend got wasted."

Our voices echo in the stairwell.

I cross my arms and give him a level look. "You're admitting to having something to do with it?"

He nods sideways, as if not wanting to admit it.

"So what was the purpose of outdrinking him?"

Leaning on the rail, he glances down the stairs, refusing to meet my gaze, as a sheepish smirk overtakes his face.

"All right," I say, reaching for the door. "Thanks for the apology. I can totally see why it couldn't wait until *morning.*"

Suddenly, he grabs me, pushes me against the door. His hands grip my upper arms and I feel an unwelcome rush of heat as his hard, muscled torso presses against me. "The thought of you two alone—the thought of you two fucking, especially after waking up in your bed this morning . . ." Not finishing his thought, he draws in a deep breath. "It was either beat his ass or get him drunk."

For several long moments, I can only stare at him. Then something in me snaps. "Really? You're jealous?" His jaw tightens as I continue. "Why would you be jealous?" I ask, my tone incredulous, my heart thumping.

His grip on my arms intensifies. "I can't stand the thought of him touching you, much less the two of you having sex."

His words cause a rush of anger. Instead of admitting he may have feelings for me, he's skirting the issue to focus on jealousy. "We're hardly friends, you and me," I snarl. "Who I sleep with, much less what I do with my boyfriend, is none of your business."

"Friends?" he repeats, ignoring my anger. He leans down, and one of his hands releases my arm and begins sliding up to my shoulder. His heated gaze, more than his touch, pins me to the door. "We're friends, Peyton. I care about you. You seem to care about me."

"You're drunk," I whisper with a tremble, evidently affected by his lips hovering near mine, by the soft stroke of his hand skimming up my neck that freezes me in his grasp, and by the intensity of his stare.

"No. Yet I'm not entirely sober," he says as his hand comes to my jaw. His fingers brush the tender skin behind my ear. His lips come nearer. "But as far as being 'hardly friends' . . . maybe you're right. I don't want to *fuck* my friends."

I gasp and he drinks in the breath with his mouth. His lips move over mine gently as both of his hands cup my jaw. His tongue is a soft caress that lures me into the kiss and arouses a passion that drains my thoughts.

Giving in, I slide my hands up his shoulders as my tongue twists with his.

The slow, intoxicating kiss steals both my breath and my mind. I'm immersed in the sensations of his full lips, the soft glide of his tongue, the gentle stroke of his fingers along my neck. I inhale the clean scent of him. The dizzying press of his growing need on my stomach. The desperate longing his mouth and touch convey.

When Sam pulls back to look down at me with a smoky half-lidded look, my hands grip his neck, my fingers dig into his skin, and I try to bring his mouth back to mine.

His eyes bore into me. "Does it feel like that when you kiss him?"

I'm frozen for one long moment. Bryce, my boyfriend, is passed out less than a hundred feet from us as my lips, my body, scream for more attention from Sam. Angry with him but more angry with myself, I push him away.

"You've made your point." I wipe my mouth with the back of my hand. "I'm guessing that was the point," I say in a miserable tone as I open the door to the stairwell.

"Peyton," Sam says, his hand on my shoulder.

I shake his hand off. "Leave me alone," I say vehemently. I rush to the door to our room. Though he softly calls my name again, I slide the key card into the lock without looking back and slip inside as quickly as possible.

Leaning against the back of the door, I'm about to burst into tears. What the hell just happened? Why does it feel so familiar to the past?

A loud retch echoes from the bathroom, followed by the splash of spewing liquid. The threat of tears ceases as I thump my head once, twice against the door before I turn toward the bathroom. I suppose that after kissing Sam, not helping my drunken, puking boyfriend would be pure evil.

Chapter 22

It's late afternoon, and Central Park is full of people: bicyclists, joggers, walkers, walkers with dogs, and tourists. The day is bright and sunny. The trees green and lush. Using the camera hanging around my neck, I randomly take pictures of sculptures, plants, and bridges, but I have a particular destination in mind. "Come on, Bryce!" I call over my shoulder.

Hungover, he has parked his butt on a bench yet again. Wearing shorts that hang low, untied high-tops, and a rumpled T-shirt, he looks like a slob. With a look of irritation at me, he pushes off the bench and slowly follows.

I had a long list of places I wanted to visit today. However, Bryce didn't get out of bed until after eleven. Trying to be a good girlfriend—instead of the bad one I was last night, who sucked face with Sam—I've kept the pace easy for him all day. We went to lunch, then to the top deck of the Empire State Building. Now we're in the park, and I have a little more than an hour before I have to report to the booth. The concert is in the park, so to save time I'm already dressed in a Luminescent T-shirt, my cowboy boots, and a jean skirt—the shorts are getting a bit too raggedy, even for concerts.

I round a bend and the sign STRAWBERRY FIELDS comes into view. I pause and take several pictures of it. Bryce is behind me, moving at a turtle's pace. I keep strolling along the walkway and taking photographs. Eventually, I come to the famous mosaic, a stone flower of geometric shapes that contain just one word in the middle: IMAGINE. Giddy to finally be seeing it, I move around it slowly, taking picture after picture. Other tourists are gathered around it too, snapping shots.

Bryce catches up and stands with his hands on his hips next to me. "This is it? This is what we had to trek across the damn park for?"

"It's a tribute to John Lennon." I snap another picture. "You know, the Beatles?"

His lip curls as he looks down at the mosaic. "It's stupid."

I lower the camera. "He was shot over there." I point to what I think is the location of his apartment building, The Dakota. "He used to walk through this park right along here."

Bryce shrugs.

"His music has inspired millions of people. He sang about *peace*."

Bryce grunts and pushes sweaty blond hair from his forehead. He has been sweating out alcohol all day. Very lovely. "Who cares?"

Okay, I'm fuming. Big time. Yesterday at dinner, Bryce had stated he wanted to go to Yankee Stadium. Though I have zero interest in baseball, I had agreed. Of course, hungover and dragging ass today, he'd changed his mind, yet I wouldn't have been bitchy if we had gone.

"Go sit down and wait," I snap, pointing to the benches at the edge of the walkway.

He looks like he might snap back but instead sighs, stretches in the middle of the walkway, and finally moves to a bench. I take more pictures, even swap cameras with another tourist so we can take pictures of each other sitting at the top of the circle that says IMAGINE.

Done, I pull a map of Central Park from my bag and search for SummerStage, where the concert will take place. With my index finger, I'm tracing possible paths to take when someone steps close to me and says, "Hello, Peyton."

Glancing up, I almost drop the map.

"Guess great minds think alike," Sam says.

I've tried, somewhat successfully, to keep him out of my mind all day. But now that he's standing in front of me—with his sky-blue eyes looking slightly mischievous, his dark curls a mess on his head—flashes of our kiss zing through me. Then I recall the words he said right before the kiss, about wanting to "fuck" me, and a sharp pang of lust hits me. I've been keeping that locked up tight, especially since I've spent the day with my boyfriend, who is edging on the line of losing that title.

I concentrate on slowly folding up the map. "What are you doing here?"

"Same thing as you," he says, nodding toward the mosaic. "Came to see Lennon's memorial." He lifts his phone. "Thought I'd get a picture with it." Then he gestures to my camera. "But maybe you could, with your awesome photo skills?" He smiles at me, his teeth so even and white that he looks like a model for toothpaste or something.

I've always known Sam is good-looking. Right now he's coming off as can't-resist hot. It's like he's my crack. But crack is whack. And I'm not whacked.

"Sure," I say, and point to the line of people on the other side. "Get in line."

He lifts a brow. "Wait with me?"

"No," I say, then glance over to the bench where Bryce is dozing. "I'll wait here."

His gaze follows mine. His eyes narrow on Bryce. "He's sleeping?" he asks incredulously.

My eyes narrow on Sam. "He's a bit tired."

Sam shakes his head sadly. "You'd think he could pull through a hangover for his girl."

"Go get in line," I say through clenched teeth, irritated. "I have to get to the booth in thirty minutes."

He looks to Bryce one last time, shaking his head—which irritates me more, because though Bryce should have known better, his condition is partly Sam's fault—then he goes around the mosaic to the end of the line.

Four people are ahead of him, so I click through pictures on my camera and ignore him staring at me. But I can feel his stare and it's doing weird things to my insides. Things that should not be happening, especially given our proximity to passed-out Bryce. At last, Sam steps up to the mosaic. He stands above the IMAGINE looking down, and I catch the shot. Him pensive, eyelids lowered. He looks up and I quickly catch the shot of him gazing at the camera, his expression a mix of openness and yearning. The sight jerks at my heart.

"What's he doing here?" Bryce asks from my side. Apparently, he woke up. Just in time, I suppose.

"Same as me, he's a fan of Lennon."

"You're both musical nuts, so interested in stones in a sidewalk."

Ignoring Bryce, I ask Sam, "Were you going to smile?"

He lifts a brow and I take a picture of that. I lower my camera. "Other people are waiting, and I need to get going."

Sam walks over to us. "Hey," he says to Bryce before turning to me. "Time to sell the T-shirts?"

"Yup," I say, twisting the strap on my camera so it hangs at my side, then grabbing Bryce's hand. "Guess we'll catch you later."

Sam stares at the clasp of our hands. "Yeah, later."

Dragging Bryce down the path, I can feel Sam's gaze burning into me. I don't look back. I'm not playing his games. Even if I'm starting to question our connection, Bryce is my boyfriend. Sam is the friend/enemy/sexy rocker I can't seem to refuse.

An outdoor concert has a different kind of energy, a different sound. Uncontainable, the music blasts and floats out into the night. The stage looks different. There are no seats or sections. The lights reach through the darkness and never end. Here in Central Park, the backdrop behind the stage is a stand of lush, towering trees. Even the fans are different—their vibe feels more gleeful and carefree. Or maybe that's just New York.

On the side of the stage, Bryce and I watch Griff. Mike offered to close up the booth for me tonight since my boyfriend is in town. I stayed at the booth halfway through Luminescent Juliet's performance, though, because it was so busy. Of course, Bryce wasn't any help. He sat in a folded chair off to the side in the shade, looking annoyed and bored.

He also stayed backstage during most of the band's performance while I took pictures. Because they were the first onstage, their set started in the setting sun and ended at dusk, which created an unusual lighting situation and the chance to get some unique pictures. I refused to consider Sam in any other way except as a member of a band I work for, even when he winked directly at me.

Now that we're together watching Griff, Bryce is whining in my ear about being tired and wanting to go back to the hotel. He's irritating the crap out of me. Our spot on the side of the stage is like being in the first seat directly behind the catcher at a Yankees game. Even hungover, he wouldn't consider leaving that game. Griff is one of the hottest rock bands in the country right now, but Bryce wants to go back to the room instead of watching the amazing show that's happening ten feet away from us.

His disregard for music is beyond annoying. His indifference for what I love feels like disrespect to me. But since I can't take the whining much longer, I tell him that once Griff is done we'll go.

Our walk back to the hotel is quiet. I'm sure Bryce senses my crankiness. It's kind of hard to keep it off my face and out of my voice. Once we're inside our room, as soon as I set my camera and purse down on the dresser, he pulls me into his arms.

"Look, I'm sorry I've been such a dick all day. I seriously felt like shit." He presses his lips to my forehead. "I want to make it up to you," he says in my ear before his lips slide down my neck.

I'm guessing he's thinking we should have make-up sex, but the whole situation feels foreign. Bryce and I never fight. We get along. But we usually go out for a few hours and then back to my place—since he lives with three other guys. We've never been together for an entire day. And I've never been mad at him enough to consider withholding sex.

He presses a kiss to my chin. "Let me make it up to you, baby?"

Standing stiff, I tell myself this is my boyfriend. He came all the way from Michigan to visit me. He's been hungover all day. He was excited to surprise me. He got us this room. Took me out to dinner.

Fingers digging into my back, he tugs me closer. His body molds to mine and his mouth covers my lips.

And it feels wrong. My insides scream that I don't want his mouth on mine. He deepens the kiss but I can't make myself respond. It feels wrong, wrong, wrong.

After a minute of my nonresponsive reaction, he breaks away. "What's going on?"

I shrug. Never having been so turned off by him, I'm not entirely sure. I'm thinking my body's rejection has something to do with being pissed off. Or maybe that's what I'm hoping.

"I said I was sorry," he says, his mouth twisting with anger.

I gape at him. Unfortunately, his apology doesn't wipe away my irritation—and it doesn't feel very authentic either. Suddenly fuming, I jerk out of his arms. "So you say you're sorry and that's it? We step into the room and start fucking like bunnies?"

"What the hell, Peyton?" He falls onto the end of the bed. "I came here to see you, got us this room, took you out to a fancy dinner, and followed you around all day doing stupid shit."

I step back as the implication of this confession hits me. "So, like some prostitute I owe you a screw now?"

"I didn't say that," he mumbles, staring at the floor.

"No? You sure as hell insinuated it."

His blond head pops up and he glares at me. "Now you're just being a bitch."

My eyebrows arch to my hairline. Fury erupts within in me. "A bitch? A bitch!" I grab my purse off the dresser. "Say good-bye to this bitch, bitch!" I slam the door behind me and march down the hall. I'm so pissed, I can't see straight.

"Peyton!" Bryce yells from the doorway.

Without looking back, I flip him off. I use the same finger to punch the down button for an elevator, then climb in. No one is in the elevator. I pace back and forth, my hands fisted at my sides. When the doors open, I rush across the lobby, then past the fancy entrance to the spa center to a back hallway. The seating alcove near an exit door is empty. I fall onto a small couch and start to cry like an idiot, my tears a mix of anger and confusion.

Chapter 23

The dam has broken, and though I have little control over my tears—I'm vaguely aware of a few people coming and going behind me—I strive to keep my sobbing quiet. I'm living in a corny, sad song. Getting control of myself, I force myself to slowly stop crying, but I'm still hunched over, a ball of stupid despair, when someone taps on my shoulder.

Fearing it's Bryce, and afraid of what I might say to him in the moment, I don't look up.

"Peyton?" a familiar voice asks.

I look up to see Gabe frowning down at me. A girl connected to his hip frowns at me too.

"What's going on?" he asks, his frown deepening.

I'm very embarrassed—my eyes have to be red and my skin splotchy—and my lip quivers, but I shrug.

His frown deepens even more. "Where's your boyfriend?"

I look away.

"You two fighting?" he asks, and my lip quivers again as I barely nod. After letting go of the girl's waist, he bends down in front of me until his elbows are on his knees, his brown shoulder-length hair falling forward. "You going to sit out here all night?"

I shrug again.

His expression turns skeptical. "Want to come to the after-party and watch us sign more shit?"

A party would be horrible in my current state. I shake my head.

Sighing, he reaches behind his back and draws out his wallet, then flicks his hotel card in my face. "Then here. We actually got a semisuite this time. The couch is all yours."

The couch sounds like paradise. My fingers reach for the card but pause. "Will Romeo care?" I ask since they always room together. "And how will you get back in?"

"Why would Romeo care? And I'll just get a new key."

I grab the card. "Okay."

He slowly stands. "Do you want us to walk you up?"

The girl smooths a hand over her short dress, looking irritated.

"No, that's all right," I say, shaking my head again.

He doesn't look convinced yet says, "Room 1229."

I stand and force a slight smile. "Thank you, Gabe."

"No problem," he says, the crease between his brows intensifying as he again takes in my puffy face. "Maybe you need to think about what you really want, Peyton," he says, pulling the girl toward the door. Over his shoulder, he adds, "Because I'm seeing something totally different than what you got."

My nose wrinkles at his insinuation. Bryce and I had a fight. It had nothing to do with Sam. Before I can comment, he whisks the girl out the door. Thankful *and* irritated with him, I start my trek to the room. Bryce and I are on the tenth floor, so at least there will be a couple of floors between us.

The suite has a small living room with a table, couch, and chair. After rinsing my face and using the toothpaste on the counter and my index finger to brush my teeth, I find an extra blanket and pillow in the closet across from the bathroom. From the shadow of the bathroom light, I can see that one of the beds is messed up, which causes me to realize why Gabe came back to the hotel. Obviously, he had a booty call in between the concert and the promotion party.

Back in the living room, after shutting off my nonstop vibrating phone without looking at it, I remove the little couch pillows and spread out the blanket. The couch is shorter than most. I just fit. Once I lie down, confusing thoughts of the past two days tumble through my head. Sam cuddling with me overnight on the bus. Bryce showing up. Bryce getting drunk. Bryce being a jerk all day. Sam's passionate kiss. Bryce's lifeless kiss.

Needing the thoughts to stop, I reach for the TV remote and watch infomercials for over an hour. I finally fall asleep, pleasantly dreaming of vacuum cleaners and omelet pans.

"Peyton," someone whispers. I try to ignore it and stay in my mindless dreams. A hand gently shakes my shoulder and the "Peyton" whisper sounds again. I slowly open my eyes. The TV is still on, casting the room in shadows. Someone is bent over me.

I gasp slightly, but the shadow of curls on top of his head gives my tired brain the only clue I need. I quickly scramble up into a sitting position. "What are you doing here?"

Sam lowers himself onto the small coffee table and we're face-to-face. The light from the TV illuminates one side of him. Shadows form under the curve of his cheekbone, beneath his full bottom lip, and below one muscled pectoral. With all the curves and ridges, he's like a living sculpture. Why is his shirt off?

He leans just the slightest closer. "This is my room."

"Really?" I say in a confused tone, pulling my gaze from his chest. "Gabe rooms with Romeo."

His smirk flashes in the grayness. "Apparently, Romeo woke in the middle of the night to a woman screaming Gabe's name. Since we're the single ones, he booted Gabe to my room this morning."

"Oh," I say, staring at the lush curve of his lips. The urge to reach out and touch them to see if they're as soft as they look overwhelms me. The urge must come from the fact I'm half asleep. *Wake the hell up, Peyton!*

He leans a little closer to me. "I should ask you the same thing. Why are you here?"

Because my boyfriend thinks I owe him sex pops into my mind. "I-I don't want to talk about it."

I can't help notice his intent look of interest. "Well, though it's past four in the morning, I thought you might want one of the beds. Gabe went home with his lady friend."

The girl in the short dress flashes in my mind. "Um, no thanks. Gabe and his lady friend already used one bed."

"Oh," he says, his full lips turning down. "Then take my bed. I'll take the couch."

I shake my head. "It's too small for you. I barely fit."

"I've slept on worse. I insist."

"Go to bed, Sam. I'm fine."

"Peyton, take the bed."

"Go. To. Bed. Sam," I say, my jaw suddenly tight.

"You still mad about last night?" He sighs and leans back. "Listen, I was drunker than I admitted, and there's too much between us already. Your boyfriend, my brother, the past . . . making things worse was stupid."

I look away into the shadows of the room as my chin starts quivering. Damn. I'm becoming an emotional mess.

"What's wrong?" he asks.

My chin quivers more at the concern in his tone.

Sam kneels in front of me, pulling me into his arms. "Shit, Peyton. Don't look like that. It's killing me." He brings me closer to him, rubbing his damp curls along my collarbone.

I put my hands on his shoulders to push him away, but somehow I can't. The sensation of skin against mine—why the hell is his shirt off?—and the way his hands span my back renders me immobile. The sleepiness of my body disintegrates and I'm more than awake. I'm alive. With a sudden burning lust.

"Forgive me?" he asks, and his lips brush my neck, sending a wave of tingles across my skin and down to the bottom of my belly.

Without thinking, I slide my hands over his shoulders, using my palms to caress the curve of his muscles.

"Peyton?" he whispers, raising his head.

His whisper and the memory it invokes cause chills to run along my skin. I close my eyes, hoping that not responding will be enough to stop what feels inevitable, to stop what I suddenly desperately want. Beyond the desire, a warm rush of tenderness for him flows through me.

"Peyton?" he repeats, and the word whispers air across my lips. The soft breeze of it on my skin is like a prelude to a kiss, like an intro to a lush, pounding, sensual song.

He doesn't move, though. Yet I can sense him. Feel him close. Too close. Unable to help myself, I lean forward and brush my lips against his, so softly and so quickly that aside from the jolt of want it creates inside me, it's as though it may not have happened.

The arms around me tremble, and the air snaps with tangible energy as his chest rises with a huge inhale before his mouth crushes mine.

A sigh escapes me. This feels right. Perfect. Wonderful.

We kiss and kiss and kiss. At each touch of our lips and tongues, we grow more frantic. With each kiss, he moves up and closer until I'm lying over the arm of the couch, his muscled weight pressed into me, his belt buckle pressed into my stomach, his hands slowly running up and down my sides. His gentle touch paired with his desperate, fierce lips makes me feel cherished.

I slide my hands from his contoured back to his damp curls—he must have showered, I think wildly, which is why he's not wearing a shirt—then down again. I can't get enough of him, his touch, his lips, his smooth muscled skin, and his boyish, just-showered scent. With one leg and foot pinned in between him and the back of the couch, my other foot lowers to the floor. I use it as leverage to arch my body against his.

He releases a groan.

We stare at each other for one long sizzling moment before his lips find mine again as his hand touches my bare knee. The kiss is fast, fierce, and frenzied, a tangle of tongues and lips and teeth. The slide of his hand along my thigh is slow, tantalizing, and magnetic, an intoxicating caress that has me yearning for more. His fingers move higher, brushing my panties, and my entire body jumps at the contact.

He breaks the kiss, breathing hard and burying his face in my hair as his fingers slip beneath my underwear from the side. We both pant above the muffled sounds of the TV. His fingers rub and slide against me, and my hips move to the pulse he sets. I'm moaning and clenching his arms, my body bowed off the couch.

He pauses for a moment, breathing harshly against my skin. I become wild, tearing at his belt buckle, then ripping open the line of buttons on the crotch of his jeans. Spurred by my frenzy, Sam pushes up on one arm and helps me yank the jeans off. When I push my hands inside his boxers and grasp him, his entire body stills as a low growl reverberates from his throat.

"Holy shit, Peyton," he gasps, then reaches for his jeans on the floor. A second later, he's tearing a condom open with his teeth, pulling from my grasp, and rolling it on in seconds.

We tug off my underwear together. Poised above me, he lifts my skirt and grips my open thighs.

Nearly tearful with want, I clutch his biceps. "Please, Sam," I pant.

He comes closer until he is pressed against me. "Tell me you want *me*. Say you want *me* inside of you," he says from a tight jaw, muscles straining in his neck.

His tip rubs up and slides against me, causing me to gasp, "I want you, Sam. Now. Inside."

"Sam and Peyton. Finally," he says wistfully, gripping my thighs tighter and sliding in.

I'm insensible. My body is in control as my head falls back and I push up to meet him. He jerks my T-shirt and bra up above my chest, spreads his hands under my back to hold me up, then he kisses my shoulders, my throat, and my breasts as we move and gasp together. As the tempo builds, faster and faster, I lose control. My fingers go from gripping his arms, his chest, his back to scratching him as I climax. His mouth goes from kissing and sucking my skin to an open moan, held between my breasts.

Our heavy breathing fills the room. Lust spent, the situation, so very much like the past, hits me. I'm in his room, on his couch, with my skirt around my waist, my shirt and bra up to my neck, and my panties on the floor. When he raises himself up on his elbows, I'm expecting Bryce to charge into the room. Mortified, I quickly scramble out from beneath him.

"Peyton?" he says softly.

Tugging on my underwear, I ignore him. I can't believe this. I can't believe what I did. Again.

He rolls onto his back and repeats my name. I tug my boots on and grab my purse. He sits up.

"Don't do this to me," Sam says. "Don't run again. Don't say it was nothing."

"Oh, it was something," I say over my shoulder, heading to the door. "I lost my mind for a bit. Now it's back." I open the door. "I have to go."

I shut the door as he angrily says my name louder, then I rush down the hall to the elevator.

Chapter 24

The morning is gray and shadowy as I walk. The dark sky brightens slowly, hinting at the sunrise soon to come. I don't stray far from the hotel, instead walking the same blocks around the hotel over and over again. Traffic is strangely erratic this early in the morning, yet it's obvious this city never sleeps as taxis, trucks, cars, and a few people pass by me. At first, I stroll and refuse to think, just try to let my mind clear. But facing what I've done over the past couple of days is inevitable.

As the anxiety loosens in my chest like the release of a knot, I rationally accept some basic facts. Some people have soul mates, theoretically at least, even if I don't quite buy the idea after what I went through with Seth. However, I do have a sex mate—I can't help but smile as this phrase pops into my mind—and his name is Sam. I'd seriously questioned if my memory was playing tricks on me about how good my first time with him had been. It wasn't. It was as good this time, perhaps even better. I'm not a sex fiend, but sex with Sam could make me one. When we have sex, I don't feel self-conscious.

Beyond the mind-blowing, can't-stop-myself sex, I force myself to admit that I do have feelings for Sam. Though they're mixed up with my music awe, pity for his relationship with Seth, and serious lust for his hot body, I can't deny my feelings if I'm being honest with myself.

And while the sun slowly rises and casts shadows across Manhattan, I'm trying very hard to be honest with myself, and rational. Very, very rational. If I were letting my emotions dictate my behavior, I'd be back in Sam's bed in a hot second.

As far as Bryce is concerned—deep calming breath—I finally, completely realize nothing ever grew past our initial attraction. He was fun and attractive but now that I have real feelings—even as messed up as they are—for someone else, the shallowness of our relationship is so evident that his showing up for a weekend of sex doesn't seem as callous as I first thought. I mean, other than dating and drinking and screwing, what else is there between us?

I round a corner and the hotel comes into view.

I'm still trying to be honest with myself. And I have to decide how honest to be with Bryce. Should I be entirely honest and tell him I slept with Sam? Or would that be too hurtful? Should I tell him I've realized there was never more between us than that initial attraction?

Ugh. My internal questions are starting to make my head hurt because the fact is, I cheated on Bryce just like I cheated on Seth. And no matter how I try to sugarcoat it—Bryce being an asshole or Seth getting paranoid—I'm still at fault. Twice. Cheater times two. The thought not only hurts my head and my heart but also stabs at my self-respect. What little I have left at the moment.

Tired of walking, I slowly make my way toward the hotel entrance.

Okay. A breakup with Bryce is imminent, yet that doesn't automatically mean I'm about to officially be with Sam. Even if I knew how he felt about me—for all I know he might consider last night nothing more than a step above his usual booty call with a groupie—I'm not ready to go there. I need time, and perhaps a shitload of beer, to get a grasp on my emotions. Logic tells me I'm having a hard time separating the awesome sex from my emotions.

Our connection is a tangled web that I can't dissect clearly when that earth-shattering climax is still so fresh in my mind.

All right. First things first.

Bryce.

The hotel lobby is empty, but I'm grateful to see that the small coffee shop off to the side is open. After waiting in a short line, I buy two coffees. I don't have to travel far to give Bryce his. He's on the other side of the lobby, talking with a bellhop. He doesn't notice me until I step next to him.

When he turns to me, his look is flat.

"Hey," I say, lifting the coffee and trying not to let the guilt running through me show on my face.

He doesn't take the steaming drink. "Where have you been?"

"Around. Walking, thinking," I say, ignoring the gray-haired bellhop watching and listening to us.

Bryce pulls the suitcase on the floor at his side. "Walking around New York in the middle of the night? What the hell, Peyton? I called you, texted you, and left a dozen messages."

"I turned my phone off. I needed to think," I say, lifting the coffee higher. "It's a mocha latte." Bryce doesn't like coffee unless it has chocolate in it.

"You have the room until eleven," he says stiffly, then swipes the coffee from my hand and marches with his suitcase rolling behind him toward the front exit.

As he surely expected, I follow and find him outside, waiting on a bench.

"I don't get it," he says, staring out at the street as I sit down at the far end of the bench. "We've never had problems. I come here and everything blows up in my face."

"Um, well, we go out once a week. Maybe have lunch once or twice. I'm not sure if our relationship was ready for prime time."

He turns and pins me with a glare. "I'm busy. You're busy. We always get along."

I take a deep breath and turn to him. "Bryce—"

"Don't say it." He scoots across the bench and grabs my hand, a strange desperation crossing his face. "We can pretend this trip never happened. You'll be home in a few more weeks, and we can continue like we were."

I shake my head and tug my hand from his grip. "I'm really, really sorry you came and things turned out like this, but the last two days put everything into perspective for me. I don't want to go back to the way things were."

He looks dejected. "Why?"

Not wanting to hurt him and not wanting to admit I've done something vile, I bit my lip. Deep down, Bryce must know we're not meant to be.

He lowers his chin and asks in a deep tone, "Is there someone else?"

"Not really," I say, cringing inside. But does it matter if he knows?

"What does that mean?"

"You were such a jerk yesterday. And well . . ." I take another deep breath, getting ready to spit out that I cheated on him, that I'm an awful person regardless of the mess of our relationship. The knot in my chest feels like it will loosen if I'm honest.

"Oh shit. This must be my taxi," Bryce says, standing up.

I stand too. "Bryce—"

"I have to go. We can talk about this when you get back."

I shake my head.

"Don't let one day of me being a dick destroy seven months." He bends and kisses my forehead. "Think about it, Peyton."

I draw in a deep breath. "It's over," I say, but he shakes his head and rushes to the taxi.

Standing still, I watch him get into the taxi, then wave to me as it heads away. After taking a long pull on my coffee and another deep breath, I turn and notice Sam standing to the side of the lobby doors.

He's smoking, and from the short length of his cigarette, it's obvious he's been out here a while, watching us. He stares at me, his striking face lined with a tension and distress that eats away at my conscience. Then his expression changes into one of casual indifference. He nods a hello before dropping his butt into the ashtray nearby, turning his back to me and going through the doors.

Longing has me nearly running after him, to explain and then beg for forgiveness, if required. Instead, I stay rooted to the sidewalk. Sam was right last night. There are tons of issues between us. Issues that I need to consider, like that we're together only when I'm cheating on someone. Plus, working through our issues during a tour isn't the smartest idea. I'm not sure working through them—the past, Seth, our differences—is possible.

As I watch Sam stalk off, I assume he thinks Bryce and I are still a couple. Funny, I suspect Bryce does too. But I'm sticking to the plan I made during my sunrise walk. Bryce and I are over. I need to distance myself from Sam and figure out my emotions. I may already be in too deep. That doesn't mean Sam is.

Chapter 25

The heavy smell of grease hangs in the truck stop diner. Since it's hours past the lunch rush, less than half the tables are occupied. We're all crammed in a booth. Outside, Gary is filling the bus with gas and water, and dumping the tanks. It's been a week since we left New York, and we've been staying on the bus the entire time. Providence, Boston, and Albany flew by. Tonight we're in Rochester. Tomorrow we'll finally check into a hotel. We're all whipped. This second continual concert run has been more grueling than the last.

The waitress comes back with our drinks, setting them at the front of the table, and Justin hands glasses back to Gabe and me in the corners.

"Can someone pass the sugar?" Sam asks from the front of the booth. His jaw is tight. He doesn't look my way. Though we're all crabby, he has been the worst, snapping at his bandmates and ignoring me.

Since the words were said in a general way, I don't count them as having been spoken to me. I shove the sugar basket down to the middle of the table and Romeo pushes it along to Sam, who has talked to me exactly seven times in three days. "Excuse me" three times. "Watch out" twice. "You gonna eat that?" once. And "Where's the mustard?"

Curls falling over his forehead, he stirs sugar into his iced tea. The tightness of his jaw reveals his agitation. Lately, he always seems irate.

Holding in a sigh, I glance down at my hands clasped in my lap. I'm still confused about my feelings for him, but the tension between us needs to lighten up. Though I'm scared shitless of the outcome, I've been drumming up the courage to talk to him. It's just—the past three days have been so busy. At least that's what the coward in me offers as an explanation for my inability to start the conversation.

Sam sets his spoon onto the table and glances at Romeo, sitting next to him. "Peyton should stay with you and Justin."

Glancing up from his phone, Romeo gives him an odd look. "Why?"

With my hands now clenching my thighs, I echo Romeo, "Yeah, why?"

Across the table in the other corner, Gabe smirks, looking from Sam to me.

Next to me, Justin keeps texting someone. Probably Allie.

Ignoring me, Sam turns fully to Romeo. "Gabe and I are single." He gestures across to Justin. "You two are pussy whipped. Why should we have her in our room? Makes it kind of hard to bag chicks." The last words come out with a sly grin.

My nails dig into my thighs so I don't go off on Sam in front of everyone. Of all the low-down things to say in front of me. I'm angry and more confused than ever. Is he doing this to get back at me? Or is this what he really wants? Here I'd thought it was time to bridge the gap between us. He's thinking of bagging chicks.

Gabe is now silently laughing across from me.

I resist kicking him under the table.

Texting more, Justin shrugs. "Doesn't matter to me."

Romeo frowns at Sam in confusion. "I could see Gabe bringing this up but you've been pretty tame this tour." He leans back against the vinyl booth, glancing at Gabe. "Did you put him up to this?"

Gabe puts his hands up and shakes his shaggy head. "Dude, this is news to me too."

I wrap my hands around my water glass, then glare down the table at Sam. "Well, I don't want to be stuck in a room with group-ies coming and going."

He holds my glare with one of his own, and I sense everyone at the table looking from him to me. Oh crap, I'm not bringing this drama into the band. I let out a huff and look elsewhere, only to find Gabe still smirking at me.

Would a tiny kick be that bad?

Romeo reaches into the sugar basket and yanks out a tiny container of creamer. "Peyton can stay with Justin and me. I just thought you two were friends from before." He glances at Sam. "You told me she'd be more comfortable in your room since you two go *way* back *and* she dated your brother."

Romeo's words settle in my gut, then blast inside me. Red-hot anger erupts in my veins and pounds through me until my fingers itch.

"What?" I screech so loud that almost everyone in the diner looks my way. I'm off my butt, leaning over the table and ready to dive at Sam. In addition to the bagging-chicks comment, I can't believe he told Romeo about our past after we'd both agreed several times to leave it in the past. "You're an asshole!" I hiss at him as Justin holds me back and Gabe catches his Coke before it spills.

"Whoa," Justin says, hauling me down by the waist. "Slow down. You're going to get us kicked out of here."

As I resist getting pulled down, tugging at the hands at my waist, Sam glares at Justin. "Get your hands off her."

Justin blinks at him, his hands loosening on my waist.

"Now!" Sam says loudly, snarling.

Justin lets go and puts his hands up. "Whatever, dude."

Romeo's head whips toward Sam. "You're not helping," he says in a low tone.

People are still staring at us, but leaning across the table, I snap too, "What the hell, Sam? I can't believe you!" My cheeks are heated. Not as much as my insides. I'm so angry, I could spit. In Sam's face.

Sam's jaw tightens again as he stares ahead. "Then that makes two of us," he says loudly.

"Both of you, quiet down!" Romeo hisses. "And you—he points at me—"sit down." After I sit and the table is silent for a few seconds, he asks in a neutral tone, "Is there something I'm not getting here?"

"Yeah," Justin says, his brow creasing, "what the hell is going on?"

Both of them are staring at me as Gabe opens his mouth, and I do kick him in the shin. He yelps.

I grip the edge of the table. "Sam is an asshole. That's what's going on." I scoot over and my hip hits Justin's. "Let. Me. Out."

Justin doesn't budge. "Our order should be here any minute."

After eating only sandwiches and cereal for the past three days, even the lure of real, hot food can't keep me sitting at the same table with Sam. I bump Justin's hip again, harder this time. "Have them box mine up."

Putting up his hands in surrender, Justin slides out of the booth to let me out.

I slide out too, glaring at Sam.

He stirs his iced tea again and stares into his glass. Refusing to look at me, he mumbles, "Overreact much?"

My hands clench into fists as Justin slides back into the booth. Maybe I am overreacting, but I feel so betrayed that achieving calm isn't possible.

"Not enough," I say bitterly, grabbing Justin's ice water. Sam still doesn't look at me until the cold splash of water hits him in the face.

Sputtering at me, he gasps. His blue eyes are an angry flash of ice.

"There," I say, smiling smugly. "Now I'm overreacting." As Sam stares at me with fire in his eyes, the water continues dripping down his face. I drop the empty plastic cup into his lap, then march out of the diner.

Chapter 26

The crowd roars on one side of me, music blaring on the other. Since New York, Luminescent Juliet's popularity has soared. Earlier tonight, the booth was busier than ever—luckily, Romeo had ordered more T-shirts. He also hired Mike to help me the entire time, and even the two of us together could hardly keep up with the preshow line. I can't help but notice that during the first part of the tour, usually only half the seats were full when the guys kicked off each show. Now, the seats are nearly three-fourths full, which is pretty good for an opening band. Their album has also skyrocketed on the indie charts.

I take pictures of both the band and the mass of screaming fans, already thinking through the best way to highlight the surge in sales and the increasing crowds. Of course, Sam is his usually flirty self, winking at the girls in the front as I take pictures. I have a suspicion he pours it on extra thick when I'm out here.

Asshole. We haven't spoken since the incident at the diner this afternoon.

Attempting to ignore Sam, the way he does me, I try to let the energy, the music, the lights, the rumble in my chest, and Justin's vocals take me away from my jealous thoughts of groupies. Then the band starts the fast notes of what has become my absolute favorite song, "Trace," and I move to the side of the stage in the shadows to watch Sam. He's not as frozen as he was last time I watched them perform it, but there's still a noticeable shift in his demeanor. Maybe nobody else would notice, but I instantly pick up the sadness that overtakes his posture, reminding me of the incomplete song lyrics I typed into my phone. I want to know why this song has such an effect on him.

The song ends and the first notes of "Inked My Heart" begin. I start heading back to the booth.

The time after their performance is as busy as the initial rush, but the crowds instantly thin as Griff goes onstage, and I help Mike pack the booth up. Then I head to the green room, grab a plate of fruit and crackers, find a quiet spot in the corner, and start filling in the lyrics of "Trace" on my phone.

I know the bus would be quieter, but I'm sick of the bus. So I munch on fruit and crackers, listen to the song again and again, and fill in the missing lyrics. Done, I pull out my earbuds and read over what I've typed into my phone.

I remember your laugh
I remember when
When you were real
Before everything changed
You fell into a nightmare
Leaving me alone
Holding on to traces of you
Gone, gone, gone
Nothing left but traces of you.
Gone, gone, gone
But still holding on to these traces of you

Life is so empty
No one understands

You're lost forever
Leaving half a man
My whole word has crumbled
Meaningless I stumble
Holding on to traces of you
Gone, gone, gone
Nothing left but traces of you.
Gone, gone, gone
But still holding on to these traces of you

Still I wait
I'll always wait
However hopeless
You're my other half
Caught in your shadow
Here I stand
Holding on to traces of you
Gone, gone, gone
Nothing left but traces of you
Gone, gone, gone
But still holding on to these traces of you
I'll always hold on to these traces of you

I grip my phone as the reality of the song hits me. Probably like most people, I thought "Trace" was about a girl, especially with the chorus, *I can't let you go.* Now reading the lyrics in their entirety, I'm very aware of what they mean, and who wrote them.

Romeo didn't. Sam did. And the song isn't about a girl. It's about missing a twin brother lost to a disease. Lost to schizophrenia.

It's about Seth.

My empty plate falls to the floor as I look over the lyrics again, and my lip quivers. When Sam explained his pain, I thought I understood, but the lyrics, the desolation and sorrow of them, and the realness behind them, tear at my heart and make it hard for me to breathe.

Poor, poor Sam. Poor, poor Seth. The stupid fucking tragedy of it sucks.

Searching the room, I find Sam on the far side. Through watery eyes, I watch him laugh, his curls bobbing, at something the girl wrapped around him says. He takes a swig of beer, looks up, and catches me staring.

Damn. I'm caught in his gaze and my lip trembles more as tears start rolling down my cheeks.

Overwhelmed, I'm up in seconds, running for the exit. I'm halfway down the long hallway leading to the back parking lot when a strong hand catches my shoulder.

"Peyton," Sam says, turning me around.

I wipe at my tears and lower my head.

"Oh shit, Peyton," he says, guiding me into an alcove. Gently gripping my shoulders, he turns me until we face each other. "I'm just messing around. I'm not going to do anything with those women."

A wild laugh escapes me as I wipe my cheeks. "That's not why I'm crying!" I want to add that, yes, being honest, girls hanging all over him pisses me off, even if I don't have a right to be pissed. But I don't go there.

Frowning, he leans back, studying me. "Bryce find out about us?"

"I already broke up with him," I snap, frustrated that he assumes I'm crying over Bryce. Bryce has sent a few texts. I've ignored them. I refuse to have a text war over our breakup.

Sam is suddenly very still. "When?"

"The morning he left."

His eyes widen as they search mine. "Why didn't you tell me?"

I wipe away a tear. "Why would I tell you?"

He winces. "Oh, I don't know. Maybe because a few hours before, we had sex?" he says in a tone dripping with sarcasm.

I grit my teeth. "So having sex with you means I tell you everything?"

"Peyton," he says, his jaw tightening.

"I didn't break up with him because of that. Though it helped my decision, okay? We didn't ever connect on a level that made the relationship worth keeping up."

"Why wouldn't you tell me?" he demands.

"Maybe I needed a little time after breaking up with my boyfriend of seven months before—before considering anything else," I say, keeping whatever is between us as vague as possible.

He glares at me. "You could have told me. I wouldn't have been such a dick this past week."

I clench my hands into fists. "*Nice.* You seriously think you had a right to be a dick. Nice," I repeat with a shake of my head. At least my tears are starting to let up.

"After the way you left and went back to him . . ." He sighs and leans close again. "Never mind. Just tell me why you're crying."

At the thought of why, my stupid eyes start tearing up again.

His hands come back to my shoulders. "What's going on?" When I draw in a deep breath, his fingers grip me tight. "Peyton?"

"I figured out the lyrics," I say, my voice choked.

He cocks his head. "Lyrics?"

"To—to 'Trace.'"

"Oh." His eyes widen in surprise. He lowers his hands from my shoulders and looks down. "I wrote that two years ago," he finally says.

"Do you feel any different now?"

He swallows, then says in a hoarse tone, "No."

The look of pain on his face has my tears flowing again. "I'm sorry, Sam," I say, stepping forward into his chest and wrapping my arms around him. "So, so sorry."

His arms encircle me. "You have nothing to be sorry for." He draws in a deep breath. "No one does. It's something I have to learn to deal with. To accept." He releases a whoosh of air that blows the hair on my shoulder back. "It's just damn hard to let the old Seth go."

"The whole thing sucks," I mumble against his shirt.

His arms crush me as he holds me tighter. "I miss him so fucking much," he says into my hair, his voice cracking with pain.

Both crying, we stand holding on to each other, drowning in sadness together because there's nothing else we can do.

Chapter 27

Though I can't make out the words, I can hear Justin in the hotel bathroom as he facetimes with Allie. Romeo sits at the desk, intent on shuffling papers. I lounge in a chair and flick through TV channels. There is tons of stuff to do in Pittsburgh but I'm too whipped to leave the room. After I did my daily blog stuff, Justin and I spent most of the afternoon fighting over TV channels. He likes to watch stupid reality crap on MTV; I prefer the old-style videos. At least now that he's busy with his girlfriend, I have the remote to myself. Romeo looked at sales numbers in between phone calls that he took out on the balcony. Apparently, we're all too tired to do anything away from the room. And obviously, after the tiff Sam and I had the other day at the diner, Romeo put the rollaway in his room when we checked in.

My phone on the table next to me dings, signaling an incoming message. I pick it up halfheartedly. Gabe texted, *Come down to the bar. I'm bored out of my mind, sitting by myself.*

I reply, *Too tired.*

Please! pops up right away, then, *Just one drink before dinner.*

We're all supposed to meet in one of the hotel restaurants for dinner.

He sends several more begging messages, until I text back, *Fine!*

I slip on my flip-flops and grab my purse. "Heading down to the bar for a drink with Gabe," I tell Romeo, trying to be polite.

Without looking up from his spreadsheets, he shrugs.

I exit the room with a huff. Fine, so he doesn't give a crap where I go. It just seemed impolite to get up and leave.

Sam's room is right around the corner, so I tiptoe down the hallway to the elevator. Facing him has become uncomfortable. We've come full circle after the other night of crying together about Seth. Both of us are being distantly polite. Now that I have internally admitted my feelings for him, his proximity is far more painful than before.

Lucky for me, the coast stays clear of Sam all the way down to the lobby. I find Gabe sitting on a stool in the bar, picking at a bowl of nuts on the counter. There is a couple at a table in the far corner. Other than that, the lounge is empty.

"Hey," Gabe says with a wide smile, and pats the seat next to him. "Let me buy you a drink."

The bartender comes over and I say, "A Diet Coke with a lime."

Looking up from texting on his phone, Gabe shakes his head and smiles at the guy. "How about a little rum in it? Vodka? Whiskey?"

"Just a lime," I repeat. I'm planning on going to bed early and getting a good night of sleep. Rollaways suck, but they beat the couch on the back of the bus any day.

His expression is exasperated as he reaches for his beer. "So what are pussy-whipped Thing One and Thing Two up to?"

The bartender sets my drink in front of me.

"One is going over sales." I reach into the bowl of nuts. "The other is busy on FaceTime."

Gabe's eyes light up. "Phone sex?"

I toss a nut at him. "Don't put shit in my head like that."

Suddenly, Sam is on the other side of Gabe.

My fingers pause inside the bowl. My pulse goes up a notch at Sam's nearness, and I'm instantly, embarrassingly nervous.

"Thought you were alone and bored," Sam says tightly to Gabe before his eyes flash to me.

Gabe stands. "I was." He finishes his beer in one long gulp and throws a ten-dollar bill onto the bar. "Need to hit the restroom." He turns to go but as Sam turns too, he puts a hand on his shoulder. "Dude, you two need to figure this shit out. If I'm sick of the tension between you two, it's gotta be way worse in your shoes." With a hand on Sam's shoulder, he steers him toward the empty bar stool next to me.

When nerves have me shoving away from the bar, Gabe pushes my stool in. "Come on, Peyton. You're tougher than this."

Then he's gone.

Sam and I both stare forward at the wall of glass shelves filled with liquor. Stupid Gabe and his stupid games. Things need to settle between Sam and me. But time, not conversation, is what we need.

Sam finally breaks the silence, saying, "So he bombarded you with texts too?"

"Yup," I say, sipping my drink and wishing I hadn't come down.

Sam orders a beer, and I keep my gaze on the bartender reaching into the cooler for a bottle. With the beer now in front of him, Sam draws in a deep breath, sighs, and says, "Haven't touched anything but alcohol since that night you helped me with the nosebleed."

Though I'm aware he's trying to break the ice and get on my good side, my nerves disappear at his news. Immediately understanding that he's implying I helped him get off drugs, I turn. "That is awesome. Has it—has it been hard?"

"A little," he says with a wince, reaching for the bottle in front of him. "I knew using was a crutch, but that night and your reaction to it made me realize how close I was coming to addiction. It had become habitual to use when I was down."

My eyes widen as I realize how close to the edge he had been. "I'm really glad to hear you've stopped."

He nods.

Silence reigns as we both stare at our drinks until Sam says in an absent tone, "Why does it feel like we're back to where we started?"

"Because we are?" I say, my voice a low grumble.

"I'm trying to do what you asked for. I'm giving you time, Peyton." He takes a long swig of his beer, then sets it down with a clunk. "I'm not sure for what, but I'm trying."

I twist my drink on its coaster. He's not giving me anything to go on. I'm clueless where I stand with him. "I'm not sure either."

"Obviously," he says sarcastically.

"Back to being a jerk?" I ask, sliding the lime around the edge of my glass.

"Back to screwing me and running to your boyfriend right after?"

I resist throwing Diet Coke in his pretty face. By sheer, momentous will. "That's low, even for you."

"It's the truth," he says.

"If I'm such a coldhearted bitch, why are you giving me time?" I grumble.

Shrugging, he turns to stare at the shelves of liquor again. "Well, you're only a coldhearted bitch to me. And only sometimes. Like after we have sex. Otherwise, you're usually sweet and caring and giving. Beyond that, you're extremely brilliant at what you do—several of your photos and blog posts have blown me away—and you're hotter than hell, especially in those cowboy boots and shorts. Fuck," he says, running a hand down his face. "I've imagined peeling those shorts from you inch by inch a million times."

He takes another long swig. I stare at his chiseled profile, my mouth frozen open. I would have never guessed he paid attention to the blog or the photos on it. And the image of him peeling off my shorts slowly? Yeah, unfortunately, just the thought is getting me hot.

He sets the beer down and turns to me. "Maybe I'm waiting to see the real you, because I truly like the person you are most of the time. I've always felt a connection to her. From the start."

My mouth is seriously stuck open, like in a permanent O. He has put himself out there, maybe not as eloquently as the romantic in me would like, yet he has stated his feelings. Clearly.

He lifts my chin and his touch sends stupid tingles through my body. His gaze radiates a sadness that hits me harder than his words. "But, then, maybe you don't like me."

"I like you," I say in a stunned whisper as he lowers his hand.

He raises an eyebrow.

Biting my lip, I try to collect my confused thoughts. "It's just . . . There is so much that's complicated about our past. And you're kind of a jerk to me sometimes too, but—"

"You two coming to dinner?" Justin asks, popping his head in between us.

Justin's appearance axes whatever confused crap was going to come out of my mouth next.

With his hands flat on the bar and his elbows up, Sam pushes his stool back. "As long as Romeo's paying, I'm in."

Romeo is actually not paying with his own money. He is using band funds for this dinner, but yeah, after five days on the bus, everyone needs some kind of bonus, even Romeo. Too bad Sam has me so confused all over again that the prospect of a nice dinner doesn't hold the excitement it might have earlier, when I was watching my third hour of bad reality television.

Justin looks to me.

"Yeah, I'm coming too," I say, scooting off my stool and refusing to meet Sam's stare.

The hotel has several restaurants. No surprise that after being inside a bus for so long, instead of choosing the most expensive and fanciest, we all wanted to eat in the inner courtyard since it's outdoors and more casual.

Justin leads the way past the elevator, then down a few steps to French doors that open onto a flagstone patio. Linen-covered tables are situated among small trees and overflowing flowerpots. Justin takes us to a partially hidden table on the far side from the entrance. Romeo and Gabe are already seated and looking at menus. Once Justin sits, I pick the spot in between him and Gabe. Unfortunately, Sam is across from me.

I order another Diet Coke. Romeo orders a bottle of champagne, I'm guessing to celebrate the near end of the tour—there's only a little over a week left for the tour. While we order dinner, I fidget whenever Sam's questioning gaze falls on me. The others don't notice as they obsessively talk about winding up the tour.

Once the bubbly is poured, Romeo raises his fluted glass. The rest of us follow his lead.

Romeo taps the edge of his flute with a knife. "Though just a group of college kids, beyond landing this tour, we've kicked ass."

"Fuck yeah," Gabe says.

Justin grins.

Sam stares at me.

"And now," Romeo says, lifting his flute higher and then looking at each of his bandmates individually. "We have two labels offering a contract."

I almost drop my flute at the news.

"Holy shit," Justin says, slowly lowering his flute. "Are you kidding?"

Romeo takes a gulp of champagne, then grins slyly. "Nope."

Gabe whistles lowly. "That is fucking awesome."

Sam is now staring at Romeo too. "When?" he asks. "When did they offer?"

"Today," Romeo says. "We got the first offer around three. The second one followed shortly after."

"That is fucking awesome," Gabe repeats.

That they now have offers from two labels is beyond awesome. It's mind-blowing. My eyes must be as wide as saucers as I slowly realize the possible implications: money, fame, travel, and an even longer string of available women.

Justin leans forward. "So what are the offers?"

Romeo shakes his head. "Both are vague right now. I'm not sure which is better. We'll have a meeting in my room tomorrow morning and get into logistics."

"Are we going to sign?" Gabe asks.

Romeo nods. "With two offers to choose from, I would hope so."

Sam raises his flute again. "To Luminescent Juliet," he says before downing the champagne.

We all lift our flutes and drink too.

Shocked conversation continues around the table, even after the waiter brings our dinners and another bottle of champagne. They joke about shooting a real video, maybe eventually having their own tour, and going to the Grammys. Though they're laughing, all of it seems possible, suddenly. Lucky for me, the news and the subsequent conversations deflect Sam's attention from me.

Listening to the guys' excitement, I eat my risotto and sip champagne, truly hoping that all their jokes become reality.

After dinner, they want to continue the celebration a few blocks away at a local bar where Brookfield is playing a short acoustic set. Justin asks me to go, then Gabe. I decline. Twice. Sam gives me a level, knowing look each time, and while he is part of the reason I decline, I'm also very tired. My confusion over him adds to my exhaustion.

So when the guys go out, I head upstairs.

I call Jill and we talk awhile. She's been supportive about my breakup with Bryce, which is not surprising. She doesn't hate him or anything, just thinks he is too boring for me. I haven't said anything to her about Sam. I don't know how to explain the mess. I also don't tell her about Luminescent Juliet possibly signing with a label. I'm more than aware Romeo will want to keep the news under wraps. And though I love Jill like a sister, the girl has one big mouth.

After we hang up, I go out on the balcony and watch the lights from the boats along the dark Ohio River. The conversation with Sam at the bar plays over and over in my head. Though it's hard for me to believe—after everything we've been through—I accept that Sam has feelings for me too. His feelings aren't a guarantee that things won't turn to shit, but it's nice to know that what we've got going is not just about couch sex for him either.

My fingers absently drum on the rail.

And maybe I drank too much champagne.

My fingers stop their drumming to grip the rail.

No, I'm finally thinking clearly. Staring at the slow-moving boat lights, I realize how silly and cowardly I'm being. The thought of Sam warms me up from my toes to the hair on my head. I don't *want* to feel this way about him. I just do. And I can't seem to stop. To ignore our connection because I'm afraid of getting hurt seems beyond cowardly. It seems stupid.

I'm sick of thinking the mess between us is all there is, when what I truly want is to be with Sam.

Besides. He wants to be with me.

So why the hell am I here on a balcony alone?

Chapter 28

Oh crap. I pause outside the bar where Brookfield is about to start playing, looking at the long line that's stretching down the block. In the middle of my balcony revelation, my stupid ass hadn't thought about getting inside without the band or some kind of backstage pass. Through the glass window in front, I can see the bar is packed wall-to-wall. I walk along the length of the huge glass window, looking for anyone I might know, from Sam to a roadie to even Rick. But all I see is a blur of strangers.

Halfway down the length of the window, there is a brick ledge below it. I step up to the glass. With one hand pressed to it and the other shading my eyes, I search above the heads of the people inside. All I can make out is that the bar is long and narrow. Though I can't see a stage, the spotlights in the back have me guessing the performance is at the end of the long room. It's totally packed, and almost completely dark.

I only walked a few blocks to get here, yet it's like I traveled miles. I suppose emotionally I have. Yet, confronting this sea of unknown faces is immediately sending me to the edge of doubt. Maybe I shouldn't have come.

After several minutes of looking, I'm about to give up and get down when a hand on the other side of the glass forms to mine. Pressing to the glass, the bigger hand overlaps mine, and pushes on the window as if wanting to melt through the glass and touch me. I slowly raise my gaze from the hand to a muscular tattooed arm and the clear blue eyes above it.

My doubt begins to fade at the longing in his stare.

I smile softly and lean forward, pressing both of my hands to the glass. He matches me with both hands. We stand, staring at each other, face-to-face, hand-to-hand. Understanding and acceptance flows between us.

Sam starts moving. I follow him, our hands still matching on the glass as we walk, our gazes locked. My confusion floats away into the night sky, little by little with each step. Our connection feels natural, inevitable, and adrenaline charged.

When we reach the end of the glass, Sam disappears. Lost in the moment, I stand on the sidewalk, blinking in confusion and wondering why he would leave me just as everything suddenly feels right.

Then he comes out the door and strides over the ropes that keep out the people waiting in line to get into the bar. Eyes only on me, he steps so close I have to look up to keep our gazes locked. We stare at each other, and everything clicks into place. Sam and I belong together. Though both of us are strong and determined to carry on, life has left us each a bit damaged. But we fill in each other's cracks and make the other whole.

Leaning down, he gently grasps my jaw, fingers caressing my skin, and gives me a fierce, sweet kiss. His mouth claims me, declares I'm his, and my lips respond as my body agrees. I'm light-headed from his kiss as he takes my hand and we start walking. After crossing a busy street, we turn onto a walkway along the river. The lights on the bridge in the distance appear violet, spreading a ghostly purplish glow on the water. Lit-up buildings rise behind the bridge. Trees edge the walkway, hiding it from the adjacent busy street. Benches and bright lampposts line the path.

He glances down at me. "I remember seeing you the first time on campus. Somehow, with everything that Seth was dealing with, I'd forgotten you were going there too."

"You hated me," I say sadly.

He shakes his head. "It was never hate, just hurt that felt so deep it made me crazy. Sometimes I think I unconsciously followed you to our college."

When I looked back at that night, I had guessed he might have had feelings for me, but we didn't see each other until almost a year later. Surely, he would have been over me by then. But following me? That blows my mind. "Why?"

Looking over the water, Sam says, "I was crazy about you before, you know."

"Before?" I ask, confused. I'm still riding the high of acknowledgment between us, and the kiss in front of the bar.

He leads me to the rail near the water. "I wanted to ask you out the first time Jill brought you to see the Bottle Rockets at that old falling-down barn. Seth beat me to it. So I tried to be content with being friends."

My free hand grasps the rail. "We *were* good friends."

"Until that night," he says, looking out over the water. "When you ran back to Seth."

Letting go of the rail, I turn to him. "Sam, I was a young, insecure girl who thought that dating Seth was like winning the lottery. My longing to be wanted, to be loved, had me imagining there was more to that relationship than there was, but I truly thought you and I were just friends. Even after that night, I blamed what happened on alcohol and my fight with Seth."

He shakes his head. "Think about it, Peyton. Except for the few dates you went on, you and Seth weren't together much. He was too busy being the life of the party. While he entertained the crowd,

you and I hung out, talked music, and joked around. I never understood why Seth took you for granted. I thought you were perfect,
pretty, intelligent, and funny. That you were into music was only a
bonus. I couldn't understand why he wouldn't spend every second
possible with you, because as we spent more time together, I wanted
to spend every moment with you."

I stare out over the water in confusion. Although I believe his
words, I'm having a hard time remembering if he's right about how
much time we spent together. Once again, my memory fails me.
Or is it my denial kicking in? I do recall talking with Sam but not
that much. I was usually thinking about Seth or watching Seth or
waiting for Seth. I was in the grip of a girlish obsession. I shake my
head slightly. "I don't know why I was so obsessed with Seth, but
my feelings died long ago."

"I've slowly realized that. It's not easy for me to let it go. Your
rejection, Seth's anger at me, then his disease . . . It's all wrapped
up together in a ball of hurt that I couldn't get rid of. When you
showed up at my apartment to tell me you were coming on tour
with us, it ripped open those old wounds." He brushes at a strand
of hair that the breeze blew across my face. "Then I started to get
to know you again, and in many ways, you're the same Peyton, the
same amazing girl who drew me in years ago."

I look at him incredulously. If anything, I've gone from naive
and bitchy to just bitchy. "After the way I treated you? You thought
I was *amazing*?"

He smiles faintly. "You've gained an edge of toughness, but
inside you still have that soft heart. You have basically taken care of
the band this whole tour without once complaining. And you were
absolutely livid at the idea that I'd abandoned Seth. And you're still
unbelievably lovely." He pushes a wayward strand of hair behind

my ear. "A week into the tour, although I tried to avoid it, I found myself becoming obsessed with you all over again."

I reach up and catch his hand, press it to my cheek as I shake my head. "I was in crazy denial back then," I say, pushing up on my tiptoes so my lips are inches from his. "I'm not that blind self-absorbed girl anymore. This time around, all my attention is on you."

His fingers cup my face and he kisses me again. Long and slow until we're pressed against each other. Gently pulling away, Sam grasps my hand. "Come on, Gabe won't be back for hours."

We step out onto the street, and I'm startled to see the hotel across the way. My sense of direction isn't usually so bad, but then again, paying attention to my surroundings is my last concern at the moment. I'm preoccupied with Sam.

On the sidewalk in front of the hotel, I teasingly say, "Why does it matter if Gabe won't be back for hours?"

In a whirl of movement, I quickly find myself pressed against the building. "Because ever since I've been with you, you're the only woman I truly want," he growls into my ear.

"It was just last week," I gasp as he rubs against me and drags his lips across the skin of my jaw.

He steps back, his gaze burning into me. "It's been years."

I nearly gasp again, shocked that he's wanted me for so long. I'm suddenly warm all over; my knees have the consistency of pudding, as wobbly as the zabaglione I make at the restaurant.

He grabs my hand again and we rush through the lobby to the elevator. Sam glances with evident irritation at the other couple going up as we're forced to wait as they slowly exit at their floor with suitcases. When the doors slide open again, we make it down the hall in seconds. He quickly slips the card into the lock, pulls me inside, hooks the chain, and pushes me against the back of the door.

His hands hold mine, pressing them to the door above my head. His mouth on mine is slow, his tongue languid as he seductively explores my mouth. His hold on my hands keeps me up, keeps me from sliding down the door and collapsing onto the carpet.

He breaks away, continuing to grasp one of my hands. "We're going to do this right for once."

I blink innocently and let him gently pull me along. He backs up, leading me farther into the room, which is lit only by the lamp on the desk. As we move, I step out of my flip-flops. "We've been doing it wrong?" I run my fingers along the low-riding waistband of his shorts. "Because it felt pretty damn right. Both times," I add with a naughty grin.

After placing a condom on the bed, he grins back at me and reaches for the bottom of my shirt. "It's going to feel more right *naked*." He pulls the shirt off over my head. With the tank top hanging from his fingertips, he stares at my lacy bra. "Very pretty."

He drops the shirt, then starts to slowly run his fingertips from my belly button to the clasp in between my breasts. His touch on my skin drives me wild but I try to stay still. He unhooks the bra with slightly shaking fingers. While he watches, his hands millimeters from my skin, I tug the straps from my shoulders and the bra drops to the floor.

"Even prettier," he says from a throat that sounds dry.

Between his stare and his tone, I'm already flushed. It's so easy being with him, so natural, we may not make it to fully naked for the third time. But I'm really, really liking this naked thing. I tug on his T-shirt, desperate to feel his skin against mine. I'm utterly, totally, unconscious about being naked in front of him. I trust him. I feel safe, accepted, and desired. Every time his hot blue gaze lingers on me, I feel like the sexiest woman on earth.

He bends down and catches a breast in his mouth, and without thinking, I jump toward him. He holds me by one hip as his mouth moves to my other breast. His free hand lightly caresses my ribs, spreading more fire. As his tongue and teeth wreak havoc on my breasts, my hands wind through his curls and grip his head. When he releases a nipple, I reach for the bottom of his shirt again.

"My turn," I say, yanking his shirt. He lifts his arms, bending forward and letting me pull the fabric up and over his curls. I step back and take him in. Smooth skin over defined muscles. All male. All hot. "Very pretty," I say, copying him. I'm not surprised my voice sounds as dry as his did.

Sam's eyes become heavy lidded. His gaze burns into mine as my hands roam over him. His skin is as hot as his stare. After exploring the contours of his chest, my fingers trail over the ledges of his abs and reach for the button of his shorts. His stomach muscles ripple, but he doesn't move as I push his shorts and boxers down.

He kicks off his shoes, then steps out of the clothes around his ankles and stands naked before me.

I break our locked gazes to get a look at him. Damn. He's gorgeous. All muscle and obvious ridged desire for me. Naked is good. Real good. Awesomely good. I reach for him, but he grabs me, *his* hands diving for my waistband.

"My turn," he says, unbuttoning my shorts. Like me, he pushes both my shorts and underwear down. Unlike me, he kneels on the floor, his gaze slowly moving up my body, as I stand naked, basking in his admiring stare.

"Beautiful," he says, looking up at me, and my breath catches. Standing, he slides his hands from my ankles up to my thighs. His thumbs brush my mound, and the jolt of desire hits me like the blast of music when I come around the stage. His thumbs tease me.

I begin to quiver and sway. Then his hands settle on my hips, and I can halfway think again. He gently pushes me until the back of my knees hit the bed.

Grinning, he wraps his hands around my waist. He gives me a wet hot kiss, then twists me around. He falls back onto the bed, dragging me with him. Gasping at the contact of his warm skin on mine, I sprawl on top of him. I push up on my palms, but he grips my head and pulls me down again until our lips are inches apart.

"I've spent a lot of time imagining this. Your luscious body on mine," he says hotly against my lips. "But being skin to skin with you is even better than I imagined." He catches my lower lip and sucks on it for a moment until we're joined in a full, deep kiss.

Lost in the sensation of his mouth, I groan slightly as his hands slide over my back to cup my butt, causing my skin to burn with desire. With a slight shift of my hips, he fits me to him, and we both groan at the contact. We kiss and pant and rub until, with shaky fingers, he slides on the condom, then slides into me.

With me above him, I try to move slowly but a building pressure quickens our motion. Like before, I'm mindless, with the needs of our bodies having us following and answering each other without thought. When he rolls us over and rises above me, his arms cradling my head, his gaze boring into mine, my lust-crazed mind not only reads but accepts what his eyes are telling me. I'm his.

I've always been his.

Chapter 29

I stare at the dark skyline speckled with the lights of Pittsburgh as Sam runs his fingers through my hair. Sitting on a patio chair on the balcony, we're wrapped in a sheet. I'm in his lap with my back pressed to his chest and my head on his shoulder. Both content, we've been sharing the view in silence.

Sam digs his nose into my hair and breathes in the scent. "You know you're perfect, right?" he asks, breaking the silence.

A deep, self-deprecating laugh escapes me. "I don't think so."

He pulls me closer, places his warm hand on my breast, and gently squeezes. "Perfect."

"Breasts do not make a woman perfect," I say with a nervous laugh, and push his hand away.

"They're the first of many perfect things." He kisses me behind my ear.

Though we're in shadows from the light coming from the lamp inside the room, I twist my head and look up at him. "Don't put me on some crazy-ass pedestal. I'm *so* not perfect. We both know I can be a bitch."

He wiggles his eyebrows. "I like a woman with spunk."

I roll my eyes. "I'm stubborn."

"I'd call it principled, strong," he says, grinning.

"I'm oblivious and totally dense sometimes."

His teeth shine white as he smiles down at me. "That's just plain cute."

I shake my head. No, it's not. Being oblivious to everyone's feelings except my own is partly why I unknowingly hurt him in the past. As he grins at me again, I realize I want him to know everything about me, even the self-absorbed parts of me. Being with Bryce was just about having someone around to have a good time with. Being with Sam is all or nothing.

"It's not, Sam. You of all people should know I can be obsessively selfish."

The grin on Sam's mouth disappears, and I'm suddenly a bundle of nerves. Does he really view me as perfect?

"Peyton, you're one of the least selfish people I know."

I shake my head again. "No, I'm not. Look at the way I treated you."

He shrugs. "You were just a high school girl thrilled by the idea of the most sought-after band member wanting you."

"Yeah, and nothing else mattered in my little world."

He rolls his eyes.

I sigh and look out over the city. "Sam, sometimes I'm obsessed with myself to the point of being completely superficial. I worry about my future, my grades, my weight . . . to the point of ridiculousness. Other people get cancer or have to mourn the death of a loved one or have a brother with schizophrenia." I turn, looking at him gently, then point to myself. "And me? I'm worried about the size of my ass. Not exactly humanitarian of the year."

He grabs my hand and holds it. His thumb draws circles over my knuckles as his gaze searches mine. "If you were actually superficial, you wouldn't have these worries," he says. "Everybody worries about the future and getting good grades. There's nothing wrong with that. Besides, you care even though you *haven't* gone through any of those awful things. And you do care. Do you remember chasing after my brother in Charlotte, Peyton? You never for one second thought about not coming with me. You care about Seth and about me, and look how we've treated *you*. You're even nice to the guys in the band. You do our laundry, cook for us, and even pick up after us. But as far as your ass . . ." He slides a hand under the said body part. "It is definitely perfection."

My brows rise. "And when it gets bigger?"

He squeezes. "More perfection."

"Yeah, that's not what all the guys in my high school thought," I say before I can stop the self-deprecating comment.

"Like I said before, blind fools. Thirty pounds more would never take away your beauty."

"Well, wow." I groan and fall back on his shoulder. "Now I'm sure I don't deserve you."

He snorts against the skin of my neck. "Like I haven't been a dick. We're here together. Finally. And all your imperfections are perfect to me. I was crazy about you then, and I'm even crazier about you now." Sam pulls me closer with the hand on my butt and kisses my bare shoulder. "Don't try to talk me out of it."

There is another imperfection I can't help bringing up—especially since guilt over the way I broke up with Bryce has been lingering. After a nervous dry swallow, I say, "And what about the cheating? I heartlessly cheated on two of my three boyfriends."

Sam's gaze whips to mine. "Who was the third boyfriend?"

"Just a guy from my journalism class who I went out for about three months during sophomore year. But are you listening to me?"

"Well-l-l," Sam says, "since both times you cheated were with me, I'm not going to complain."

I draw in a deep breath. "Aren't you—you worried that I'll cheat again? On you?" The last question comes out in a squeak.

He shrugs. "No. Not really." When I pull away from his shoulder to give him an incredulous look, he asks, "Do you know why?"

Truly bewildered, I shake my head.

His hands follow the curve of my hips to my thighs. "You. Me. We're meant to be together. I've felt it from the beginning."

My expression turns skeptical but he ignores it.

His head tilts in thought. "Being an English major, I've read just about every kind of love story there is, from Shakespeare to Fitzgerald. Some end happily, others in heartache, and most in tragedy. But I've connected with each one, even the sappiest"— his hands tighten on my thighs—"because you're my star-crossed lover, Juliet. Because I've been cold, proud Mr. Darcy pining in torment for you. Because you've been Estella Havisham, blindly refusing your feelings. Because, like Jay Gatsby, I've been obsessed with my former lover." He lowers his head until his gaze is even with mine. "But together we're Buttercup and Westley riding off into the sunset on white horses. We're Lucy and George whispering from their room with a view. Jane and Mr. Rochester reuniting amid the burned ruins of his estate."

Air is caught like a fluttering butterfly in my throat. I'm overwhelmed by the comparisons and can only stare at him opened mouthed until he adds, "Superman and Lois Lane flying in the night sky."

The butterfly escapes as a laugh bursts from me. "*Great Expectations* to comic books?"

He smirks. "Some comics are classic too."

Feeling semidrunk on his words, I twist around and grasp his jaw. "Do you know how many times over the past weeks I've wished I would have fallen for you back then instead of Seth?"

He stares at me for a few silent moments before asking in a hoarse voice, "How many?"

I lean forward, my hands slipping into his curls. "Countless," I say against his lips before kissing him long and slow. Kissing him is so right, I can't imagine kissing anyone else ever again.

His hands move down my back to my butt, jerking me toward him. At the touch of his hard heat between my thighs, I'm thinking forget the bed—right now, it's about this patio chair. We need to try everything at least once.

But a loud clunk and a voice yelling "What the fuck?" interrupts us. Someone beats on the room door and yells, "Sam!"

Realizing Gabe's trying to get in, I scramble off Sam's lap, drawing the sheet with me. "What time is it?"

Sam reaches for my waist. "Who cares?"

I step away from him and into the room, searching for my clothes. The clock on the nightstand reads three eleven. Gabe keeps pounding on the door. I'm tugging my shorts on when Sam comes in and kisses my neck.

"He'll go away eventually," he says softly, then runs his tongue over my shoulder.

"Get dressed!" I hiss, pushing him away and trying not to laugh. "We're not leaving Gabe in the hallway." Gabe has opened the door a sliver and is rattling it back and forth to try and free the chain that Sam—very smartly, I think now—must have fastened before we came outside to the patio.

"Fine." He reaches for his shorts but pauses with one leg in as I clip my bra on. "You're staying, right?"

I snatch my shirt from the floor. "And sleep with you while Gabe's in the next bed? Ah, I don't think so."

He finishes pulling his shorts up. "Gabe won't care."

I pull my shirt over my head. "I'll care."

Before my arms are down, Sam's wrapped around me. "Come on, Peyton. Please. Stay."

The feel of his arms around me tempts me to.

"Come *on!*" Gabe rattles the door harder.

I try to envision sleeping next to Sam all night with Gabe snoring a few feet away or, worse, Sam getting me hot with Gabe snoring right there. Ah, no, it's not happening. Untangling myself from Sam, I say, "We can meet up in the morning."

"Morning, shmorning," he grumbles as I toss his shirt at him.

"Put it on," I say, moving toward the door after slipping on my flip-flops. I hesitate before removing the chain. Gabe isn't dumb— he knows why the chain is up, and I'm not in the mood, nor will I ever be, to hear his shit. But this is his room, so after checking that Sam put his shirt on, I reluctantly let the chain loose and open the door.

Gabe's fist pauses midair. "Well, hello, Peyton. Strange meeting you here," he says with a sarcastic grin, breezing past me. "Oh look, Sam's bed is all messy, even missing some sheets," I hear Gabe say. His laughter follows me as I fly out the door.

Sam catches up with me in the hallway and pins me to the wall. "Don't I get a good-bye at least?"

"Good-bye," I say sweetly.

"And a kiss?"

I raise an eyebrow.

He raises one of his.

"Fine," I say, leaning toward his lips, then give him a quick peck.

"That's not a kiss," he says flatly as his fingers tighten around my arms.

"My lips touched yours," I say wryly. "That would be the definition of a kiss."

He huffs in annoyance, jerks my body to his, then covers my mouth in a long, searching, hot kiss as his hands roam over my body. He breaks the kiss with a smirk, and has to untangle himself from my arms to step away. "Good night, Peyton," he says softly.

"Night, Sam," I say dreamily, watching him saunter back to his room.

Once the door closes, I stumble like a drunk to my room.

Neither Romeo nor Justin wakes up when I enter the room. Still in a daze, I wouldn't care if they did.

Chapter 30

The next night, as soon as I get to the green room, Sam catches my gaze and nods toward the exit. After doing an interview for a local radio station, he and the rest of the band are surrounded by fans. Most of them are female. Pretending not to notice him and his gestures, I fill a plate with mini sandwiches, a heap of fruit, and a few chips, then I go sit in the back, where the roadies are coming and going as usual. Sam keeps moving around the fans, trying to get my attention as I listen to TJ and Chris bitch about their day.

Finishing off my chips, I almost spit them out in laughter when Sam's text comes in.

Either get me a crowbar to remove these women, or meet me in the bus.

After wiping my hands on a napkin, I text back, *One of the roadies should be able to find a crowbar.*

Chris and I talk music for a bit after TJ leaves.

PEYTON! pops up on the screen of my phone.

I respond, *Crowbar incoming in two seconds.*

Chris leaves and I'm packing up my trash when Sam texts. *First you leave me with Gabe and now you're ignoring me for roadies.*

I dump my trash in a bin before typing, *You shouldn't have tried to molest me in the laundry room this morning.*

Sam's eyes narrow at me from across the room as a girl wraps her arm around him and her friend takes a picture. I smile wide and wink.

I'm loading my bag with bottled waters—I started snagging waters at each event so we never run out anymore—when another text comes through.

I'm going to molest you in this room. Presently.

Suspecting he's not kidding, I race out of the green room and head to the bus.

Gary is sleeping on the couch. We'll be leaving tonight, starting the last run of concerts. I tiptoe past him, deposit the water bottles in the fridge, and go to my little cave in the back.

It doesn't take too long before Sam comes into the room quietly and tugs the curtain shut. The only light is from the computer screen as I load pictures from my camera. His eyes gleam at me in the near darkness. He dives at me and I slap a hand across my mouth, stopping a laugh from escaping as I scoot across the couch. He lands over me, the leather of the couch squeaking under his spread knees, his hands braced on either side of me. I'm caught sitting up with his body like a gorgeous cage around me.

Leaning forward, he brushes his lips against my ear. "Playing games, Peyton?" he asks, and the rush of hot breath into my ear sends lust tingling over my skin.

I push at his hard chest. "Trying to order me around by text?"

He nibbles at my ear. "No need now. We're on a couch."

A laugh does escape me. Obviously, he has thought about couches and us too.

"Shh," he whispers near my mouth. "Can't wake Gary."

His lips hover millimeters from mine, and Gary, games, and everything but sensations are forgotten.

After dragging his lips across mine, he kisses the corner of my mouth, tracing a thumb along the line of my neck. He nips at my lower lip, then sucks on it before kissing the other corner of my mouth as his fingers follow the line of my collarbone.

The touch of both his lips and fingers fills me with breathless anticipation. My hands twine in his curls and grasp his head as I try to catch his lips for a full kiss. He chuckles, then traces my upper lip with his tongue.

"Sam," I groan in frustration. I've never wanted a kiss so bad. I'm practically salivating with want, aching for his mouth to cover mine.

"Thought you liked games?" he murmurs, then runs his lips along the curve of my chin as he tips my jaw back with his thumbs. His wet mouth traces a path down my neck. I gasp. He chuckles. The hand holding my jaw shifts and his thumb rubs across my bottom lip in a soft, teasing caress. "Paybacks are hell, right?" he asks against the skin of my neck before he gently sucks.

Recalling saying those words to him in his apartment, I release his curls, push at his chest, and twist my body until he flops over.

Grinning, he wriggles his eyebrows.

I smile wickedly. Now that we've switched positions, he has no idea what he's in for. I'm a dessert maker. I know how to wait and let things rise. "Oh, I like games," I say, grabbing the hands on my thighs and holding them to his chest.

His grin dwindles and his eyelids lower as I settle myself on his lap.

I drop kisses along the line of his jaw and the strained cord of his neck while my free hand slips under his shirt. My palm traces the hard curve of his chest as my tongue traces the curve of his ear. His taste is like the best dessert, fresh out of the oven.

His chest rises in a deep breath, and it's very, very hard not to kiss him. Instead, I kiss along the curve of his cheekbone and over the bridge of his nose to the other cheek while my palm rubs circles across his ridged abdomen. When my hand gets to the waistband of his jeans, I trail a finger across the skin above at the same time my tongue trails across the seam of his lips.

A moaning sound comes out of Sam, from deep within, and before I can blink, I'm on my back, his body pressing mine into the couch. The kiss is explosive, his mouth demanding against mine, his tongue delving. My fingers pull him closer.

When the main door bangs, Sam lifts his head. Our breath is heavy as we both listen.

"Screw you!" Justin says, laughing from the other room, and my hands instantly let go of Sam's curls and start pushing at his chest.

He smirks at me.

"Sam!" I whisper, shoving harder.

He slowly pulls himself away, and once I'm free, I scoot to the end of the couch.

And just in time too, because a second later, the vinyl curtain opens and Gabe pokes his head into the room. "Thought you two might be in here," he says, grinning. "Romeo's still looking for you guys inside." He pulls out his phone and starts tapping on it, doubtlessly texting Romeo. "I told him you were probably on the bus." He glances up. "I expected you to be sucking face or something else," he says with a smirk.

Lucky for me and my burning cheeks, the room is shadowed except for the soft glow of the computer screen.

Sam whips a pillow at Gabe. "Go away, asshole!"

Lifting an arm to deflect the pillow, Gabe asks in an incredulous tone, "You're not playing?" He's referring to their habitual after-show video games when we're on the bus.

Sam shakes his head. "Nope. I'm hanging back here."

"Of course you are." Gabe rolls his eyes at us and takes off.

"I don't mind if you want to go play," I say nonchalantly.

Sam looks at me like I've lost my mind as he scoots closer. "I've been playing stupid video games for weeks, imagining you back here in various stages of seminakedness." He grips the bottom of my shirt. "I'm not going anywhere."

My hands cover his. "They'll be no stages of nakedness." I push his hand away. "Not with three other guys roaming free on the bus."

Sam stares at me for a long moment, then looks around the small room. "All right, how about some TV?"

"Sure," I say, leaning back into the couch cushions. But once he turns on the TV, he unfolds the blankets, throws the pillows on the far end of the couch, yanks me to his chest, and wraps us up—then we lie down together.

"Sam," I say, trying to disentangle myself, fearful of Gabe popping in again.

He holds me tight. "Forget it, Peyton. If we can't do the sucking stuff—" He pauses at the elbow jab I give his ribs. He catches my earlobe and sucks on it. "Unless you want to do the sucking stuff?" he asks, his teeth lightly scraping my skin.

"Stop it," I say, trying to elbow him again as he pulls me closer.

His lips release my earlobe. "Then let me hold you."

"Gabe's going to come back here again."

"Who gives a shit about Gabe?"

Blinking up at him, I realize he has a point. Though it's a bit weird cuddling with him while the guys are up front playing video games, I let him tuck me against his chest. He just holds me and within seconds, I relax.

He flicks through channels and nuzzles my neck intermittently, which is quite nice. The bus starts rolling, and my eyelids grow heavy.

Warm and content, I realize I could happily fall asleep like this every night.

Chapter 31

The next afternoon, Sam's head lies on a pillow next to my thighs. I'm hunched over the computer on the couch, typing in a post. If I weren't working, my lap would be Sam's pillow. My elbow knocks into the book he's reading. Instead of bitching, he adjusts the book from above his face to over his chest.

"Sorry," I say, clicking open a picture file from the previous night.

He shrugs and keeps reading.

I've noticed Sam can block out the world when he reads. Like totally. The guys could be next to him shouting and playing video games, or Gabe and Justin could be in a heated argument, or a volcano could erupt. Sam would keep reading.

I look him over as he reads with his curly head on the pillow. He's in one of his plain white T-shirts, baggy worn shorts, and a flip-flop teeters from his foot at the end of the couch. His chest rises with a slight shake. He does this often. Obviously, he's reading another "funny" book.

An obnoxious thought enters my head as I watch him read. *Don't do it, Peyton!* my conscience yells. If he ignores me, my ego might read too much into his dismissal, but my wayward fingers have already dug into his curls. My thumb brushes at his temple. My other hand moves to his jaw and caresses his scruff.

For several seconds, he continues to read, until he finally glances up, his lips forming a soft smile. "You bored?"

I shake my head.

"You done?"

I shake my head.

"You need a little attention?"

I smile slightly.

He carefully sets the book on the couch and lifts up on an elbow, reaching up behind my neck. He pulls me down gently. The kiss is soft, sweet, and filled with longing.

"Damn," he whispers against my lips, "I'm starting to hate this bus."

I nod, brushing my nose against his, then he lets go of my neck, settles back onto the pillow, and picks up his book.

I start clicking through pictures. Low music and snippets of conversation vibrate from the front of the bus but not loud enough to drown out the occasional turn of a page. I get back to typing again.

My little cave has become a place of contentment.

I wake up in the middle of the night to the rhythm of the bus moving and a tightly muscled body holding me. Gazing into the darkness, I recall falling asleep on the bus while the guys were stuck in interview after interview in Kansas City. Apparently, Sam skipped his bunk and came right to me.

For a nanosecond, I wonder what the guys thought of that.

Then Sam's warm breath rushes over my cheek, and I realize I don't give a shit.

I wrap my arms around the ones holding me and fall back asleep.

• • •

"So what magazine is your dream job?" Sam asks, bumping his elbow into mine as we stare out the window, gawking at the mountains on our way to Salt Lake City. After that, it's back to California, where the tour had started before Luminescent Juliet even joined up, for the last concert in Fresno. "*Vibe? Alternative Press?* Or *Rolling Stone?*

I break my gaze from the view of endless mountains—the part of Michigan where we grew up is pretty much flat—to look at him kneeling next to me on the couch. "Any of those would be awesome. I mean, maybe if I land a job and build a big enough reputation to be picky, I'd probably go for something like *Alternative Press,* but with the way the Internet is screwing journalists at the moment, I'm not sure being picky will ever be an option."

"Ah, the joys of technology," he says, then grins. "I knew you'd give the *Press* special treatment, punk fan that you are."

I roll my eyes. "What about you?"

He raises an eyebrow.

"What do you plan on doing with that English degree?"

"Maybe add a teaching certificate? Maybe write?" He gives me a pointed look. "Maybe edit you?"

Edit me? Please! I return his pointed look.

"Maybe I won't need my degree." He glances out the window. "Maybe I'm going to 'Beverly Hills,'" he sings, his pitch perfectly matching the song by Weezer.

"Is that what you want?"

"To play music? Write songs? And party until I'm fifty? Stop cutting lawns from April to October? Hell yeah."

"Party until you're fifty? Okay. I didn't know Keith Richards Jr. was the type to run to the back of the bus to snuggle instead of hanging in the green room to party." He laughs but my expression turns hard. "Unless you haven't given that shit up."

The lines of his expression smooth out as he becomes serious. "I didn't lie to you, Peyton. I would never lie to you about that. I've been clean since that night." He shakes his head as my features soften. "And you're right, it's not about the partying. But just like you, I love music, and I dream of being able to make it my real career. To be able to write songs and play onstage for years . . ."

I gesture behind us to the bus. At this point, it's starting to feel like a well-furnished prison on wheels. If it weren't for him, I'd be pulling my hair out by now. "What about living like this?"

"Sometimes," he says, shrugging, "you have to take the good with the bad. If the good is that freaking good."

It's obvious he loves to perform and play. It was obvious when I watched him in the Bottle Rockets. But songwriting? It's kind of established that Romeo is the band's songbird. I stare at Sam's stunning profile against the almost equally stunning backdrop of mountains. "Exactly how many songs have you written?"

He turns slowly to look at me. "Well . . . um, I've helped Romeo a bit with the melodies, so maybe about twenty percent there, but more than half of the album's lyrics are mine."

"Why?" I ask, knowing he'll understand that I'm asking why he'd hide his contribution.

He turns back to the scenery. "Like 'Trace,' most of them are personal. I don't like the idea of people getting a peek into my soul."

I'm thinking I'm going to have to figure out some more Luminescent Juliet lyrics when an awful thought occurs to me. "Are any about me?" My tone sounds pathetically fraught.

His lips twist into a frown.

"Sam?"

He glances out the window while I try to stay patient. He finally says, "There's one."

My teeth clench and grind until I let out a deep breath. "How bad is it? How bitchy am I painted? How—I mean I get it, I hurt you and you had every right to speak the truth, but . . ." My mind starts flipping through songs. None of them are about a heartless bitch. But I haven't dissected all the lyrics yet.

"Hey," he says, as his knuckle lifts my chin, "it's not that bad. Really not bad at all. I wrote it remembering the sweet girl who'd filled my thoughts and spent time talking and joking around with me. Not the girl—"

"Who left you in the barn without a glance," I say, finishing for him. "I'm sor—"

His fingers cover my mouth as he shakes his head. "No more sorry. You were right. The past is the past." He scoots toward me, his knees sliding across the leather. "We're here now. I want to live in the now, and let the past go." His hands cup my face. "You were my first, and now you're mine."

Am I? When we're intimate, there's no doubt. Outside our passion, things aren't as clear. I search his steady gaze, and drown a bit in the bright blue sea of it. Okay, fine. I am his. I rub a thumb over his bottom lip. "You're mine too."

He smiles softly and leans forward.

The swish of the curtain opening has Sam pausing.

"Hey, lovebirds," Gabe says. "Lunch is served. Hot lunch. As in Gabe's simmered steak and potatoes. The Crock-Pot with the battery inverter thing worked like a fucking charm."

Sam's gaze stays on me while he tells Gabe, "Great. We'll be there in a second."

"One last smooch?" Gabe says with a laugh, walking away.

"Several," Sam says, reaching for my face so he can kiss me thoroughly. Standing, he grabs my hand. "One and a half more days, and we're off this damn bus."

"Wait," I say, pulling him back. He looks down at me. I bite my lip, then ask, "When you said I was your first, what did you mean?"

A ghost of a smile crosses his face. "You were the first girl I ever slept with."

I blink at him. "Really?"

He sits down. "Seth was the playboy." He points to the book on the table. "I was the geek. We didn't do the band thing for real until senior year, and, well, I wasn't used to the attention." He adds with a frown, "Yet."

"You were my first too," I blurt.

He cocks his head. "You and Seth?"

I shake my head a bit too violently. "No, never."

"But he said . . ."

My gaze turns glaring.

"Yeah, well, it never mattered even when I thought that you two—" He slaps his forehead. "Fuck. How did I not know that you were a virgin?"

He looks so unhappy with himself, I reach for his hands. "Maybe because you were a virgin too?"

"Still," he says, wincing.

"And we were kind of lost in the moment and drunk. I mean, we didn't even use a condom."

His hands tighten on mine. "I would have stood by you if you were pregnant. Seth falling off the deep end or not."

"I know. I knew it then," I say, realizing that I did. Sam would have been there for me.

He nods, but his eyes are troubled.

Probably because I'm slowly seeing the past through a different, more mature lens, my emotions are as troubled as his gaze.

"Hey, assholes!" Gabe yells from the front of the bus. "I didn't peel potatoes for nothing!"

I stand. "We keep saying it, but we really need to let the past go. We've got now and the future," I say with a bright smile, and tug him out of the room before Gabe loses it.

After performing, signing a few autographs, and having pictures taken with fans, Sam leads me to the bus. He drags me past snoring Gary to the back of the bus, which is parked behind an arena in Salt Lake City. And after shutting the curtain to our little cave, he drags me to the couch and pulls me onto his lap.

"We've got about forty minutes," he says, pushing his hands under my shirt.

He goes to kiss me but I turn my head. "We're not having sex with Gary sleeping in the front room," I whisper.

His lips slide along my cheek. "Who said anything about sex?"

"Sam," I warn.

"Just want some semi-alone time." He tugs my head down and kisses me.

Though the kiss pulls me into the passion his mouth always creates, I push at his chest. "Wait, wait," I gasp. "I need to tell you something."

Sighing, he falls forward, his forehead against my shoulder. "What?"

"Well . . ." I say slowly, trying to collect my thoughts, even though the topic I'm about to bring up has been on my mind all day. During their sound checks, while I ran the booth—and as I shot photos of them performing, of Sam performing—that was when the lightbulb clicked on and everything made sense. "I know we both said to leave the past in the past, but . . ."

He looks up at me, his lips turning into a thin line.

"I slowly came to realize something today. I didn't ever truly like Seth. I was in love with the idea of him. The idea that the lead singer, the guy all the girls wanted, wanted me. Don't get me wrong, I wasn't a total airhead, there were times that Seth *was* charming—"

"I don't want to talk about my brother and you," Sam says, interrupting in a tight tone.

I put my hand up. "Wait. Let me get to the point. Seth and I were superficial. He'd call and text me all week, then ignore me until the end of the night at the parties I rushed to."

Sam groans against my shoulder.

"During most of those parties, I was with you. Until today, I'd forgotten about the party at the lake, where we lay on the dock, looking at the stars, talking about music and college. Or the time you drove me all the way home when Jill took off with some guy. You introduced me to the Violent Femmes and Moby. Remember that night we lit those firecrackers—"

Sam leans back and looks at me. Despondency lines his features. "Peyton, are you telling me that until now you didn't remember any of our time together?"

"I had . . . maybe not forgotten, but I tried to block everything after the fallout. I felt guilty because why would I sleep with you but not my boyfriend? I didn't understand myself at all. I know that now."

He grabs my shoulders. "We need to leave this shit alone. We were kids."

I shake my head. "I *was* superficial, Sam. I'm certain, looking back, I was falling for you, but I was blinded by what Seth represented—the attention, the other girls being jealous of me. It went to my head."

"I'm okay with the past, Peyton. You don't have to do this."

"It was always you." I grab his hand and clasp it to my heart. "You were here even then," I say, leaning toward him and making our gazes level. "No one else has ever been."

He stares at me, lets the truth of my words settle. His other hand trembles slightly as he pushes a strand of my hair back. "It's the same for me. The girls between then and now are a haze. It's always been you for me too."

I can't help smiling as I press my lips to his.

We're content to hold each other, kissing softly and sighing into each other's mouth, until Sam pushes gently on my back. His hands settle on my thighs. "Your boots are hot," he says in a whisper, bending to kiss a knee. His hand slides up my thigh, brushing the edge of my panties. "And I love this skirt."

As his mouth, warm and sweet and soft, slides up my inner thigh, I pant out, "Sam?"

"Shh," he says as his fingers push my underwear out of the way. "No sex. I'm just kissing you. Just kissing," he murmurs, and his hot breath warms the flesh quivering beneath it.

"Um," I whisper nervously, but when his mouth finds the center of me, I gasp, "Oh! Oh, okay. Just kissing . . ."

Chapter 32

Sam holds the hotel key card above the slot and shoots me a smoldering look. "You know I'm going to attack you as soon as we get inside, right?"

I keep my expression blank. "Well, I'd like to unpack first, take a shower, and relax."

"Screw unpacking but hell yes to a shower." He slides the key into the lock and opens the door.

I rush past him, dropping my suitcase near the closet. Since the room is a standard double, I run behind the chair in the corner.

Within seconds, Sam's leaning over the chair, with his hands bracing the wall on both sides of my head. "The chair ain't gonna stop me, honey."

I raise a brow. "You didn't just call me honey."

"I did," he says, grinning as he bends down and runs his lips over my chin, down my neck, and into my cleavage. He sucks the skin there, and my knees start turning to mush. One of his hands slides down the wall and pulls my tank top lower, giving his lips more access to the swell of my breasts.

Giving into a rising tide of lust, I am about to slip down the wall when someone pounds at the door.

"You've got to be kidding me," Sam says against my skin. The pounding continues. He stands up as a sneer twists his full lips. "Each one of those fuckers knows why I got my own room."

The pounding grows louder.

"Let me get it." I shove at his shoulders.

He steps away from the chair. "Oh no. *I'll* get it, and shove a boot up someone's ass."

"You're wearing flip-flops," I say with a giggle, coming out from behind the chair.

He glares at me over his shoulder before whipping the door open.

Both of our mouths fall open at the sight of the person standing in the doorway.

"Hey, guys," Seth says, stepping into the room. After kicking the door closed with one of his beat-up checkered Vans, he punches his brother lightly on the arm. "I always wanted to visit California, bro. More like LA but Fresno works."

Fists clenched at his sides, Sam looks like he's about to blow up, and I'm aware it has nothing to do with us being interrupted. His expression is angry and worried and desperate all at the same time.

But his brother just crosses his arms and grins at him.

The music blasts above us on the stage. It's the last show, and the fans are roaring from behind the line of bodyguards. Seth is my shadow as I shoot pictures of screaming fans. I take shot after shot as he looks from the stage to the crowd. As I switch lenses, I catch his shocked expression and understand it instantly. It's mind-blowing how much Luminescent Juliet's fan base has grown in the past six weeks. The concert seats are nearly full, and except for the extra-smalls, we're out of T-shirts today—we sold out completely fifteen minutes after the doors opened.

Sam does his bouncing thing and winks at girls in the front row. Usually, he winks and flirts with me when I'm up here with my camera, but I'm aware he's not going to go there with Seth next to me. After tearing Seth a new asshole, then calling his mother—who reminded him that Seth *is* an adult, even if he lives at home still— Romeo plays off us being together as friends once again. Wanting to keep Seth calm, I go with it.

And since Sam had sound checks and interviews for most of the day, Seth has been with me. He's been polite and kind of quiet. No crazy talk has come out of him all day. He even helped bag T-shirts and hats in the booth in between making runs to the nearest beer stand. Though he's had a few tall beers, he doesn't seem drunk, just a bit happy. He offered to buy me a drink, but essentially being at work, I declined.

The band starts their most popular and final song, "Inked My Heart." I stand in front of center stage, getting pictures of each of them one last time. They all wear sentimental expressions. Justin still appears sad and emotional as he sings. Gabe's expression is reserved as he beats out the slow tempo. Romeo looks over the crowd with nostalgia. And Sam stares at me, then Seth.

As I lower my camera, I notice Seth looking from Sam to me. But Sam's attention has returned to the crowd. I start jotting in my notepad, trying to ignore Seth's stare. I can't help imagining the direction of his mind, and suspect he's having thoughts of Sam and me together behind his back. I don't look at Sam again, just take notes about the energy of the fans.

Right before the song ends, I wrap an arm around Seth's arm and yell in his ear, "Let's go get a beer!"

Nodding, he lets me lead him by the arm, and we move to the side of the stage as the song ends. The crowd's excitement is deafening. The guys in the band move to the front, bowing and waving. Seth stops and watches, his face a picture of concentration.

"Come on. I'll buy," I say, trying to tow him backstage as the lights come on. Recorded music bursts out of the speakers, and the roadies appear to change the stage around for Griff.

The guys start coming down the ramp. We're standing a few feet from it, and though I tug on Seth's arm again, he jerks away from me. His eyes narrow and his mouth twists into a sinister snarl. He takes a few running steps, and then dives through the air at Gabe. I gasp. It's a dive of at least five feet.

Eyes wide, Gabe drops his sticks as Seth slams into him. A checkered Van flies up and lands on the ramp. As they tumble toward backstage, a gasp and instant murmur rises from fans who could see the tackle.

Security guards, the band, and I rush across the ramp.

Seth is sprawled across Gabe, hands around his neck. He chokes him for about two seconds before guards wrench him off. Sam rushes in and grabs Gabe, who looks like he is about to kill Seth. Romeo helps Sam hold Gabe back when he goes ballistic, intent on attacking his assailant. Justin and Romeo start dragging him farther backstage, and the guards holding Seth follow. He twists, spits, and kicks at them while yelling obscenities at Gabe.

Shocked, I follow behind. A man next to me is on a radio, instructing someone to call the police. I feel like a lifetime has passed, but the entire episode was less than two minutes.

Justin takes Sam's place holding Gabe, so Sam can try to calm his brother.

Seth spits in his face. "Fuck you! Fuck you!" he screams. "You won't listen! You won't listen! And you're fucking her! You're fucking *her*!"

He thrashes his body in between the guards, and he tries to kick Sam with a bare foot as I wince about being the "her."

Seth keeps yelling and spitting, but another guard comes over to Sam. Pulling him back, he says something too low for the rest of us to hear. Sam shakes his head violently and grabs the guy by his collar. "Call an ambulance," Sam loudly hisses.

The guy tries to argue.

"He's mental! Call an ambulance!" Sam says again, and lets the guy go. "And get him out of here!"

By now, people hanging out backstage are crowding around us.

The guard who Sam yelled at directs the guys holding Seth to a storage room near the exit. Seth yells and spits the entire way. Sam follows behind them. They disappear into the storage room. The remaining guards get people to disperse, and I'm left in the circus of people, completely disoriented.

The crowd finally thins. Gabe, Justin, and Romeo are gone too. Several security guards stand in front of the storage room. After picking up Seth's lone shoe, I wait as two EMTs push a gurney into the room. I'm relieved to see them and not the police. After a half hour, they push Seth strapped down on a gurney out of the room. Sam walks alongside his brother. His expression is so worried and torn, I have to stop myself from rushing to him.

Once they disappear out the back exit, I slowly make my way toward the dressing rooms as the backstage returns to normalcy. The muted thud of thrash metal comes from down the hall—Brookfield likes to get pumped up prior to going onstage. I knock several times before Justin peeks out and then lets me in. With arms crossed, Romeo leans against a wall. Across from him, Gabe punches another wall.

"Stop it," I say, moving behind Gabe and dropping Seth's shoe on a table. "He's sick, Gabe. He's delusional."

Gabe pauses and looks over his shoulder at me, through his hair. The strands lift in sync with his heavy breathing.

"He's schizophrenic. He believes you're bad, an alien or some-thing."

Gabe's fist drops as he turns toward me. "An alien?"

"Well, that explains a lot," Justin mumbles from somewhere behind me. "And I'm not talking about Seth," he adds with obvious laughter in his voice.

I lift my hands and shrug. "Like I said, he's delusional. His brain doesn't work right."

"An alien?" Gabe repeats, then starts laughing so hard he has to reach out for a table to support him. "He thinks I'm a fucking alien! That shit is too funny!"

I look around the room to find Justin and Romeo grinning.

Suddenly, my phone vibrates in my pocket. I dig it out in a rush to hear Sam's voice asking, "Has Seth been drinking?"

"Ah, yeah, he had a few beers."

"He shouldn't be drinking," Sam snaps.

"Um, I didn't know," I say slowly. I know he must be freaking out, so I'm trying not to let his angry tone affect me.

"How many did he have?"

"Maybe three or four?"

"Sixteen-ounce drafts?" Sam asks incredulously.

"Yeah," I answer in a small voice. "I didn't know he couldn't drink," I repeat, though I'm not sure I could have stopped Seth from doing what he wanted, anyway. "I'm sorry."

Sam sighs. "It's all right, Peyton, I'm just—they have him in straitjacket, and even drugged up, he's flaming pissed at me right now."

"Where are you? Do you want me to come find you?"

"I wish," he says, his voice sad. "But I don't think that's a good idea. I'll call you later, okay?"

"Is Seth going to be okay?"

"After they regulate his meds, he should be as okay as he gets."
The phone is quiet until he says, "Shit, I miss you already."

"I miss you too," I say tightly, hearing a forlorn tone in my own
voice that matches his before I hang up.

I sincerely hope Seth gets better, but he has always been the
wild card. His disease and its implications were things Sam and I
haven't talked about over the past week. We ignored the world outside the bus window, yet Seth has long been an unspoken issue.

That I used to date him is odd enough. However, I'm aware
Seth's schizophrenia adds an entire new layer of difficulty to Sam
and me being together. And the instability of his disease, his obvious dislike of our being together, could come between us.

I sit in a row of chairs in front of the huge glass window at the
Fresno airport. Justin and Romeo are a few chairs down. Both of
them are on their phones. Gabe is hungover from the huge end-of-
tour party last night—a party that was totally lame for me because
of Sam's absence. He's on the other side of the walkway, lying across
several chairs.

Sam isn't with us.

His mother flew in yesterday. They're staying at a hotel near the
hospital. They hope to fly back, with Seth, by the end of the week.
Sam says Seth's doing better, but the doctor doesn't want to release
him until his new medication is working effectively.

I haven't seen Sam in two days. I miss him every minute, yet
him being with his brother is more important than my melancholy,
obviously.

As a 747 taxis by the window, my phone vibrates, and a picture of Sam lying on the couch in the back of the bus flashes on
the screen along with the text: *Can you find somewhere private and
call me?*

Why? I text back, confused.

Just do it! Please!

I'm suddenly scared that Sam is going to share bad news—Seth isn't doing well, Sam's letting me go, or who knows what else. So I stand on shaking legs and head to an area of unoccupied seats. After setting down my carry-on and taking a deep breath, I call Sam.

"Hey, Peyton," he answers.

"What's going on?" I quickly and nervously ask.

"I wanted to send you off with a memory of me."

"Huh?"

"I'm going to put the phone down. Just listen until I pick it back up, okay?"

"Um, okay."

I hear him set the phone down, then the chords of an acoustic guitar echo. I'm trying to place the familiar tune when he starts singing:

Even amid falling leaves
She was brighter
Than the summer sun
Fell under the spell of her
Smiling brown eyes
Faster than a breath
And when she's gone
It's always night
And I'm under a bleak moon
A bleak, bleak moon

She's more than beauty
She's a generous soul
Rich with laughter

She makes me
High on life
She makes me whole
But when she's gone
It's always night
And I'm under a bleak moon
A bleak, bleak moon

He rolls into the instrumental, and overwhelmed by the song, I draw in gulps of air, imagining his fingers flying over the guitar stem, imagining the tender look on his face, and wishing he were here with me. Then he starts the last verse, and my throat burns.

From the shadows
I watched her shine
Trying to be content
That she'd never be mine
Never touch the sun
Never hold her brightness
Now she's gone
It's always night
And I'm under a bleak moon
A bleak, bleak moon

The song ends and I wipe the lone tear rolling down my cheek. I don't deserve such a beautiful song now, much less years ago when he must have written it. I recall being worried about being portrayed as a bitch, but the way Sam sees me fills me with pride, hope, and fear—I want to be what he sees. I want to be what he needs.

"Peyton? You there?" Sam asks, breaking me from my turbulent thoughts.

"Yeah, um, wow," I say in a rush of air. "I'm sure that's really not me but thank you."

"That's you. It was you even then."

Someone pokes my shoulder, and I turn to see Gabe. "We're boarding," he says loudly.

Nodding to Gabe, I reach for my bag and say, "I have to go. We're—"

"I heard. It's okay. I told my mom I'd meet her soon at the hospital." He sighs sadly into the phone. "Though it will be the middle of the night, text me when you land?"

"Yes. Text me when you wake up?"

"The moment I open my eyes. Have a safe trip, Peyton," he says in a desolate tone before hanging up.

With a sigh, I turn my phone off.

It feels like I'm turning my connection with Sam off.

Chapter 33

Go out with us!" Jill says, falling onto my bed next to me. I shake my head. "Don't feel like it."

What if Sam was to call? Classes start in three days. He has to come back soon. I haven't seen him since the night Seth freaked out at their last concert, three weeks ago. There have been a few calls and texts to each other, but I hate the distance between us. He is at his parents' house right now, but I can't stop worrying about the last text I got from him. It was days ago, and I've been preoccupied with it because it was so utterly impersonal. The short lines won't stop running through my head and making me apprehensive: *Home now at my mom's. Still straightening things out. Hope to call you soon.*

Jill elbows me. "You can't stop your life and wait for Sam." The day I came home, I told Jill about Sam and me. Strangely, she wasn't all that surprised, and admitted she knew back in high school there was something between us. Too bad she couldn't have told me then, when I was blind to it.

"True," I say with a sad sigh.

"Forget about the asshole!" Jill says, sitting up. "Let's go out!"

I smile weakly. Sam being there for his brother does not make him an asshole. Even if Sam decided to end things with me because of his brother, he wouldn't be an asshole. It would destroy me, but the only thing I'd be angry about would be the unfairness of Seth's stupid mind-twisting disease. I couldn't be mad at either of the brothers. They're both hurting too.

Jill tugs at my arm. "You've been moping around for a week now. Enough!"

I let her pull me up, and she goes to my closet, flicking through clothes. Once she's done, I raise an eyebrow at the outfit laid out on the bed. "Really?"

She nods vigorously. "Hell yeah. Nothing better to get you out of a funk than a multitude of guys hitting on you." She bends over to search for shoes.

I frown at the tiny skirt and bustier top. "I don't want guys hitting on me," I say miserably.

"Peyton!" Jill flies up to face me. "You're going out. You're going to have a good time. I'm tired of looking at your sad little face."

It probably has been annoying for her to deal with the despondent expression I must have been wearing constantly the past week.

"Fine," I say. "But I'm not wearing those." I gesture to the heels in her hand.

"Deal," she says, tossing the shoes over her shoulder and back into the closet. "You got twenty to get ready and then the party bus is outta here."

"Your piece-of-shit car is hardly a party bus," I grumble as she marches out of my room.

"Twenty minutes!" she yells from the hallway.

Of course, twenty minutes later, Jill is applying more makeup to my features. I didn't put on enough, apparently. Then she's taking out my ponytail and flat-ironing my hair because "ponytails aren't sexy." And then she's threatening to throw my flip-flops out as she shoves wedge sandals on my feet.

Forty minutes later, we head out the door.

Opening the front passenger door to Jill's car, I notice someone walking across the parking lot toward us.

My heart starts beating and my body breaks into a sweat, even though I'm barely dressed. Somehow I stay where I am instead of running across the lot.

"Fucking really?" Jill says, following my gaze. "He'd better not be here to hurt you," she grumbles under her breath. "Or so help me, I'll bitch-slap his fun bags."

"Shh," I say, my heart pounding in my ears as he comes nearer.

His gaze glued on me, Sam steps onto the sidewalk. "Hey," he says a little breathlessly.

"Hey," I say, also as if slightly out of breath. Shocked, I stare at him in the coming dusk of night.

"You busy?" he asks.

I start to shake my head, but Jill snarls, "Yeah, we were just leaving. Going out."

Sam glances at her.

"Sort of," I mumble.

"Dammit, Peyton," Jill says. "Don't play hard to get or anything."

"You have time to talk?" Sam asks, ignoring Jill.

"Sure, of course," I say, surprised I sound halfway normal, given the anxiety coursing through me. A "talk" doesn't necessarily mean what I want. And I want Sam.

"Could we go inside?" Sam takes a step closer to me.

Sparks fly through my body at his close proximity, his piercing blue eyes, and the tight swell—I can tell he's holding his breath—of his sculpted chest. My body wants to jump into his arms, but I simply nod and turn around toward our apartment while reining in the emotions—hope, fear, and love—tumbling through me.

Behind us, Jill yells, "I'll go over to Mindy's! Three doors down. Call me if you need anything. My boxing gloves are on my desk, ready to go. You know exactly where I'll punch him if I have to!"

I bite my lip to stop a giggle, but the moment I step inside, and Sam and I are alone, I feel weighed down and worried. I turn on a lamp by the couch, then move toward the fridge and grab a beer next to the tiramisu I brought home from Tony's for Jill. I need something to calm my nerves. I hold the beer out for Sam. He shakes his head and watches me from the living room as I pop the top and take a sip.

"So," I say slowly, "what's going on?"

He steps closer to the kitchen as his eyes roam over me. "You were going out? Dressed like that?"

I set the beer down with a clank. Now anger mixes with my fear. "Really? I didn't know I needed to check with you on how to dress. Even if you hadn't ignored me for the last week, you wouldn't have a say in my wardrobe."

He stops at the counter across from me. His fingers grip the edge. "Shit, Peyton. I don't care how you dress. It just looks like you're going out on—on the prowl or something when we . . ." He frowns. "I'm not sure what we are, but I didn't mean to ignore you. Everything just feels so fucked up right now."

His words pound in my head. *I'm not sure what we are . . . I'm not sure what we are . . . I'm not sure what we are.*

I take a sip of beer and say nothing. He's too close, even with the counter in between us. I want to run my hand through his curls and feel his strong arms close around me but it seems impossible. He's only feet away but might as well be miles from me. Untouchable. Unattainable.

He runs a hand over his curls. "I want to be with you so bad . . ."

As my throat tightens, I somehow whisper, "But?"

He draws in a deep breath and slowly lets it out. "Seth's adjusting. His meds have started to work, but he still obsessively thinks that we're cheating on him. The thought of us together makes him angry. I'm not sure if it's part of his disease, but he just can't seem to let that grudge go. I want to be with you," he repeats, looking down at the counter. "Yet I'm being torn in two."

I swallow tightly, and will myself not to cry, not to make this harder for him. Yet my heart is sinking, shriveling, drying up as I stand in my kitchen holding a beer. I'm staring at the person I finally realized I'm totally in love with, but he's not mine, and there's nothing I can do. It may feel like he is choosing his brother over me, but it's far more complicated than that. And his decision is something I have to respect, accept, and somehow get over. However, the sadness and loss crushing my heart at the moment doesn't feel like it will ever end.

Slowly sitting down on a stool, Sam says, "I told you things were all right between Seth and me before. They're not. I've spent the last three years mostly ignoring him. I have to start accepting who he is now. I have to let the old Seth go. And I need to be there for him. My mother feels that my absence is related to some of the way he's been acting out recently. I don't know if she's right. But I've promised her to come home every other weekend if possible."

"That sounds like a good plan," I say tightly, because it is. Sam should be with his brother more, and should accept him, disease and all. Though I understand him missing the old Seth, this brother needs him now.

He grips the back of his neck. "The people he works for at the diner are allowing him to come back. The girl he dates on and off"—he shakes his head—"who I knew nothing about, really cares about him and is trying to help. Seeing him with her made me aware that he has a chance at a good life. I suspect it will always contain drama, and maybe even periodic hospital stays, but I want him to have a family of his own."

Feeling cold enough to shatter into a million shards of ice, I force myself to say, "He should have as normal a life as possible."

He sighs. "And then there's you. The girl I've always wanted." His tightened lips signal a deep sadness, but there's a sliver of hope in his eyes. "As things stand, Seth will always be an issue. He could show up at any time, acting like a crazy, jealous idiot and throwing a temper tantrum. I can't see how being with me is fair to you with my commitment to him. I can't even take you home to meet my parents. You deserve much more time and devotion than I can give at this point in my life; between my commitment to him and the band signing with the label, I'll be gone more than I'm here."

My chest hurts as I take in his twisted, torn expression. I hold the tears in somehow, but slowly, ever so slowly, as I start to understand what he's saying, what that touch of hope in his gaze means, my desiccated heart starts coming back to life. I set my beer down and a laugh escapes me. "That's it?"

He tilts his head. "What do you mean?"

I lean over the counter toward him. "I can deal with not meeting your parents. And I can deal with Seth's tantrums and your commitment to him. I can deal with your absence so you can be with your brother." I now push myself up onto the counter and crawl across it, my barely covered butt in the air. Inches from his lips, I insist, "I'm not sure I can deal being without you."

He doesn't kiss me. Instead, his gaze searches mine. "Are you sure? Think about it, Peyton. If we do this, I'm not going to let you go. I know we're young, but I'm certain that you're the girl I want to marry someday. My brother is never going to be easy. He'll be a constant thorn in our sides. But he'll always be my brother, so when you get me, you get him and all his shit too."

Well, if that isn't a fuckload to contemplate, I'm not sure what is. Marriage to Sam and a lifetime with his crazy brother to boot? And wait—my palms suddenly feeling sweaty—did I just imagine it, or was he actually just talking about a wedding? Wow. Yikes. Wow.

I take a deep breath, but before I can speak, Sam says, "I never want you to regret being with me."

Peering down at him, I try to stay rational even though I feel like swooning after his words. "Here's the thing. Your brother is a huge pain in the butt, but it's not his fault," I say, knowing it's the truth. "Maybe he'll cause a rift or two in your family, maybe sometimes he'll get crazy and screw things up with us. Yet being without you will feel so much worse than any of that." I lean forward and bury my hands in his curls. "I'm not expecting everything to be rainbows and butterflies, Sam." I lower my head, my lips centimeters from his, as he sits there staring at me, still as a photo. "I'm expecting to be with you whenever possible, and that's all I need. You once said 'sometimes you have to take the good with the bad. If the good is that freakin' good.'" I grab his jaw and our gazes lock onto each other's. "Being with you is just that good," I say, before pressing my lips to his.

He's frozen for several too-long heart-thumping moments until he pulls me onto his lap, tugging my legs around his waist, and wraps his arms around me. He holds me tight as his mouth claims me. The press of his lips, the strong embrace of his arms, and the touch of his fingers on my back all express a mixture of joy and relief.

My own heart sings.

Soul mates. I've come to believe in them again.

As our lips separate, he stares down at me, his pretty blue eyes lit with happiness. He runs a thumb across my cheek, whispering, "'Lovesong.' The Cure."

Wrapping my hand around the one caressing my face, I whisper back, "'Never Tear Us Apart.' INXS."

Author's Note

I'm quite sure that schizophrenia comes in various forms and degrees. I wrote the disease as I know it, and sincerely hope I did not offend by doing so.

My maternal grandmother has schizophrenia.

I have many wonderful memories of my grandmother. From the time I was very young to this day, she has showered me with compliments—most of which I probably don't deserve. She has tried to make every occasion special, from Christmas dinner to a simple barbecue. She has always gone the extra mile. I've never seen anything to match her Easter egg hunts. I could go on and on, but she simply is a great grandmother.

I have some peculiar memories too. My grandmother telling me the FBI was taping her. Or that aliens had landed in her backyard. Or the time we went to Sea World, and she wanted me to change my shirt. *"Purple is the color bad people wear."* I took this all in stride. My mother had told me about my grandmother's diagnosis.

My mother has had a hard time dealing with my grandmother's disease. Not only because it was and is *her* mother saying and thinking these bizarre things but also because my grandmother's paranoia sometimes became all-consuming. My grandfather didn't always make sure she stayed on her medication. He tended to believe her—maybe out of desperate hope—every time she said she was better. Off her meds, she would alienate fellow workers, neighbors, and friends with her threats and accusations. Unfortunately, my grandfather tried to hide her disease from others, thinking she'd be embarrassed if others knew. I don't believe having a disease should be embarrassing. The people closest to my grandparents might have been more forgiving—my grandmother could be cruel in her paranoia—had they known the truth about her diagnosis.

Drama was inevitably part of my grandmother's life. Sometimes her worst episodes ended in strapped-down trips to the psych ward after erratic behavior that included things like turning most of the furniture in her home upside down or becoming violent with my grandfather, whom she usually adored. Her life was a roller-coaster ride and included some heartbreaking times, but with the support of her husband and children, she made it through each fall off the deep end.

Even though my grandmother has had a challenging life, she has also had a full life, including a loving husband, four children, and now, almost a dozen grandchildren. She worked as secretary, then later in life ran her own antique shop. She's been to Europe twice. She lived in Florida for several years before returning to Michigan because of my grandfather's failing health.

She's now in a nursing home. Her medication is regulated, and she hasn't gone off the deep end in quite some time, but there is an occasional nurse or patient who she accuses of prying into her business or taking something of hers.

Shrug. I accepted long ago that here will always be some drama with my grandmother.

She drives my mother crazy sometimes, and I truly understand my mother's frustration, but I love my grandmother, aliens, accusations, and all.

Acknowledgments

I'd like to thank everyone who helped pull this book together. Thanks to Lisa, again, for always reading my early drafts and offering unbiased suggestions. Thanks to Kate Chynoweth for her awesome story editing and spot-on suggestions. I always like to thank every reader who gave this story a chance. I'm honored that you would spend your time with my imagination. You all rock! As usual, a huge thanks to my husband and son for all their amazing support. None of this would have happened without it or them. And thanks to my grandma for just being herself. Her life is an inspiration.

About the Author

J ean Haus is the author of the Luminescent Juliet series, which revolves around a sexy, talented indie band from a small college town. She lives with her husband and son in Michigan, where she spends almost as much time teaching, cooking, and golfing as she does thinking about the tough but vulnerable rockers featured in her books. Visit Jean online at http://www.jeanhaus.com.